About the

Emma Jones was born in 1975 in North Wales. She lives in London with her partner, four kids and two cats. *Supernova Hangover* is her first novel.

SUPERNOVA HANGOVER

SUPERNOVA HANGOVER

EMMA JONES

Unbound

This edition first published in 2018

Unbound

6th Floor Mutual House, 70 Conduit Street, London W1S 2GF

www.unbound.com

ISBN (eBook): 978-1-912618-21-7

ISBN (Paperback): 978-1-912618-20-0

Design by Mecob

For Sonny, Raya, Connie and Clara

Dear Reader,

The book you are holding came about in a rather different way to most others. It was funded directly by readers through a new website: Unbound.

Unbound is the creation of three writers. We started the company because we believed there had to be a better deal for both writers and readers. On the Unbound website, authors share the ideas for the books they want to write directly with readers. If enough of you support the book by pledging for it in advance, we produce a beautifully bound special subscribers' edition and distribute a regular edition and e-book wherever books are sold, in shops and online.

This new way of publishing is actually a very old idea (Samuel Johnson funded his dictionary this way). We're just using the internet to build each writer a network of patrons. Here, at the back of this book, you'll find the names of all the people who made it happen.

Publishing in this way means readers are no longer just passive consumers of the books they buy, and authors are free to write the books they really want. They get a much fairer return too – half the profits their books generate, rather than a tiny percentage of the cover price.

If you're not yet a subscriber, we hope that you'll want to join our publishing revolution and have your name listed in one of our books in the future. To get you started, here is a £5 discount on your first pledge. Just visit unbound.com, make your pledge and type TOOTS18 in the promo code box when you check out.

Thank you for your support,

Dan, Justin and John
Founders, Unbound

Super Patrons

Jane Austin
Henry Austin
Robyn Benson
Diane Burke
Joe Cusack
Marianne Fonteyn
Michele Foulger
Luke Hyams
Graham Johnson
Dan Kieran
John Mitchinson
Joshua Mowll
Judith O'Kane OBE
Lauren Oldbury
Julie Oldbury
Aneesha Pandya – the best assiduous niece
Danielle Peppiatt
Justin Pollard
Lauren Price
Richard Scrivener
Kerry Symington
Mike Scott Thomson
Dominic Toms
Dan Waddell
Judith Walters
Brian Walters
Kate Williams
Cherina Wynne-Williams

Prologue
The Funeral Show

St Paul's Cathedral, London, March 2007

The anthem rings through the church, a hymn for our times. I can't resist a smile. Me and him naked in a field. Ecstasy-fuelled haze, arms outstretched, belting out the words at the top of our voices, to no one or nothing, except the stars in the sky.

A lifetime away now. Clay Allison is dead. This is his funeral song. His goodbye. But it was ours, too.

The gathered-here-today probably assume it's a battle cry, or a salute to Cool Britannia. But what if I wasn't the only one? I glance around at the other faces. Beautiful faces, grieving with effortless panache. Is every woman imagining a similar vision with him, their own special moment?

The rational part of me pulls me back. I wasn't like them. That was my attraction to him. And of course, his to me was easy. The promise of all the good things life could offer. My passport to a place where nothing was impossible.

Eight years later, all that late Nineties hedonism stuff feels exhausted. But today is like revisiting that place one last time. Only I'm not that person any more, I'm grown up, married, responsible for a child.

Opening my bag, I forage for the lipstick I'd thrown in earlier. Inside, a screwed-up Tesco receipt. My diary, the cover scribbled on with blue biro. A tampon with half the wrapper hanging off, bulbous and unusable. A stray library card. Turning the smooth surface of the plastic over in my hand I think, do any of these people own a library card? I find what I delved in for – Lancôme Rouge, a gift from Rach. One beautiful thing.

'Remember – reapply regularly,' she'd told me, with well-meaning insistence (she cares about this stuff), placing it in my palm, then folding my fingers around the capsule.

'I'll try, Rach, I'll try,' I'd assured her, bemused by the earnest expression on her face.

Rach put together my look for today. Rachel: my first and best friend in London. We'd been on this journey together, crashed and burned as one. So it was only right that she should be the one advising me what to wear, or not, just as she'd always done when we were sharing a flat all those years ago. Next thing, the music was on, the vodka out, just a shot for nerves. Felt a bit like the old days, getting ready for one of our car-crash nights. She'd done it to cheer me up, take my mind off Clay, like she always did. That was Rach. We gave each other the courage to dare.

Earlier, we stood in front of the mirror in my bedroom, as she circled me, eyeing me from all angles, like a pro. Brushing down, straightening me out, pretending not to notice while I pulled a disgruntled face.

'It's a funeral – but it's going to be like sitting on the front row at Chanel, Toots. So you need to look divine.'

'Divine is a tall order, Rach. Do I look divine? Like fat drag queen Divine or...?'

'Proper, not a trace. You do. You are.'

We opted for a classic wool coat – belted and black – and a softer silk dress underneath. I wore my hideously expensive Agent Provocateur underwear because, as Rach has it, 'a girl has to feel good on the inside too.' Prada court shoes in deep, dark purple. 'Bit kick-ass,' she assured me.

Looking around, most of the other mourners have opted for a more exotic statement of pain. I spot one in a Philip Treacy hat made up of a bird in flight; it positively screams, 'Look at me, I'm grief-stricken.'

Lady Floris Van Eyck arrives. She stages a theatrical entrance, flouncing into the chapel like Lady Macbeth. I catch the rustle of her layers and gently raise my eyes to clock the spectacle in full flow. Like the bride of death, her billowing cape, six metres long. Striding out from the layers of material, her stick-thin legs, naked to the thigh. Block-heeled platforms on her feet forge her forwards like a mechanical spider.

At the front of the congregation I spot Erin, Clay's wife – her platinum-blonde hair perfectly coiffed. A plastic replica of what a film star's wife should be. To see her now though is a shock. I feel raw. It's real. I'm not just a spectator.

I was always fascinated by pictures of Clay with his wife. In the glossy pages, he and Erin looked like an immaculate couple: golden-brown skin and pearly whites gleaming from the front of *Hello!* or *OK!*. Springing off the supermarket shelves, catching me off guard as I was going about my day.

I played a game when I saw pictures of them. In my head, I'd contrast my reality with theirs. Them: A Winning Pair in Las Vegas – Living the High Life for a Good Cause. Me: Late Night in Londis – Winning a Fiver on a Scratch Card – Blowing My Winnings on a Bottle of Jacob's Creek. The mundane nature of my everyday activity only seemed to add to the alluring, otherworldly quality of their image.

But that was an age before. I'd heard he'd gone off the rails again, no surprise there and anyway my life had moved on too, I was busy, happy. And I had someone to make me feel better too, someone who wouldn't give credence to that sort of rubbish.

Despite my nagging doubts, when I look at these staggering, gleaming examples of not just her but all his womankind, there is a part of me that feels privileged. Like I'm rising above them all. He had chosen our moment. Our song.

The final words fade out; a string quartet fades in, almost crushing me with the beauty of its impact.

He would have buzzed off the magnitude of this place. Not that Clay had ever been religious – flirted with a couple of the cults, got bored, moved on, sure. Worshipped at the altar of his own magnificence. Didn't we all?

The priest knows the chosen ones when he sees them. He's cupping hands like he'd been a dear friend. Although it's far from his normal order of service, he seems happy to act as compère, a sort of holy DJ for the day. Through Clay, I'd become an expert at decoding the rituals of the famous. We reinvent their folklore; we reinforce their mythological authority when they die.

I'm getting on fine with the acerbic me, when suddenly I see something that brings it all back, rips down my guard. I squeeze the hand I'm holding so tightly that it lets go of mine. Feels like my head is being held underwater. My jaw clenches, my nasal passages sting.

The coffin. The one concession to normality that I've seen so far. Its levelling force flying in the face of everything else, obliterating any other sentiment. Leaving only loss. Clay's body. The one I'd lain beside, legs wrapped around and into his. His perfect form: a blessing and his curse.

On its red lacquered surface a floral tribute rests, spelling out the word 'Son' in white roses. The flowers are strangely out of place: humble really. Poignant and human. Clay Allison was, after all, someone's son.

Lily. Her face comes into my mind and I find myself scanning the rows in the church. She wouldn't be at the front, of course not, I remembered the words she'd said to me when we met, 'He was my dirty secret, now I'm his.' She would be hiding somewhere in the shadows.

Feeling a tug on my arm, my search is interrupted, I reach into my bag again. Automatic. I grasp amongst the rubble for the packet of Smarties I've been keeping there on standby.

'I'm hungry, Mummy,' Ray's little voice pipes up. I greet him with a knowing smile, finger on lips. 'Shhh,' I say, passing him the hexagonal tube, which he takes with a happy grin.

He's quiet for a moment, opening the lid on his sweets, dropping them through the hole, into his palm, then cramming them into his mouth. The sound of his crunching soothes me.

'What happens when you die, Mummy?' my son asks me. I don't want him to think.

'You go to Heaven,' I reply, shaking my head a little, trying to regain my composure, get back to my boy.

'What's Heaven like, Mum?'

'Well, it's very beautiful, and nice things happen all day, and you get to do what you like and eat what you like, and sleep in silky sheets in a massive comfy bed. At least, I imagine that's what it's like, darling.'

'Do famous people go to Heaven, Mummy?' I think about this one for a moment because it's an unnatural question and I brought him to it with my shit.

'No, sweetheart. For celebrities, Heaven is probably more like a place on Earth. So when they die they go somewhere ordinary instead, like Warrington, and get to act like normal people. Only for them, it feels a bit like Heaven, darling, because they've had the heavenly stuff all their lives and to them that's boring. So it's nice to get a bit of normal.'

'Oh,' says Ray, half satisfied, half understanding I'm being quippy and weird and maybe not altogether nice. He gives me a knowing look, like I can't be serious. I knock one back and I squeeze his soft, sticky, warm hand, happy to have my beautiful boy next to me.

A man stands up at the pulpit to read. My heartbeat quickens in anticipation. His body, the way he holds himself. It's him. Only it isn't him. He has that oddly familiar look of a celebrity sibling. Right but wrong. Same gene pool, or some at least, just not drawn so perfectly by nature as his younger half-brother had been. Enough to make his whole life feel inconsequential.

To add insult to injury, he's gone down the route of trying to look as much like his brother as possible. He's dressed like an off-duty film star, only on him the scruffy long hair and body-conscious shirt are more Dad Rock than God's Gift.

I'd seen Paul before, of course, years ago. He'd been a fully paid-up member of Clay's entourage back then. Family members were always on the payroll, just to be on the safe side. Even blood ties need business contracts, especially where his father's legacy was concerned.

'In the event of his death, Clay asked me to read these words.'

Paul's voice echoes Clay's slightly: same deep drawl, just missing some of the swagger – and the transatlantic accent. Even so, it makes me want to listen even more, to close my eyes and imagine it's him.

'He wanted me to share them with you all . . .

"We are all stardust, each and every one of us.

"Particles of magic dust from an exploding supernova.

"When you look at the stars, think of me.

"When you look at the moon it shines for me."

"I am the light and you my friends were mine."

"Shine on."'

Clay had one sick sense of humour. And how typical of him. Even today of all days, he's on a power trip from the grave. Playing with the people who, right now, aren't sure whether to laugh or to cry.

Am I wrong? It seems to have hit the right note among most of the mourners, some of whom are ditching the sunglasses, looking suitably dewy-eyed. God, he knew how to work the crowd. He was so astute; written the headlines for them. Leaving his trail of stardust; still makes me laugh.

Brushing down Ray's miniature military jacket (his choice), more out of habit than anything else, he stiffens, cross. Then burying my fingers in his soft hair, which he likes, his body softens. 'Come on, let's go home, soldier.'

We let the camera worshippers go first. We can follow in a minute. Making our way through the bustle, I catch sight of a few ex-colleagues from my magazine days. Oh please, not today.

Then in the distance I see her, tiny, wrapped up in a black coat, hat pulled down over her face. 'Lily,' I call out. 'Lily, it's Toots, Lily. There's someone I want you to meet.' But she can't hear me. I try to pull Ray's arm a little to encourage him but he's not having any of it. Shit. Ray's staring at a man who is grinning like he's about to tell him he's won the golden ticket.

I recognise him instantly. Roddy. Panic. No. The habitual feeling, trepidation, creeps in. How can he turn up here, after everything that has happened? He's irrepressible. He catches my eye and grins, teeth bared. Dog face.

'Hey, Toots, long time no see.' He always did speak in headlines, like he'd rather carve the world up, make it behave in the cretinous way he understood. I shoot him a quick glance. 'Smile,' he mouths at me, squeezing his thumb and forefinger together like a camera clicking. 'Toots,' he jeers, 'if you ever want to do that story, you know where I am. Remember, the dead don't feel it no more…'

I can't believe he's said that out loud.

'What's he gonna do now, sue you?!' Roddy, the shameless bastard. He morphs the camera charade seamlessly into a mobile phone.

'Call me, OK. You might need to. Just sayin', babe!'

'Do you know that man, Mummy?' Ray asks.

I pause.

'Yes, I did know him, once. I knew him a long time ago. Come on, darling, let's move. You must be hungry; I want to go home,' I say, leading him by the wrist.

Air, that's what I need. The warm lunchtime sunshine hits my face as we step outside onto the iconic steps of St Paul's. A stark contrast to the cold darkness of the church. I blink to prepare my eyes for the glare, but instead they flicker, unable to adjust. It feels like I am walking into a tunnel of light. But this isn't sunlight, it's the harsh spotlight of hundreds of wildly flashing camera bulbs. Then realisation dawns. They are all pointed at me.

1
Thatcher's Hungry Child

The beauty of desire is you don't know where it comes from or where it will take you.

Almost as long as I could remember I had been coming to live in London. Staring out the window in our cul-de-sac, I had set my sights on it. I was Thatcher's child all right. She took our milk bottles and left us wanting. Looking back now, it was less to do with what was going on in the outside world and much more about what was going on in my mind. I was an itching, squirming, creature.

Leaving became my point of fixation. Not that I had any idea what the reality would be. It was more a fantasy I could escape to, which gave me hope there was a future away from the four walls and the tensions of the family. That house taut with the strain of someone else's robbed desire.

Home was a semi-detached in Nantwich. Our compact house held the lost ambition of one woman. My mother. Ellen Silver. Clever, beautiful and stagnated by her lot. Family, class, illness.

Nasty, vicious, unrelenting illness that ate away at her immune system and stopped her being able to do so many of the things her wonderful imagination craved.

My parents are normal people. Two children. One cat. If it wasn't for mum being ill, we would be a textbook family. And for the most part we were, certainly we could pull it off, because it wasn't the sort of sickness people talked about, or were even aware of. Despite the fact that in our house it hung there like an omnipresent dark cloud, waiting to overwhelm us and take her with it at any given moment.

For her, desire became a series of thwarted attempts to change her environment from within. An obsession with Arts and Crafts furniture and design, redecorating our home which we didn't appreciate, or care for even. The wish to travel, expressed through learning languages, French, then German, on a course of audio cassettes. Never in actual adventures to those faraway exotic places she would have loved. My dad always put paid to nonsense like that. Money, worries about her health. 'It wouldn't be good for travel now would it love? What if you dip again?' He always had a good damp cloth to pat down her fire with. It wasn't that he didn't love her, he loved her completely. The problem was he'd never worked out what to do with her.

Childhood memories consisted of mum serving up overly ambitious dinners to a man who was happy with egg and chips and my brother Marc, a human dustbin. I used to look at her sitting at the kitchen table while they ate, staring into space. And I swore that wouldn't be me.

'What do you want to go to London for, Toots?' my dad would say. But I remember the look in my mum's eyes when he said it. A little flicker of something there, a twitch of her mouth. She wanted me to try. Even in her state of unrest she still had her dreams, it just so happened they would have to be fulfilled another way. By watching me take flight.

The 10.37 to Euston was packed, people cramming themselves into carriages, pushing to get in the doors and rushing for the unreserved seats. The train had already left the station as I struggled down through the carriages with my stuff, a holdall in one hand, a carrier bag wound round my fingers cutting off the blood, in the other, banging people in the head as I went.

'Sorry, sorry, sorry 'bout that,' I muttered in an 'I'm not really arsed' sort of way, enjoying the look of surprise on people's faces.

Eventually I came to a quieter carriage with free seats. 'No heating in here, luv,' said a man in a grey anorak sitting next to the door.

Carrying on through the coach, I spotted a table with three free seats and headed towards it. The back of the passenger's head was female, not male. Good. My dad had told me to only sit with women. 'Perverts on trains,' he warned, matter of fact.

'Is this seat taken?' I said, sidling in without waiting for an answer.

'No, it's fine.' She smiled a massive big-toothed grin and my heart leapt a little, as I realised it was a girl I'd spotted at the station earlier by the ticket machine. She'd stood out somehow.

Her dark hair was madly curly but cut into a super-smart blunt fringe. She was wearing a finely striped black-and-white blazer, floral-print blouse and cuffed jeans.

In my washed-out vintage Vivienne Westwood cowboy T-shirt and no jacket, I was cold. But it was worth it because the T-shirt was classic, a real find, so I was dead chuffed I wore it the day I met Rachel. Someone who looked like she knew the difference. But apart from her gear, mostly I noticed she had a great mouth. A curling, lovely mouth that was just so fine I couldn't help staring at it.

Five minutes in and I was telling her my story in real time: 'I'm on my way to London for an interview.' I was aware I was talking too fast. 'No going back, that's the plan. I mean none of it's set in stone, but hey, there's got to be more opportunities and how do you know unless you try?' There was a silence, not awkward exactly but even so I was anxious to fill it so I motored on. 'How hard can it be? Do you think I'm mad?'

'No, not mad.' Big smile, reciprocated by me. I was so relieved she said that; my plan felt legitimate now. 'Unless I am as well. I'm going for a job as a merchandiser at the Lowndes flagship store, in Bond Street, you probably know it, right? It's my dream job, except for the pay. That's lousy... of course, and I've nowhere to live, oh and the position is for a sales advisor, but I've been told there's potential... so.'

Only later would I learn that this was Rachel demonstrating her most admirable quality: the ability to look for the best in every situation and turn it into a positive.

The drinks trolley came down the aisle and Rach flagged down the fella. 'Tea, coffee, refreshments ladies?'

'Nah. Hey, fancy a can of lager?'

'Yeah, sure, why not?' I was pleased Rach was a girl who liked a can of lager in the morning.

We treated ourselves to a couple of Carlsbergs and three packets of cheese and onion crisps for our lunch. Rach didn't get on with her mum's boyfriend, got kicked out. She'd negotiated enough money off them to leave. It struck me as harsh and dramatic but exciting too. A world away from the stagnant unspoken troubles which made me run.

Our defences down now, we talked and laughed all the way to London. We'd decided, based on hope rather than actual knowledge, that between us with my savings and the little bit Rach had, we should have enough for the deposit on a flat. Reaching Euston, we were high on cheap chemically enhanced refreshments. 'Shape of things to come, hon!' said Rach with a grin.

Would it end up that way? Neither of us knew. Fact was I had two interviews lined up, the first one was with an agency and the second one was at a sort of small-time music trade magazine. I'm not sure I would have promised to move in with someone I had just met if I wasn't on my second can of lager but hey, at least it was someone to share the burden of looking with, and there was just something more plausible about it all if we did it together. We were less likely to fail.

Looking back at the young me on the train that day, it seems ludicrous but I'm almost envious of the person I was back then. Able to make a life decision based on the way someone wears their jeans, and if they have a nice way about them, a great smile. As a mother now, with a small child, the complexities and risks of a situation go through my mind like a virtual reality spreadsheet before I do anything, and the idea of making a decision based on a gut reaction is unthinkable. Funny though, I was right about the mouth: Rachel was a gem.

2
Believe Innit

'What do you believe in, Toots?'

The question was a gift, the one I'd practised all my life.

'I believe in everything.'

'Shirley MacLaine,' Roddy smiled.

'Yes, she's an icon isn't she? Sharp, beautiful, witty,' I replied.

Four long soul-sapping weeks of failure. Up until now, every job interview I'd had had been the same: a grey, airless room, two spindly chairs and a desk in between the interviewer and me. Last Tuesday's with the publishing house had been a disaster, the woman on reception was called Tabitha and had a double-barrelled surname. From then on in I'd convinced myself I wasn't posh enough and flunked the interview badly. Afterwards, I dignified my performance in my head as class war, although really I was irritated with myself for letting negativity cloud my vision.

Then there was the depressing media agency, more of a form-filling exercise. At this point I was ready to give up, pack my bags and return to the look of quiet triumph from my dad and the resigned disappointment of mum. But it was there I'd seen the advert for this pinned onto the corkboard in the office. The reason it caught my eye was what it said in big black letters.

All it said was 'Are YOU something else? Work should be passion. We are looking for a Creative Mind to go on a Journey. Can you Come?' Then a name, Roddy's, and a number underneath. His assistant's it turned out. The last-chance saloon.

That's how I got here. True enough, this was different. Delivering his first question, Roddy's artful technique had already gleaned more about me than all the rest of the interviews. Maybe it was the location: a mixture of intrigue and romance in the air, the beautiful decor designed for furtive conversations, not formality.

'Have you seen that film from the Sixties, *The Apartment*? She has that magic, lights up the screen. She's a girl's girl. My kind of star.'

'It appears, Miss Silver, like you're my kind of girl too.' Roddy winked provocatively, clearly not caring how conspicuously slick he sounded.

That answer was one qualification that got me the job. Done deal.

The meet was at Kensington Park Hotel bar. It was early afternoon, empty. I was early.

Sitting at the bar, I tried to look relaxed, but as the only female in the place, I felt self-conscious, out of place. I drank a glass of water with ice to make it last longer. I didn't have the money for a proper drink. I wondered how Rach was getting on. She was pissed off first thing, due to a shoe malfunction, followed closely by a phone call from her mum who had yet to send her the rest of the money she'd promised for our deposit. We'd only been in London five minutes, but already we were both of us slaves to money. I didn't even have a job yet.

I was about to call her again when Roddy arrived. I knew it was him. Like a smart version of Keith Moon, with a Nineties version of a mop crop and one of those loud, proud Ozwald Boateng suits, which transformed his basic raw goods into something much more attractive. He was talking fanatically into a mobile phone.

'Ange, Ange, just do what I told you to do and I'll talk to you when I'm back in the office later. I need to go now,' he shouted.

Roddy's face transformed in one motion to a charming grin when he set eyes on me sitting there. Without introduction he turned to the barman and ordered a bottle of Veuve with two glasses, turning swiftly back and planting a kiss on both my cheeks. He smelt good too, like figs and spice. Definitely not Lynx.

'Miss Silver, thanks for coming. So, tell me, what's happening in your world?'

'Just hanging out, erm, you know, contact-building,' I said.

Contact-building? What did I know about networking? I only knew Rach and Saeed from the lettings shop.

Should I show him my portfolio now, newspaper cuttings from the local paper? This was my fourth interview and in all honesty I still hadn't worked out how to play this stuff. The bar set-up was a new one on me. Shit, only one thing for it. I took a massive slug of my drink: this would work better pissed. He looked me up and down, giving me the once-over, a bit of a virtual undress.

'What do you believe in, Toots?'

'I believe…'

Job done.

Thank God he asked that question. Thank God for Shirley. The rest of the evening disappeared into a fog. Roddy was playing with me after that. He'd got his kill. The smile on his face as I'd answered told me I wouldn't be needing to unzip my portfolio.

We drank more Veuve, and Roddy chatted hungrily about the new magazine he'd established. Told me I would be his deputy, learning the ropes, then, in six months or so, if I played my cards right, editor for a new, revamped version. All of this despite my having no experience of editing a magazine whatsofuckinever unless you counted a freesheet at college.

'If you prove to me you can make this work, that you can do the shit, then we relaunch with you as editor, Toots. What about that, hey? Name in lights. Fancy it? Course you do. You see, I think you're the girl with the golden touch, you'll be the one the stars want to talk to, am I right?' At this point Roddy reached into his bag and pulled out a file of magazines. He started flicking front covers in front of me with glamorous film celebrities on them. I recognised most of them.

Then he paused for a moment on one picture. I knew the face. Clay Allison. Human stardust. Did time stand still for a moment? He was beautiful. My eyes gazed at the picture for a moment, before Roddy whipped it away again and I realised he was looking me straight in the eye. 'Are you?' He didn't wait for an answer.

'That's what my hunch tells me, and guess what, I need that golden touch working for me.'

'Yeah,' I said.

The memory of Roddy showing me that picture of Clay still haunts me occasionally. Was it a plan? He planted a seed in my head right there. I was young and green, he knew it. I'd even gone home and stuck a photograph of Clay Allison on my fridge, like a reference point or something. Rach and I had laughed about it. How every time we went in the fridge, Clay Allison would be an incentive not to eat too much shit. He became my fixation. What was that about? Or was it just my fate that things unfolded the way they did? It's hard not to believe, knowing Roddy as I do now, that he didn't have something to do with it. But even Roddy couldn't have known it would have ended up quite like it did.

'You've got six months to give it the magic it needs to take it from a good steady magazine to a market leader to the hottest title on the market. Got it?'

'Got it,' I repeated back to him, like a disciple.

He talked like a presidential candidate and you had to buy into it, go with it, vote with your feet. 'We are going to capture the new culture. Celebrity is the new politics. Our magazine will blaze a trail. Toots, this is a new dawn. And you can be the trailblazer. What do you think, Miss Silver? Are you on board for the big win?'

'I am, for sure, this is the job I was made to do,' I said, soaring in confidence and suspending all reasonable doubts, thanks to the champagne.

The thing is, the way this guy was talking I couldn't help but believe my own hype. I sounded Great. I wanted to be that Great-sounding person, and if I wasn't her right now, I was going to make myself be her. I would be Great.

The bar was still quiet, so Roddy, sensing an opportunity, invited me into the men's toilets for a line of coke as 'a little mood-enhancer.' Hell, it had all been going so perfectly, it would have been a shame to spoil things with a negative vibe:

one line wouldn't hurt, surely? We were getting on so well. 'OK, sure, why not?' I needed this job.

There was a moment after I'd snorted the line in the toilets that I realised it was probably a bad idea. Then the coke kicked in, and a surge of gratification washed through me. I wanted more of this, I wanted it all. Roddy nodded at me – 'another line?' – and I couldn't help thinking what a lovely boss he'd make.

On the way back in Roddy's car, my head was spinning with the thrill of the job but also with a lingering feeling. I had conspired with him, which felt odd, or was it cool, was this the way things got done?

Roddy planted a kiss slap-bang on my mouth as I went to get out of the car. I felt the lingering wetness on my lips.

'See you soon, Miss Silver.'

'Goodnight, Roddy, and thanks.'

I watched his car disappear and wiped my mouth off with the back of my hand, where the spit hung on.

Although we knew it wasn't glamorous, that it wasn't the life we would lead one day, Rach and I met in Wetherspoons. The reason for this lapse in judgment and taste, this wrong turn in our path to cosmopolitan living, was simple. We were skint. We needed to eat. And at Wetherspoons, it was possible to do so for £2.49, including a pint of lager.

'It's a diversion until we get to the free drinks phase of our existence,' I said, toasting Rach with my pint. 'For now, it's burger, chips and a lager. Sorted.'

'Later, we will dine on fish – posh fish with a surname, what's it, John summat, and a choice of hand-baked breads in a basket,' she replied, finishing off my chips one by one, dipping them into a sachet of salad cream, twirling them round and popping them in her mouth while I lamented the success of the interview with Roddy.

'I mean it was totally cool. It's an amazing opportunity,' I said to Rach. 'It's just I'm not exactly sure what the protocol is. Do I call him, does he call me? If I do call, is that too keen?'

'How long's it been now Toots?'

'Two hours.'

'You wait.'

Rach laughed like she was used to it. Part of her attraction was that she was more worldly wise than I was and although, when she described her background, it was far from romantic, the evictions, her mum's breakups, overfriendly boyfriends, I was beguiled.

Regardless of my romantic vision of Rachel's unconventional life, the taste of it I'd just experienced in the form of Roddy was uncomfortable. That's the trouble with interviews like that, where portfolios are left unzipped and the only thing that's out on the table is a line of coke.

Truth was, the nagging voice had returned and it was getting on my tits.

'What's the problem? Do you – y'know – like him?' Rach asked me, smiling.

'Roddy? No, I do not. Listen,' I said, 'and I know this sounds weird, I just appreciate the skill. People underestimate what it takes, but I don't. I mean, I'm a sucker for the sales patter, 'cos I know it's an effort. That's what journalists do too, isn't it? Charm you, sell you a good feeling. That's what I want to do too. I want to be an operator like that. And Roddy is an exceptional operator. He just freaks me out a bit.'

'Sounds exciting and dangerous, I'm not saying I don't know what you mean. That boss thing is intoxicating,' said Rach, reaching for the last chip and burying it in her mouth. 'But where do you draw the line with a guy like that? He'll have you doing all kinds.'

'Yeah, maybe, still I just wish he would call.'

Roddy didn't call: Ange did, half an hour later, telling me a contract would be biked over tomorrow along with a mobile phone. It was real. I had a job.

Rach and I let out a collective screech of joy across the pub and promptly downed the rest of our pints.

'Let's go shopping!' she said. 'You need to be stimulating, but not slutty. Great shoes, you need great shoes.'

'No Rach, we have no money remember. Home.'

Our home was Lillie Road. On the outskirts of posh, close enough to feel like it was within reach. Not Hammersmith, but not Fulham either. Above our flat, number 257A, lived a real Russian princess. We knew that because sometimes we got her post, addressed to Princess Anastasia Nikolaevna. 'Either that or she's a prostitute,' Rach said.

Two doors down, one of the houses had been converted into a bar where in the garden you could drink Pimm's and champagne in the afternoon. Rich twentysomethings with thick hair, in cream cord jackets, from the better half of Fulham would lap up the champers after lunch, joined in the evening by a mishmash of folks, who would take advantage of the late bar in the basement nightclub.

Over the road was a shop specialising in offbeat *Barbarella*-style lighting and furniture, which was all the more spacey because it only ever opened at night. Then it became a fluorescent metropolis. Rach and I got to know the man who owned it, Reverend Jim; we bought an ashtray off him as a housewarming gift to ourselves. It was a very cool, floorstanding Italian one – you pushed a button and the tray flipped over, emptying the ash into a vessel below.

On the other side was a row of antique shops. But not the kind I was used to, selling polished oak dressers and mahogany desks, which induced a feeling of mild inertia. These ones sold things that were beautiful only to the people who saw them as such. Battered leather armchairs, candy-striped rocking garden furniture, gigantic wire chandeliers.

The flat itself was 'small but desirable', according to the ad in *Loot*. It had colonial-style MDF wardrobes, which were a sophisticated step up from the MFI ones where I came from, and a tiny space in the back yard the size of a professional pool table. I had a shower, a room with a double bed, and there was a living room with a futon, where Rachel slept.

Choosing the flat had gone like this. Rach and I were checking out the areas we might want to live in. Our criteria were based neither on practicality nor on prudence. There was just one factor.

'Is it happening there or what?' I asked Rach as we pored over the lettings page.

'Finsbury Park, nah; Highbury, suicide bridge, no ta; Clapham, too far. Shoreditch?'

'The postcode is good. OK, well not there exactly. It's more curry row than front row.'

'But McQueen lives in Hoxton Square…'

'Yeah, but Rach, by the time his thang hits our skang we'll be robbed blind and penniless. Iron bars on a window don't say home sweet home, more like in da hood.'

'What about Camden?'

'Bleurgghh.'

'Primrose Hill?' she offered.

'In your dreams.'

Actually, we realised our criterion wasn't whether it was happening right there. We couldn't afford there, but was it happening within spitting distance of there? If so, we would consider it, damn right we would.

In the end we settled on the basement in 257 Lillie Road because, as long as we didn't want any natural light whatsoever, it was perfect. It felt and sounded right, we were in budget.

Juxtaposed with both the rough and the smooth on the way to something better. One direction led to the vibrant market at North End Road where music pumped out from the stalls. The Spice Girls on the radio; one of the vendors used to take them as his cue: 'Tell you what you want, what you really really want, come on now ladies. Pound a box the spinach, 50 pence your bananas. You know you want some. Look at those juicy tomatoes.'

There were fruit and veg vendors, and three-for-one knickers, a Cash Converters and a Woolies. 'A tenner to you, luv,' the pants man shouted at the woman rifling through the cardboard boxes on his stall. At least I hoped it was her. He couldn't mean me? I was going to have posh knickers, from

Rigby & Peller, Fortnum and Mason's (did they do pants?). They would be lascivious and lacy, and they would certainly not be cheap, and I would be buying them myself with money I would earn in my top job.

Carry on to the end of North End Road and you'd get closer to the better bits of Fulham. You could turn right into middle-class suburbia, terraced houses that cost a packet, fringed with long-standing Italian restaurants and convenience stores of the calibre that sold tinned caviar, sushi and quality champagne. Eventually, once I did start earning really good money, I learned what it was to appreciate this cultivated cosmopolitan lifestyle. Obviously knickers were a part of that, but not all.

3
The Office

It was dark outside when I got up. I paced around for a few hours waiting for Rachel's shape to appear in the kitchen so I could seize her. Then feed her Marmite toast to lessen the possibility of her going back to bed. I shut the fridge door and saw the photo of Clay Allison wink at me.

'Rach, I'm so nervous, I don't actually think I can do this. What if they don't like me? What if they find me out?'

Rachel continued to chew toast slowly and thoughtfully, barely looking up at me from the Chinese takeaway menu she'd been studying. 'It'll be cool, Toots. You'll be fine. Can't be that hard, can it?... Chilli chicken wings or chicken chow mein?'

'What? Now? Neither. I'm not hungry. It's 7.30am.'

'No, not now, I'm just thinking, compiling a personalised menu for us. Good idea or what? I'm tied between crispy duck and chicken and cashews? Ooh, spare ribs...'

'The thought of spare ribs right now is so nauseating. Why don't you just draw a line under the ones you like Rach?'

I was pacing up and down. My feet were making little squeaks as they stuck and unstuck themselves from the lino on our kitchen floor. I was thinking of my mum. She'd sounded weak last night when she called. I'd been sharp with her. I just wanted to fixate on my little bubble of opportunity. Only this morning it didn't feel like that and wanted to talk to her and see her face and make her smile. I glanced at my stolen picture of Clay Allison again and promptly brought myself back to the present. 'Hiya handsome. I'm off to work now,' I said to him.

Rach had disengaged and wandered into the bathroom shouting a breezy 'Listen, you will look amazing'. She wasn't brushing me off really, more showing she had faith in me by ignoring me.

When I arrived outside the glass-fronted building, I stopped short of going in. Instead, I crossed the road. Bottled it for a few minutes, reached for my ciggies.

Watching the people going in and out of the revolving doors, it was impossible to say what the right mode of dress was. Girls with immaculate make-up, beautiful coats and high heels swanned through the doors clutching coffees, followed by scruffy guys sporting DJ bags, low-slung for effect, wearing loose-fitting jeans barely connecting to their backsides.

Anything goes, here goes. I put my fag out with my foot.

At the reception desk, I was given a name badge in a slippy plastic folder with a crocodile clip on, until I got my proper ID. My fingers were sweating. Deciding not to put the ID onto my jacket, I clipped it onto my handbag instead.

In the lift, a smallish boy-man got in. I studied his pale, soft hands and freckly face, the mole on his neck. His face was down, headphones on.

He was dressed casually but he was wearing snakeskin shoes with silver-tipped laces. Experimenting. This was a place you could be anything you wanted to be.

Walking through the doors to the open-plan space that housed the magazine, exhilaration took over. Here I would become a world-class magazine editor.

No one saw my grand entrance. Many of them hadn't got there yet. Those that had, didn't even realise.

The editorial team were positioned in three rows: the picture desk and production at the back, with the big-screen Apple Macs, and the writers on the first two rows. The ones with the best jobs, such as the features editor, sat on the first line of computers.

Their desks were covered in detritus. Discarded prawn sandwich packets, plastic salad boxes smeared with tomato salsa, polystyrene coffee cups half-filled with gunge, stuck to the stained Formica surfaces by rings of crystalline tea residue. Strewn around were assorted freebies – Bart Simpson keyrings, comedy rubber toys, a pink wig, CDs, unread books, trays of newly launched fizzy drinks with forgettable names, Pot Noodles and Wispa bars. Housed underneath their computer stations were big blue A4 pads, blue hardbacks and half-filled reporters' notebooks, along with stacks of daily newspapers with interviews ripped out.

Walls and surface areas were plastered with pop pin-ups who'd been doctored with the usual moustaches, tits and dicks and the occasional arrow through the heart. A few of the best front covers were blown up and displayed in light boxes. There were thank you letters from Take That, Madonna and Steps, and one from Cherie Blair.

Roddy, editor in chief, had his own office: a smoked glass-fronted affair with its own windows on the corner of the building. I swear I could feel his vibe from the outside: a shudder of bad energy.

I tapped on the window, looked for movement. I was keen to get on with it. Just as I was about to try the door, he opened it straight into me, no apology. 'Miss Silver,' he said, taking me by the hand and leading me out front into the magazine hub.

By now, more people were beginning to arrive, sitting down at their desks, turning on computers and generally trying to look focused.

'Ahem, morning. Can I have your attention please, you lifeless bunch of beauts.'

Unhappy silence.

'I would like to introduce... the future. A new colleague who will be working on a special project. A project which for now we shall call Project X. All will be revealed at a later date. This is Toots. For the time being she will be assisting on the magazine at editorial level. This means she will be second in command to myself, who as editor will be delegating some of my responsibilities to her. Act like humans, and don't spit in her coffee. Claire, give her a quick tour, but don't take all day.'

Dropping my hand at that point, he stepped away in the direction of his office.

'Excuse me, Roddy, can I just ask where would you like me to sit?'

Roddy sighed. 'Claire will clear someone's desk for you. Yeah, that'll do. I want you within earshot of my door so I can shout at you. Anything else? No? OK.'

Bang. Door shut.

Claire, who was the office manager, was a breath of fresh air. She immediately put me at ease as she showed me around. 'This is Sara, production editor,' (a hand went up to wave), 'Karen, freelance, she's here till January' (obligatory wave), 'if you want a tea, Cassie will oblige, she's here on work experience this week' (shy smile). She took me around the desks until my head was full of unfamiliar job titles and names I couldn't remember. But I was canny enough to remember the ones that mattered: production, features and pictures.

I needn't have worried about the delicacies of my relationship with Roddy either. The charmer I'd met at the bar in the hotel had been put firmly back in the closet. The Roddy I encountered at work was an altogether different animal – more beast.

Mostly he'd greet me with a 'babe' or occasionally 'Miss Silver', but the way he said it somehow twisted the endearing part.

As the day went on, I wasn't exactly feeling the love in the room. Who could blame them? Roddy had introduced me as 'the future' (which he might as well have prefaced with the words 'the threat to your'). The disgust in their faces was obvious. I could see their point.

I swear to God, Stephen the art editor actually snarled at me when I held out my hand to introduce myself. 'Hiiiii Toots, so pleased to meet you.' If he'd opened his mouth and let out a low growl, it would have been more authentic.

The reaction from the rest of the team wasn't much better. Lise, the features editor, was a potential ally. But the others were going to take some persuasion.

Their first line of defence was a monumental group sulk. Later, I learned the team did everything in groups – hugs, kisses, lunch, fag breaks, whatever. This was a weakness for sure, but it could also be a strength if you could convince one of the cheerleaders that something was a good idea. It meant they were a team, even if for now it was a team united in hatred of me.

The only glimmer of hope that day came when an outsider strolled into the office. Everyone's mood seemed to lift as the guy appeared. He had a light tan, the natural kind people have when they work outdoors. He was long and sinewy with wavy, dark-blond hair to his shoulders. He had a camera slung over his shoulder and a motorbike helmet under the other arm. Coke Ad man.

The team immediately seized the opportunity to relay the gossip to a new person, bored after discussing it with each other all morning. I watched him disentangle himself artfully. He got out some pictures to show Stephen and, when they were finished, looked up towards me and walked over, holding out his hand to shake mine.

'Hi, I'm Adam, you must be Toots.'

'Pleased to meet you, Adam. Nice to see a smiling face.'

'Don't worry about them. They're OK really, they just get very excited about things. They'll come round. I guess it's just fear of the unknown.'

'Well, I hope so. Or I'm going to have to kill someone.'

'Just buy them some chocolate or cake or booze. That normally works. There you go: free tip.'

'OK, I'll try it, thanks. Kill them with kindness.'

At that point, Roddy put his head round the door and shouted in our direction, 'Good, you've met Adam. He's one of our best photographers, great guy. All good, Adam?'

'So, nice kit,' I said, looking at the camera – not that I could tell, but making an educated guess. 'Do you do a lot of stuff for us then?'

'Yeah, I work all around, but mostly for you guys. I'll see you soon then.'

'I guess so,' I said, pleased, first because he seemed human and second because I wasn't immune to the stir he'd caused in the office myself.

'Come for a drink with me next week and I'll fill you in on the inside info. They are basically puppies. They just need some treats and a firm hand.'

'You're on. That would be great.'

'Compassionate, attractive and a firm hand too, I think I'm a bit in lust,' I told Rach later.

4

Michael

A very different kind of universe. Dim blue lights, neon-blue drinks and dark blue corners of intrigue. At night I was to lead a parallel life as a professional party person. Not very professionally. In fact, extremely disreputably. The Met was the in hangout of the moment, the place to be and all that. When most people were calling it a night and hitting the sack, we would head to the Met to turn night into day again.

Rach was there already. Roddy was positioned at the far end of the bar whispering into the ear of a slim brunette in bleached denim. Roddy's name was a permanent fixture on the list too. As a master of the dark arts, he knew the right people on every door of every bar and restaurant worth knowing in the city. Seeing me here made him happy, I knew that. I was out. Working for him, dancing for him, to his tune, no matter what music was playing in the club.

Dancing wasn't on my mind. I was distracted by a beautiful man. He was tall, black, shaved hair, good suit, held himself proud. I wanted to sit and admire him. He was a pleasure to watch. I could have stayed that way for the rest of the night but I feel a tugging on my arm.

'Come on, Toots.' Rachel ignored me and dragged me from the comfort of my man-gazing and my sea breeze onto the dancefloor.

The Mary Jane Girls' *All Night Long* always got us in the mood. It was our cue to party. I could see Rach was already in a different gear, she was talking ten to the dozen in my ear while we danced. Something about a nightmarish customer with a passion for gold leather trousers.

'I mean, even Naomi would struggle to look good in them,

Toots, and she's six-foot ten or something. This woman was a four-foot Buddha. You should see these people, the money, it's ridiculous. Ri-di-cul-ous.' She repeated it for effect.

My eyes kept drawing me back to the man but my head was still wrecked from the day at the office. I needed to put all that behind me now. Relax. Dragging Rach downstairs to the loos in the basement, I was compelled to get into the same headspace as her.

The crowd at the Met was eclectic. Cool Londoners, not wall-to-wall celebrity. Just to be in was the mark. A few faces broke up the clique – a emo-ish rock star huddled up in a cordoned-off area, a couple of box-fresh, up-and-coming actors on the plush leather sofas.

Rachel and I took it in turns to snort a line off the toilet seat, squashed into the same cubicle. I felt alive again. We each had a pee, all the more tingly for the coke. Then redid our Stila lipgloss with a click-click and leered at our reflections for longer than was normal. Rachel pulled me back to consciousness.

'Looking good, babe, but we have work to do. Let's see who can pull the most interesting guy in this place; come on, it'll be a laugh.'

'Geez, Rach, I've had a long day, not sure I've got the old magic sparkly stuff tonight, and I'm seriously drawing the line at the gone-wrong Alice Cooper bloke in the corner…'

The stairs from the basement were conveniently lit up with a little rim of dazzling white bulbs on the edge of each step to guide you back up. In my chemically induced state, the underfoot display felt a bit showbiz. Like the staircase on a Saturday-night TV show the stars danced down.

In the mood for a party now, we headed for the long, silver-smooth line of the bar to put a couple more sea breezes on my tab and into our brains. We'd only been standing there momentarily when the beautiful man and his friend started checking us out.

This went on for a while, mutual appreciation, playing up to them, glancing over, making the most of it. Then, from the other end of the bar, Roddy appeared and sidled up to them. He smacked them on the shoulders and turned to the man who'd captured my attention. He and Roddy greeted each other like old mates, throwing their heads back with laughter.

'Jesus, Toots, how does he know them?' asked Rach.

'How should I know?'

But Roddy was looking over as well now; we were clearly the focus of their conversation, devious bastard.

'Oh my God, he's bringing them over.'

'Bloody hell, Rach, does he have to be involved? It all feels a bit weird now.'

'They are cute, though.'

'True. OK, maybe it's not such a bad thing?'

'Saves all the messing about...'

We put our heads down and waited for the inevitable, faux-surprised looks readily planted on our mushes.

'Toots, I have some friends I'd like you to meet.'

'Hello, I'm Michael, and this is Raph,' said the guy I'd been meditating on.

Roddy, all smiles, gave the men another slap. 'Now I'm going to leave you all to it,' he said, gesturing to the denim woman with a finger wave that he was on his way back. 'Gentlemen, ladies, have fun.'

'Like a pimp,' whispered Rach in my ear.

'Like you're bothered.' I kicked her in the leg because right now I didn't care either.

Michael was playing along with me now, looking indifferent, even though we both knew we were sizing each other up well before Roddy arrived.

Eventually he spoke. 'Don't take it the wrong way, please. Roddy knows how I feel about people who write your kind of stuff.'

'What do you mean?'

'What I mean is, is this what you do?' Michael answered. 'Chat people up for stories? I'm aware that what I do for a living might interest you, I know who you work for. Weighing things up, it would be a fair assumption to make.'

'Michael, you have a vivid imagination. But I've no idea who you are, or what you do. If I were to hazard a guess, I thought maybe you worked in the City.'

'That bad!' he laughed deeply.

Somewhere in my mind I knew that it would be a sensible thing to draw this to a close, there and then. We had only just met, and it was already complicated by Roddy's involvement.

But then I looked at his face. His dark eyes challenged me, his smooth mouth turned up at the ends in a quizzical way. He was definitely interesting. All I knew was I didn't want me to be the one to make it stop.

'So we're quits then,' I said, smiling this time, feeling like we'd reached a kind of impasse.

'Are you and Roddy old friends?' I asked.

'No, not exactly. We have known each other since university.' He tailed off as though he was about to say something, then changed tack. 'But I don't want to talk about him.'

He was being cagey perhaps.

'So,' he paused. 'Did you want a drink or not?'

The thing was, I really did want a drink.

'I'm Toots. This is Rachel. You two may have just met your match,' I grinned, slamming my glass into theirs.

Raph sidled in towards Rachel and I found myself alone with Michael. I looked at him in more detail now. The cut of his suit on his body was quality.

He smiled confidently and poured a large shot of vodka into my sea breeze. I knocked it back, a nice high hitting me, and he did the same with his shot, looking at me.

'OK, so cards-on-the-table time again. What do you do exactly, Michael?'

'I'm a specialist advisor.'

I looked back blankly.

'For the government.'

This didn't have the same rousing effect on me as his body, but I was vaguely interested. It sounded kind of important.

'Don't worry, I won't bore you with the technical stuff. We're here to relax; we had a victory today.'

'OK, for real. So what makes a specialist advisor celebrate?'

'Do you really want to know?' Michael looked at me searchingly.

'Sure,' I answered.

'Let's just say celebration is earned when a man's sense of justice is upheld, and when that same justice works for the greater good of the many. Raph and I have brought about something today which almost certainly will achieve this, I hope, for years to come. That is why we earned the right to feel victorious tonight.'

I burst out laughing.

'Wow, that sounds rather noble. Takes this to get you to the bar. You guys should ease up on yourselves...'

It had sounded honourable, annoying though it was. But right at that moment there was no way I could talk politics. All I wanted to be was dishonourable.

'Cool, I guess I'm celebrating too. I've been putting the final touches to the hottest new magazine you are ever likely to read,' I said, exaggerating wildly, the coke and the one-upmanship spurring me on.

By the look on his face, Michael definitely wasn't thrilled by the prospect of my 'hot' magazine. The words rang hollow after his talk of good works and moral righteousness.

'Not sure I'm your demographic,' he smiled.

'Sure you are. Even noble warriors need light relief, don't they? And from what I hear, everyone involved with politics is corrupt one way or another. Hey, I could debase you with celebrity! Wouldn't be the first, or the last.'

'Ah, but you see, the thing about me Toots is this, I have never been corruptible.' I was aware he was looking at me with resolve as he said this, but I'd had enough earnest stuff.

'You say that, Michael,' I laughed, 'but that was before you met me.'

At this point Rachel lurched forward, bottle of vodka in hand, her delicious grin fully formed, and she proceeded to pour a healthy double shot into all our glasses.

'So this must be a lucky night all round, I guess? Good job we have the tools we need at our disposal,' I laughed, gesturing to the refilled glasses.

There was only one problem. It was difficult to unwind with Roddy there, lurking in the background. Watching me – working me, that's what it felt like. Worse still, he was being nice – courteous, actually, sending me and Rach drinks over and toasting us from the far end of the bar. Taking a voyeuristic pleasure in our sideshow.

I could see that Michael felt it too. I caught him a couple of times nodding a polite smile in Roddy's direction, willing him to go.

It wasn't just me, something in the way Roddy operated and wielded his supremacy over people threw them off balance. When he was being treacherous, you felt obliged to thank him. Normally that was OK, but with Michael there it was different. I didn't want him for Roddy's sake. I didn't want Roddy to think this was for him. I wanted Michael for my sake. In the end, there was only one thing for it.

Michael and I were dancing now, and I could feel Roddy's eyes in the back of me. I turned and caught his eye, and he smiled, pleased I was under his spell, as he saw it.

I looked back into Michael's eyes to see him staring straight back into mine and realised that maybe something like the same thought had come to him too.

When I turned back the next time, a few moments later, Roddy was gone. The denim woman at the bar had gone too, presumably to the same place.

Feeling myself relax, I moved closer to Michael, hammed it up a bit. The DJ put on Q-Tip's *Breathe and Stop* and its hypnotic beat seemed to up the mood. Rachel and I were in our element.

She nodded in the direction of the toilets and I followed her. 'Look what Raph gave me. Isn't that nice?' she said, gesturing to the little wrap she was carrying in her hand.

In my mind I was pleased, because it meant my noble warrior had a dark side.

She locked eyes with me and smirked. She looked lovely

tonight, Rach. With numbed lips and happy heads we hit the dancefloor once more. Camp Lo came on and everyone chanted 'This is it, what?'. The rest of the evening fell into our familiar pattern of dance, drink, coke and so on and so on.

Next morning, I regained consciousness. I was in my bed. My head was lying on the chest of a sleeping man. 'Michael,' I thought, 'his name is Michael.'

Images flashed through my mind. Getting back to my place, slamming the door shut, leading him into the bedroom.

He was sleeping deeply but that just made him look even stranger to me. Lovely, Jesus Christ, he was lovely, but huge in my little bed, grown-up, manly, unknown. I prayed to God he wouldn't wake up. We didn't know each other.

Panic set in. I needed to be in work in 15 minutes. I didn't want breakfast, small talk or indeed any talk whatsoever. I just wanted to run.

It wasn't regret exactly, but that fear a hangover brings. The confidence I'd felt last night wasn't quite so buoyant now.

I eased myself slowly from his body, which dipped up and down softly as he breathed slowly and rhythmically. My hair was sweaty and sticky. Some of it was caught under his neck and I had to tug it out. The unsticking-myself manoeuvre made him stir a little bit. The shock of his movement froze me momentarily, desperate not to disturb him further.

On the floor were the telltale signs of last night: my discarded pink and grey Calvin Klein bra and pants, the dress I was wearing to work. I glanced at Michael's body and found myself staring for a moment. He was naked and his sleeping form was an awesome sight: solid and beautiful, with muscular shoulders and smooth, dark brown skin. His physicality had an ease to it; maybe it was because he was asleep, I'm not sure, but his strength just seemed part of him. Somewhere in my consciousness a memory of his body awakened in me. I remembered standing at the end of the bed in my underwear, letting him admire me for a moment, seeing his gratification, before he pulled me down onto the bed. But if he'd woken up now I wouldn't have known what to say. I wouldn't have felt I knew him at all.

Without looking, I grabbed a lucky-dip handful of underwear from my open drawer and lunged into the abyss of my wardrobe in the hope of pulling something decent out. I made a run for it. I had make-up in the drawer of my desk. I was good to go.

As I passed through the living room, which doubled as Rachel's bedroom, I noticed her bed hadn't been slept in. This unsettled me but I told myself I'd call her from work. I closed the door behind me and walked up the steps to the street. I heard the phone go off in the flat. It would be my dad, telling me how mum got on at the hospital. Or Rach? I ignored it. Hoped to God sleeping man did too and got on my way. I'd phone when I was in a better state of mind.

At my desk, swishing down some effervescent Berocca with the coffee, my hangover cure, I started to feel a bit more normal again. The dread and panic began to ease, and I began to feel like I had got away with last night. The vision of Michael's naked body as I'd left him popped into my consciousness.

But I knew Roddy had the power to spoil that in an instant.

As I ran through my emails, my inbox alerted me to a new message. Sure enough it was from Roddy, like he'd read my mind.

I glanced around to see his office door was open, he was sat at his desk. He caught my eye and grinned at me like a manic cat about to pounce. A wave of fear passed over me.

'Glad to see you and Michael getting on so well last night.'

Shit. How much did he know?

'Thanks Roddy. Yes, interesting guy. Useful too, I hope, politically speaking. Sorry I missed you at the end. You shot off without saying goodbye,' I replied in the hope he was calling my bluff, and I counter-attacked by drawing his attention to his nifty exit with denim woman, which I was sure his wife wouldn't have been too pleased about.

Then his phone rang, he picked it up and he gestured to me to fuck off out. I was sure I heard him say Clay Allison's name. My ears pricked up.

Roddy didn't email back for half an hour. Made me wait. So I could only imagine the collateral he had stored up for a future powerplay after watching me in action last night. My head was spinning, half of me fixating on the whole Clay Allison possibilities, the other half lapsing back to crazy thoughts about Michael and whether the whole thing was a set-up by Roddy.

I tried Rach a couple of times on her mobile but no reply, then just when I was thinking I might be safe I heard him bellow, 'Toots. Office.'

I stepped in cautiously. He was grinning, pacing up and down hungrily. I was the food.

'Hey, take a look on there, see if there's anyone you recognise, Toots.'

He walked away, leaving me staring at the framed magazine exclusives and career highlights mounted on the wall adjacent to his desk: the success wall. My eyes were drawn to a photograph: it was Peter Mandelson and Roddy, arms around each other at what looked like a celebration party. Behind them was Michael, a big, childish grin on his face, hair a little longer, grade three cut maybe, so you just started to see the natural wave in it. They were dressed casually in chinos, cotton shirts hanging out, champagne glasses raised. Peter Mandelson, in acid-green cotton, was criss-crossed with party streamers; Roddy, dressed in a sherbet-lemon version, was holding a champagne bottle aloft.

'Hey, very nice Roddy,' I said.

'Didn't know I played with the big boys? The big hitters Toots.' He looked at me for a reaction. I wasn't sure what to give so I raised my eyebrows and nodded to give him awestruck. But really I didn't care much who he played with, other than Michael. 'Got to be tricky in that game though. That's why I chose to do something nice for a living. Couldn't pull moves like those guys. Ruthless operators. No denying Michael's done them proud.'

I got the message. He was telling me Michael was one of them, that next to Michael he was an angel.

'Still, looks like you were all having a good time there Rod,' I said, calling his bluff as much as I dared.

'I was. Got to be able to play well Toots. Work hard, play hard.'

The object of the exercise had been a success. I felt uneasy now about the man in my bed. Fear crept in. How well did he know Michael anyway? The only thing I couldn't figure out was why did he introduce me, then warn me off again? He left me guessing and fearing the worst.

And why hadn't Roddy told me about Clay Allison?

'Hello, Toots, favour...'

Really, I knew Michael wouldn't be there, but I would have quite liked confirmation before I stepped through the front door of the flat that night. Unfortunately, it looked as though I wasn't going to get any such thing, at least not courtesy of Rachel.

'I'm locked out, I know... again... sorry, where are you, hon? Shall I meet you at the bar? Let's – could do with a drink to be honest, the day I've had. How far away are you anyway?'

'Flippin' 'eck Rach, have you not been home yet? Where the fuck have you been all night anyway? I've been trying to call you.'

'Long story.'

This set my mind at odds. Snapped me out of my fantasy world. The well-worn panic returned. I remembered I hadn't called my mum. I imagined the quiet of the house in the morning. Mum slowly edging her way round tidying up, doing her chores.

By the time I hit the sack, I'd pretty much forgotten about Michael. My mind was preoccupied with thoughts of home. Until I saw a card with his mobile number scrawled on it on my bedside table. Michael Dawson. Still, it was alluring to think of him here. I shoved my head under the pillow and went to sleep.

As it turned out I wouldn't have the chance to figure out

whether phoning Michael would be a good idea or not. Roddy had other plans for me. I got a phone call later that night from Ange. Ticket booked, car picking me up in the morning. I was going to LA to interview Clay Allison – fridge-magnet man of dreams. A-list supremo. It simply did not get any better than this.

5
Hello Hollywood

'Toots. You've arrived. It's manic here, MANIC. Uh oh!' she said, eyeing me with disgust. 'Problemo massimo. Yikes. Did you not get the dress code directive I faxed earlier?' Clay's PR was in mania mode.

It was 11am, LA time. I'd arrived in the country last night.

'Stella, I didn't get it, but I pass, don't I? Clay can't be too fussy about his interviewer's mode of attire, surely? What's not to like?' I barked back through a smile.

'But sweets, it's a pool party. A POOL PARTY. Geddit? Clay woke up this morning feeling so, you know, up there, so he's declared today is Wet and Wild Wednesday and that means biki-nis-a-gogo. I'm afraid he was quite adamant he will only do meet-ings by the pool. Now, if you turn up in that it would be sooo offbeat, I can't tell you how upset it would make him, darling. I just would not want to be you, in fact as a friend I simply couldn't allow it.'

'A friend.' Fuck me. This had to be my absolute worst night-mare. The most important interview of my life, the front cover star of *Incite*'s launch issue, my exclusive chat, and she wanted me to do it in a bikini. What a total bitch. (She wasn't wearing a bikini.) And Clay Allison: what a total pig. Who did he think he was, Hugh Hefner? What the hell was I going to do?

I glanced around the modernist boutique hotel lobby. The Mondrian – the most exclusive hotel in Los Angeles. The white marble and corian walls closed in on me in my mild panic – it looked like a sanatorium for rich people. There was no reception desk, just a golden pod, which on closer inspection I saw was actu-ally a shop selling bling, jewellery, watches, wallets and… oh dear God… no… yes… swimwear. Bingo. Except I didn't feel like I'd won anything. This was quite literally the booby prize.

On the back wall was a rail selling designer bikinis and thongs. I looked at the label on one of the tiniest pieces of gold string I'd ever seen and coughed out loud. Six hundred dollars. It must have been spun gold.

From behind the rail the pod's keeper appeared, a gorgeous young woman looking every inch the Californian dream. 'You like to try?' she drawled in a West Coast accent, assessing my capacity to buy one with a quick once-over.

The cheapest was the Pucci. One hundred and twenty dollars, it had diamante studding.

'I certainly wouldn't advise water as it would seriously compromise the diamante, but I think it would look great on you. Here, you can try it in the bathroom.'

She thrust the Pucci at me, nodded towards a door, and I limped towards the toilets ready to take on board the full horror of my uniform of shame. Standing alone in front of the smoky glass mirror in the loos, I tried very hard to be positive. Keeping my sunglasses on for a start. Actually it wasn't so bad. What they say about paying megabucks for a bikini in order for it to make your body look a million times better seemed to be at least partially true. My embellished breasts looked roughly the same size as each other: that was a first. The large blue gemstone covering each nipple actually seemed to balance them out a bit, maybe even made them look as expensive as everyone else's breasts out there in the LA sunshine. It was like they were saying, 'Look at us: we're worth it.'

They were. So was I for that matter, worth a whole lot more than this. But here we were. OK, so I could do with a bikini wax. Also, I had to be grateful it wasn't a thong. This was my body armour, the suit in which I would do battle, come back from the jaws of defeat and win, I coaxed myself. I bought a wispy watermelon sarong too, to wrap around my torso, closed my eyes when the bill came.

Pimped out in Pucci to get a story. Rach would have killed me, she hated Pucci. I remembered what Michael had said about me chatting people up for living, swallowed it down fast, desperate times. I didn't have time to weigh it up. Fuck it. It was Clay Allison. It had to be done.

I walked past Stella, who was standing outside the pod punching numbers into her phone.

'Take the lift to the top floor. He's by the water.'

'Cheers, Stella.' Had I just thanked her?

Standing alone in the white rectangular space of the lift with my image gleaming back at me from the mirrored wall.

As the bell chimed to tell me I was there, the doors opened simultaneously and I was hit with the glare of the LA sunshine. Warm air and a vision that looked like a glossy movie scene beckoned.

The pool, which was on the roof of the hotel, reflected the morning sun like a sheet of smooth metal. Black tiles made the water look like it was endless. I had a primal urge to step in and let myself sink down into the depths of icy-cool water.

A DJ was positioned in the corner and groups of perfect people with honed bodies milled around him, nodding their heads to the music. Utopia; a world away from ugliness, trouble or poverty. This was where fame transported you to.

Walking across the roof terrace, I saw him, like a silverback gorilla with his band of females. I felt drawn towards him. Perversely, it was like seeing someone I'd known all my life. The investment of my belief for him to be the person I imagined him to be.

I strode over to where Clay was lying on a black-cushioned sunbed. I sat down on the opposite lounger without being asked. Deep breath.

'Hi. I'm Toots.'

He looked into my eyes and smiled. A smile like a laser beam. Ouch. Why did he have to look so amazing? He had a sort of radiance about him, lying there like a sun-kissed prince with his shirt open. But I was determined to hate him, just the same.

'So you are the *Incite* lady, I suppose. Have you got anything insightful to offer me?' he drawled, sounding bored. 'Where do you want to start?'

'Well,' I began, enlivened by my own sense of indignation and, if I was honest, by the sight of his near-nakedness, 'I've got something I wanted to discuss with you. See what you think.'

Maybe it was the bikini thing. Or even the jet lag. Something in me had flipped out in that lift. Whatever it was, I was determined to show that I was immune to the virus of celebrity.

In my mind I was the righteous feminist (albeit in a designer bikini) in the blue corner and he was the fat porno pig of evil in the red corner, and I was representing all womankind right here right now, ready to burn a bikini in victory after I'd claimed glory.

'You're a film star, and a musician, ordained as a god, if you like. But I've been wondering what is it you get from all this.'

'Apart from the obvious,' he gloated, looking around him, smiling, waving at a couple of gazelles sipping bloody marys by the pool, and gesturing to the in-your-face splendour around us.

So far he hadn't taken the bait, so I went for it with this one: 'I wanted to ask you a question. Do you envy women? Are you trying to be more like a woman? And you doing what you do, is it the closest thing to actually being one?'

OK, so it wasn't exactly what I'd planned to say, but my indignation combined with nerves and pressure had propelled me into new territory. I noticed Adam had arrived and was taking photos. His presence banged home to me the importance of doing my job proficiently.

Clay looked blankly at me, as well he might given the bizarre line of pugnacious questioning I'd embarked upon, but he was interested enough to let me finish. I was a one-woman floorshow.

'See, I have a theory, hear me out, that men like you will always be looking for that level of consciousness women have when we use our unique abilities to the max. The power we have. After all, we are in possession of the ultimate gift of nature. We can give birth, enable life.'

Even I didn't know what the hell I was on about now. It had sounded alright when I had thought of it a minute ago; it sounded different now. What could I do other than carry on?

'The screaming fans, the buzz, the electricity of performance: it's exciting, but it will never come close to that, will it? That's why so many more men become rock stars than women, isn't it?' I said.

'What about Patti Smith, Janis Joplin? I love those leading, inspirational women,' Clay replied.

I pretended not to hear. 'We don't need the trip that you do. It's already within our grasp. Whereas you, you need to feel it.'

'But I'm not a rock star, sure I like playing music but I make films, that's my job,' he said simply, honestly. Clay looked at me in the manner of someone who had just been confronted with an agitated lunatic who might be about to do something dangerous. He shot a look behind me too, for someone to rescue him maybe?

'Yeah, but you were in a band, weren't you?'

'Briefly, babe, more of a hobby. Erm, I'm not quite sure where you're heading with this…'

Truth was, neither was I, but it was just spilling out of me as I talked.

'Is it a sense of powerlessness that drives you?'

Clay rubbed his head, perplexed, but he didn't get a chance to answer. My adrenalin had got the better of me and my rant was in full flow. I was panicking slightly, and a quick glance around the pool bar confirmed my fear: I was actually letting the side down. Adam was shooting film, discreetly and unemotionally moving around the bodies as if they were stage props, applying the same composed, professional technique he would use if he were shooting a sunset, adjusting his lens, smiling politely. Clay's entourage would make an incredible backdrop, spread around the pool, lying on deluxe sunbeds, talking on white mobile phones in one hand and sipping cocktails with the other. One of the babes blew Clay a kiss and fluttered her fingers into a little wave, which he received while half listening to me.

'Is that why you make the women around you look like idiots, sexual livestock fawning about undressed all day, so you feel a little better, and make us feel a little worse?' Another puzzled look from Clay. 'That way, I don't realise the power within my control, the real strength of my sexuality. In other words, is that why you ask me to do my job in this bloody ridiculous bikini and you are lying there in your shorts and a shirt: so you can feel a little bit more powerful than me?'

Confused, fazed and more than a little bit baffled, Clay paused, then politely framed his answer.

'Do you usually wear swimwear for these things? What kind of magazine is it you work for babe? I mean, where you gonna put your notebook and shit afterwards? It don't make sense.'

Oh my God. It hit me like a tonne of bricks. What a complete and utter idiot I was. A five-foot two bimbo, bikini or no bikini.

It was Stella, not Clay, who had dreamt this whole thing up. A trick. He couldn't have cared less what I wore, and this lot would have turned up half-undressed whether he'd asked for it or not. Why would he have wanted me to join in as well?

And here I was ranting at him like a mad person. What could I possibly say to redeem this god-awful situation?

'Come on then, Toots, I think maybe you need to cool down. I think you're crazy, maybe the heat is getting to you, right? But I like you. You're like a pocket-sized Brigitte Bardot, that's what you remind me of, and that's what I'm gonna call ya – my Pocket Bardot. And you're funny. You sure are funny. So c'mon, let's swim.'

Before I could say, 'but I left the crotch hygiene sticker on', Clay whipped off his shirt, movie star-stylee, to reveal his predictably amazing torso. He dived in with a wild cry of ecstasy.

In what could just have been happily described as a suicide bid, I followed. I jumped into the water, above my head and let it swallow me up into the black abyss.

Roddy could pay for the hundred and twenty dollars.

6
Riders on the Perfect Storm

Humbling though it was, my loss of face turned out to be a bonus. The interview went better than I'd hoped for. It wasn't exactly the way I'd planned it, but what did it matter?

Clay had taken a shine to me, like I was a new toy. To my astonishment, he invited me to be his guest in LA for the next couple of days.

After the swim, we'd actually got on really well. Clicked, even. We shared a towel. A million fans would have died to be able to say that. Much to Stella's disgust. She stared at me with evil intent from across the pool, as the interview ran on from 20 minutes to over an hour.

My bonkers line of questioning had got him thinking. He started spilling the beans. Inhibitions melted away like the organic ice in his highball. The whole situation was beyond limits. (How could ice be organic anyway?)

'Tell you one thing, Toots, no buzz I've had, no drug I've taken, has ever made me feel high enough. That's a fact. As a young guy, I was so desperate for success, it overrode everything. Like Dracula. Trying to figure out ways of sucking more blood.'

The confessional was interrupted only once. A beautiful person came over, whispering to him, reminding him that his girlfriend was arriving from New York. I'd read there was a 'someone else' when I was doing my research. She was an established TV star, younger, an American sweetheart. I felt a little disheartened now, thinking of her wholesome description, in the light of having met Clay for myself and finding him so alluring.

'I want you to stay here for a bit, we can talk, you'll do that,' he added, more a command than a request. I agreed enthusiastically; I couldn't believe my luck.

A couple of hours later, I called Rach. I had five minutes to kill before we were due to hit the streets of LA in Clay's car. I hid behind one of the *Alice in Wonderland*-dream sequence oversized plant pots in the hotel's restaurant to call her.

'Rach, he asked me to interview him here. Clay Allison asked me. My stuff's been moved down to the Mondrian today. I'm going to have a room of my own, so I can shadow him. It's good-bye Hershey Bar slot-machine supper, hello in-room dining.'

Screaming on the other line.

'I know, I know! And he's taking me in his car. Can you believe it?'

I held the phone away from my ear so she could hear the hip-hop soundtrack they were playing in the restaurant.

'Call me later. You have to call me. I have to talk to you, I need some advice.'

'OK.'

At that point I got a tap on the shoulder from a woman I recognised from Clay's team. She gestured towards the entrance of the hotel, where an immaculate Rolls-Royce Corniche soft-top was pulled up. Clay was in the driving seat, swigging from a bottle of JD.

'Are you ready to experience Hollywood?' he shouted, flinging open the door for me to get in. 'You hungry yet? Let's go eat.'

We pulled up outside a terraced restaurant. It looked smart but anonymous and had plush fake grass outside, and a sort of brass cordoned-off area at the doorway. Clay threw his car keys at the valet – 'Catch!' – and we stepped out into the roped-off carpet at the entrance.

We were led into a large dining area, which was abuzz with the lunchtime rush, but there was something else. As I glanced at the faces, it was like a strange dream sequence. I felt like I was walking into a scene from a movie.

As Clay and I were led to our table, he stopped every couple of steps to kiss someone famous. A smallish man in a black cap and glasses sprang from his seat. 'Spike, my man!' High fives.

'Hey man, long time. Call me soon, we need to swap information. You're so good, man, I'm almost tempted to make movies about the white man.' Spike yelped with laughter. 'I jest! Take it easy, Clay. Enjoy your lunch,' he said, to both of us. Spike Lee had just told me to enjoy my lunch.

I don't know what we ate. I don't know what we drank. But when we eventually left the restaurant, the sun was setting over the Hollywood Hills and it was getting dark.

'Beautiful night.'

'Yeah, it's so beautiful,' I agreed.

'But you know the best way to enjoy Los Angeles at night is looking down on it from the hills.'

'Well, I guess so. That must be incredible.'

At that point Clay's car pulled up outside, but it wasn't a valet in the driving seat, it was someone else. 'Hey bro,' said Clay. 'Thanks dude, someone I would like you to meet,' he said to the driver. 'This is Toots; she's a refined English journalist. Pocket, this is my brother, Paul, he's gonna take us on a little road trip up there,' he said, pointing into the Hollywood hilltops. I liked that he'd reserved the right to call me Pocket for himself, not giving his brother permission to use it.

The night air was sticky and we kept the roof down to let the air flow through our hair as we wound up into the mountains.

Clay was smiling to himself and occasionally nodded his head at me, to check if I was OK. I was so OK, which gave me a warm, happy feeling. We trailed off onto a narrower dirt track, which forced Paul to slow the car a little. The noise of the car was startling against the silence up there. Occasionally a flash of movement darted in front of us; I was sort of half aware it was there.

'Those right there are the Hollywood bats, babe, beautiful creatures, we got 48 different species in this country. I just dig them, the way they can hide away then spring up on you, fierce little faces they got, flying mammals, that sure is something, huh?'

'Yeah, something else,' I said, looking at his face, which was magnificent: strong jaw, an inch-long cleft in his chin, large brown eyes, everything in the right place. A real testament to mammals, he was.

In the near distance I could see a glow, and as we drove closer

I could see that must be where we were heading. Only when we pulled up did I get a clear view of what was ahead of us.

It was a Bedouin tent, lit up with orange and gold lanterns. Inside it was littered with cushions and there was the most incredible smell of burning myrrh, like amber resin. It was the smell of the spirits. There were a dozen or so people milling around, bohemians dressed like well-heeled hippies, except they hadn't got any shoes on and some of them were sitting on the floor playing instruments. Clay was greeted by them one by one. 'Nice vibes, man, nice vibes.'

Through the night, the music continued. One man dressed in a cloth shirt and breeches like the original John-Boy Walton started up on his fiddle. I became transfixed by him, staring at the twisted tuft of his beard, which he'd fashioned to a point so it stuck straight out from his chin. Everyone was singing. I joined in. Did any of us know the words? They seemed to come from somewhere. Harmonising now, I felt a sense of relaxation and joy spreading through me that I'd never felt before. I wasn't really aware of Clay or of anyone else: just the wonderful music.

I woke up later that night lying on a mattress.

Clay was gazing down on me, asking if I was warm enough. 'I'm perfect,' I said, because I was in Heaven and I would never know if that part had been a dream.

'You've got the devil inside you, same as I have, Toots. That means you can do anything you want to in life, if you believe, if you want it enough. And I know you want it, I can see it in you. It takes one to know one, kid,' Clay said.

Looking into the eyes of this man who had the ability to make crowds of girls weep with the agony of desire, it was hard not to be convinced. He had that evangelistic, saintly quality that A-list movie stars have. We had a connection. He said so.

It was only when I got back to the hotel that I came back to some sort of reality again. I lay on the bed gazing at the ceiling.The hotel phone next to my bed rang. I picked it up and a man's voice answered.

I recognised it immediately and sat up with a jolt.

'Michael. Hi, how did you know to call me here?'

'Rachel gave me the number. I called your flat, you gave me the number remember,' he replied enthusiastically. I could tell he was pleased to hear my voice, which was sweet, but he'd caught me off balance.

'Did I?'

'In the taxi you wrote it down on my hand, remember? I wanted to talk to you. See how you are?'

'I'm good. I'm in LA. It's, er, nice.'

'I know. I bet. Listen. I don't have long, I've got to go into a meeting. I just wanted to tell you I was thinking about you and, well, I thought we should do it again, dinner perhaps. Would you like that?'

My heart was beating fast. I was excited to hear from him, it was thrilling, but I remembered Roddy and then I wasn't sure.

'Maybe,' I said non-commitally. 'Shall I call you?'

There was a pause on the other end. 'You have the card I left,' he said, the enthusiasm gone.

'Yeah.'

'I'll leave it to you then.'

Something in me knew that was a big mistake. I had wanted so much for Michael to call. I just hadn't expected him to call. It was being here, I hadn't been ready. Maybe the stuff with Clay meant I wasn't thinking straight. London seemed a world away now. I'd allowed myself to become completely immersed in the world of Clay, hadn't even phoned Rach. What was I thinking? That Clay meant the stuff he said about me, really? But I was from a different place, one where ambition had to be matched by hard work and experience, and even then wasn't always rewarded. It was ridiculous to think like him.

There was a knock at the door, someone delivering a fax. Roddy was on the warpath.

'Silver, where the fuck are you? Get back to the office now. First edition deadline – can't wait!' I could hear Roddy's voice in my head.

He had the ability to switch from charming to charmless within seconds, and it was anyone's guess which one he would be at any given time. My own theory was simple. His moods were entirely dependent on cocaine.

If he had a coke hangover, he was pissed off. Equally, if he had just had a line, he was in love with the world again. He was like a chemically controlled schizophrenic warlord. Lucky old me.

The truth was Roddy wasn't the only reason I wasn't relishing the thought of getting back.

'I'm just not sure I'm ready for the next phase Adam, you know, taking over from Roddy, actually being the real editor. No one likes me.'

Sweet Adam was kindly comforting me on the flight.

'Listen, Toots, you don't need to prove anything to these guys: you're the boss. End of. And once they read the interview with Clay it will blow their tiny minds, I promise you. You just nailed the number one most elusive star on the planet, metaphorically speaking. Not only that, we have pictures of him no one could imagine. They capture him in a way never seen before: the real Clay. Respect is due, girl.'

'Thanks, Adam.'

The murky clouds over London looked grim as the plane made its descent into Heathrow, and the only remnant of the Californian sunshine was the tan mark my bracelet left on my bronzed arm. But my spirits lifted again as my black cab whizzed along the Thames. I loved this city. Being part of it. It seemed my friend the devil was back inside me again.

7

Insight and Inspiration

Back at work on the sixth floor, we were making the final adjustments to the first edition of the relaunched magazine, my editorial debut. There was palpable excitement as the cover began to take shape on Stephen's Mac. He might have had a queeny frost, but he was also a whizz at computer artistry. But seeing the image of Clay there, splayed out on the page, I couldn't help feeling the whole thing looked a little too familiar, like something I'd seen before too many times.

Incite had to jump out on the stand; its cover had to grab the spectators' attention in an instant. The predictable headshot pose coupled with a rather obvious cover line didn't ignite that sense of shock and awe I wanted the readers to feel. I called the staff around to canvass opinion.

'What does this image say to you?'

'Cooeeeer,' chirped Sara. 'It says, "Come and get me, girls."'

'Exactly. I think you are totally spot on, Sara, but not in a good way,' I replied. 'I mean, how many times have we all seen it before? Because I don't know about any of you, but I'm not interested in shovelling out the same old stuff. Stuff that pleases the PRs and keeps us in lunch tickets week in week out, if it means the sum total of our creative input is to put out something that evokes the sad sodding reaction, "Cooeeeer."'

Sara paused and thought for a moment. 'He does look fit, though, doesn't he?' she offered.

'Well yes, he does look fit, yes Sara, I cannot deny the fact he does look fit!'

No one knew that more than me, and there was something slightly unsettling about seeing those gorgeous eyes, which I had stared into while engaged in deep conversation, staring back in the same seductive way to all and sundry. Slut. But that wasn't it.

'That's not the point. Don't we have some other pictures, something that tells a different story? Something we can use?'

At that point, Anna, the picture editor, and Stephen sat up and took notice. I felt them ready to take the offensive, their hackles rising.

'The cover is amazing, don't you think, Toots? The sharpness of the image is absolutely magical. This really was a stand-out image. Stephen and I both agreed when we saw the shots, and so did you Toots, if I remember correctly.'

'Yes, Anna, there's no doubt it's a great picture. The PR and Clay will all love it – it casts him in his very best light, and I agree that, when I saw it, I thought the same thing. It's just that now, seeing it there, like that, I can't help feeling, isn't it all just a bit, you know, boring... A bit obvious?'

At that, Stephen gasped dramatically, pulling his Cher 'Believe 1998' tour T-shirt down in little jerky movements to convey his disgust. As he did so, the picture of Cher's face stretched out across his tummy, even further than her plastic surgeon could have dreamed. Freakishly, her elongated brow seemed to align with Stephen's shock, like she agreed with him.

'I've been an art editor for seven years,' he said. 'Before that, I studied for three years at Goldsmiths. Never, in all that time, has anyone referred to my art as "boring".'

'Stephen, wait...'

With that, he stormed off for a chocolate biscuit and a cigarette.

Anna was also annoyed, but was able to control her rage and direct its force at me.

'Well, Toots, if you are so keen to scrap the cover, I have to warn you it will mean us all working all night to get a new one in place on deadline. All that depends on calling back Adam, to see if he kept any shots back that you might find a little more worthy. And, of course, convincing Stephen that it's in his interest to slog all night to redo the cover.'

'I'm sorry, Anna, but that's exactly what we have to do. I'll call Adam, don't worry.'

'Adam, you have to help me, I'm desperate,' I begged.

That's how the phone call began and, within half an hour, Adam's lean frame was striding through the office to my rescue.

Watching him walk in, I felt the knot of tension in my shoulders ease. I noticed he'd had his long blond hair shaved off since I'd last seen him. It looked better: you could see his sharp features and wide jawline. He was dressed in full biker leathers, having shot over to the office on his beloved motorbike.

As luck would have it, the sight of Adam in full-on hunky biker mode seemed to soften Stephen's ice-cold demeanour.

'Hey, handsome, it's been ages. Thank you so much for answering *my* rescue call. Two kisses, mwa, one for me and mwa, deux for you.'

His rescue call, was it? This was promising stuff. I let Adam and Stephen settle into the business of selecting some new frames and tentatively sidled over when I hoped it was safe.

'What have you got?'

'Toots, you saw the best stuff, I have literally brought over the dregs. What's left looks more like reportage. I just shot this when I was warming up; it's kind of like my hobby, you know, for my own portfolio, the stuff I like doing. It's from when I arrived at the pool party, remember, you were in the water, looked like you were having a great time?'

'Uh hum, yes I know Adam, but bear with me. I just want to check we haven't missed anything.'

I remembered Adam had arrived for the shoot at the pool just after I had. I glanced through the contacts one by one, remembering the bizarre sequence of events as I looked at them. He had shot the decadent scenes around the poolside, the beautiful women drenched in Technicolor LA sunshine, which gave the pictures a filmic, super-real quality.

When I'd all but given up hope, I spotted the frame that stood out a million miles. Staring back at me were two faces, folded arms on the poolside, drenched to the bone: Clay and myself gazing into Adam's lens. Me looking bedraggled but kind of good too. It was definitely different. The shot had been taken as we swam over to greet Adam. I gasped when I looked at it, stirred by the intensity of the feeling it provoked in me. For a moment I was transported back to that moment. Clay's expression contained a look of mild amusement; it's the detachment I now knew kept his crazy existence from sending him nuts. It made me long to be with him again, sharing that glimpse he gave me inside his head. What wouldn't I give to be back there now, his body next to mine in the water?

But my objectivity kicked in: I needed to break my connection, look at the picture and see the image for what it was. Something about the water, the drenched faces and the sunlight gave it almost a Herb Ritts feel and wonderful resonance. And me, I was no Christy Turlington, granted, but bathed in the light of the pool and next to Clay... I looked pretty good, actually almost beautiful. And the simplicity of the twin head shot was great, especially the juxtaposition of someone so massively famous and primed, with someone unknown. It was intriguing.

'That's the one,' I piped up.

Stephen muscled in, 'Erm, who's the babe?'

'That's me, actually, Stephen,' I replied triumphantly. 'And that, that is our cover shot.'

'Toots, you can't be seriously thinking of putting a picture of yourself on the front cover of this magazine. Nobody knows who you are. You might look quite hot, sweetheart, but doncha think you'd be better saving it for the family album, show it to the grandkids? I mean, how narcissistic can you possibly be?'

'Stephen, you are missing the point. I know nobody knows who I am, but everyone knows Clay, don't they? That's the idea, don't you see? By putting me in the picture, we put *Incite* on the map and we show that we aren't some hero-worshipping bullshit celebrity magazine. We are serious players. You can call me narcissistic if you want to, and you'd be right, because frankly this is genius. I am a genius.'

I wouldn't normally talk like that, but I was excited and inspired. I felt it in my bones. It was the sort of decision you either go for, hell for leather, or not at all.

'Sorry Toots, I just think this is a suicide note,' replied Stephen curtly. 'An editor stays in the background. I'll explain how it works, shall I? It's dignified to write a small letter to the readers on the introductory pages. A little something about what's in the issue to tempt the tastebuds, then you fade away into the background graciously. That's it. Finito.'

'Stephen sweetheart,' I take a breath to contain the seething anger threatening to reward him with rage but manage to contain it just beneath the surface, knowing nothing will annoy him more than my calm meeting his storm, 'with respect, I am well aware of the traditional magazine format. But I did not come here to reproduce the traditional magazine format. I came here to break the mould. And yes, I agree, the readers probably couldn't care less who I was if I stuck myself on the cover stark naked.'

'God save us,' he muttered under his breath.

'But next to Clay, as a mystery girl, even if it transpires I'm just interviewing him, then… then they care. Mark my words, Stephen, it makes the story, particularly when I tell them what happened. It's my call and you're just going to have to trust me because my instincts tell me it's great.'

'Well, it's your funeral, Toots; probably mine too. Pity you didn't choose to let us go down with a little more dignity, that's all.'

Stephen marched off for another biscuit but there was definitely less flounce in his retreat.

Meanwhile, Lise, Anna and a couple of the others who were milling around were beginning to look interested and seemed a little more persuaded.

The intimate moment I shared with Clay allowed me to get an amazing photograph: Clay from a different perspective, not some hallowed Hollywood star but someone more real. I hoped to draw the readers into a more personal experience, share it with them.

Lise seemed to be having a eureka moment. 'I get it. It's like we're saying, "What is a celebrity anyway? Can anyone be a celebrity?"'

'Precisely, Lise!' I said. 'This says no more bollocks, it says *Incite* is the objective voice, the equaliser, the No Bullshit Bible, the voice of the free-thinking people.'

'It's revolutionary. I love it, Toots!' said Lise.

'Yes exactly, that's it, exactly,' I said excitedly, glad at least someone was getting with the programme.

Even Anna nodded as she put the picture on the light box and began to examine it as though she might actually be thinking about using it.

Stephen walked slowly but deliberately back into the hub, nibbling on a Bourbon biscuit in a way that conveyed hurt. 'What do you think, Stephen?' I asked. He said nothing but made his presence known by taking the occasional small, hard bite.

Adam was smiling enthusiastically, clearly pleased I'd chosen one of his more personal portraits, not the run-of-the-mill stuff. 'Hey, Toots, what do you imagine Clay will think when he sees this?' he asked. It was the one question I'd rather not have thought about right then.

'Adam,' Anna finally spoke, unable to bring herself to address me directly. 'What format are these on? I think we will need some heavy-duty Photoshopping, if that's in the budget, Toots, but OK with some processing, uh huh... There may be something I can work with.'

I took that as an endorsement, pulling Adam aside before she had a chance to change her mind.

'Thanks, hon, I think you may have just saved my life. The picture is perfect.'

'Hey, don't mention it, Toots, all in a day's work. By the way,

I don't think you need that much Photoshopping,' he grinned. 'Maybe just a bit of Kirstie Alley-ing here and there?'

'Cheers, Adam. Send me the bill, OK?'

Just at that moment, when I thought we had sealed the deal and finally put the magazine to bed, the worst-case scenario happened. Roddy arrived in the office. Typical Roddy, it was almost as if he knew the exact moment that would have maximum impact. He smelt the drama, I swear.

I glanced up at his face as he approached, to see if I could ascertain what sort of mood he was in. But it was impossible. He was smiling – that might have been a good sign. But then again, with Roddy, moodwise, the smile was often just a mask for evil intent. Unless he'd had a line, of course. 'Please, God, let him have had a line,' I thought.

'Hi, Roddy, want to see the front cover before we get to work? We just got Adam here to wrap the whole thing up.' I tried to sound as breezy and upbeat as possible, to put him at ease, but inside my heart was racing at a staggering rate.

'Course, babe, why do you think I'm here for fuck's sake? Hit me up.'

Jesus, I felt so edgy my nerves were in bits. What if he didn't like it? What if he thought I was bonkers? I knew we'd agreed on the vision for the magazine that first night, but that was after a tankful of champagne. It seemed such a long time ago now. I switched the light box back on and summoned Sara back over from the picture desk.

'It's different, I know,' I began to blather, 'but good different, I think.'

No response. After about 30 long seconds, Roddy looked up at me, scrunched his lips and nodded very slowly, like he had just eaten something strange and was coming round to the pungency. Then, for 30 more long, ponderous seconds, Roddy was silent.

All of a sudden he came alive. Looking through me, he turned to the team. Roddy surveyed them for a minute, winding his finger around in dizzy circles, deciding who he was going to stop on, like a kid in the playground choosing who's on his football team. Out of the blue, he pointed, quickfire, at, of all people, Stephen.

'Stephen. What do you think of the cover? Do you like it? Thoughts?'

I felt like crying. Just when I'd managed to get my message across to the team, just when I seemed to be winning them over, it was all going to be ruined.

Stephen's nostrils flared and he shuffled a little, rolling his shoulders and proudly standing to attention. Bloody loving it, in other words. I looked at him with pleading eyes, but he was a masterful actor and pretended he couldn't see.

'Well now, what can I say?' he began. At this point, Adam sighed slightly and I thought he caught Stephen's eye. Stephen's posture changed ever so slightly. Cher's taut face on his T-shirt eased a little. 'I think it's a finely lit, well-mastered and orchestrated photograph and I think Adam has done an excellent job,' he said.

Wow. I was flabbergasted; that was as close as I was ever going to get to solidarity from Stephen (and Cher, who was basically God). I didn't care that he'd taken pains not to mention me in any way, shape or form: that was a result. I felt like kissing him. I felt like running over to M&S and buying him a tin of celebration biscuits.

'Well, well, well. Miss Silver, that may very well be dynamite you have there,' said Roddy.

He paused.

'On the other hand, it may very well be a suicide bomb.'

Another hiatus.

'But, as luck would have it, I'm going to give you the benefit of the doubt, as I happen to think it's da bomb, baby.' A menacing look spread across Roddy's face. I attempted to smile back at him, but I was perturbed because his expression said he was about to deliver the sting in the tail. My instinct was bang on.

'But babe, you do realise if it all goes tits up, you go down with it, don't you?'

I nodded helplessly.

'It's your neck you're putting on the line with this, girl. You know that? Your picture, your neck, your tits... Ha ha, I like that.'

With that threat hanging in the air, he turned away efficiently.

I turned to the team. Adam, who was standing by my shoulder, gave me an affectionate squeeze.

'Let's go, guys. When we're done, the drinks are on me. Right?' I said.

'Too bloody right they are,' said Stephen.

8

Oooh Millennium – We Got Mick Hucknall Directing Our Fate

Rach and I had decided to spend our first Christmas together in Lillie road, to prove our independence. For the first time in our lives we wouldn't be doing the mum-and-dad thing up north. We got a little turkey dinner from M&S and even procured our own glowing neon Christmas tree from a dubious ex-display stall on the market.

It was cosy, just me and Rach in the flat. Just lacking the trimmings, that's all. The soft touches of luxury I had been cosseted with at home for Christmases past. Like the endless supply of Quality Street and those savoury fish-shaped snacks. Freedom and independence didn't feel quite so decadent now. I could definitely see the advantages of sitting around at home and letting the goodwill come to me.

The guilt was niggling away at me too. The thought of mum managing without me. Not being there to help if she had an off-day. Consoling myself with the thought that my brother was on leave, and that he and his wife would spend Christmas with them.

Marc had joined up as a soldier when he had just turned 17 and never looked back. Northern Ireland, Cyprus, then part of the first British deployment to Bosnia in 1993 with the Cheshire Regiment. Resourceful, good with people and quick to pick up the language even, they'd sent him back on a second tour 18 months later with the Paras, where he'd won lots of medals.

Like me, he'd wanted to get away from humdrum but that's where the similarities stopped. Marc was straight as a die and he actually wanted to help people, make a difference, serve his country. All that.

Earlier this year, even though he was married, he'd volunteered to go back for a third tour but this time his detachment had detoured to Kosovo. Now he was home on leave for Christmas with his wife. Just having him there would make mum happy, but it would be harder for her. She wouldn't ask them for help like she did with me, she'd have been too ashamed to ask – would want me to be the one helping them. Bending down and finding a hair-brush under the bed, the intimate stuff. Helping her get her tights on right when she felt wobbly. She would have pushed herself too much. Dad was useless at spotting when she overdid it. I'd been half thinking about going home until Ange called.

She was phoning me on Roddy's behalf.

'His Highness is giving you his VIP invitation to the ultimate Millennium New Year's Eve party, at the Dome. Aren't you a lucky girl? The Queen will be there and the prime minister.'

'Only 'cos they have to. Anyway, I don't like royalty. I only like Prince.'

Ange carried on, undeterred, 'and you get to invite a friend.' That did it, I couldn't hold it in any longer. 'Rachhh, you won't believe this…' I yelled.

It looked like a UFO had landed in the middle of the desolate swampland, exuding a purple neon light from its core. Gleaming yellow spikes pointed up to the night sky in flashy provocation, like a cabaret girl in fishnets lying on her back giving it 'you know you want me' to the world.

'Do you think if we go in there it will be like… forever, that we'll never come out, you know, like in *Close Encounters of the Third Kind*?'

'Er, no, Rach,' I said. I spotted a steward talking into a walkie-talkie and made my move. 'Excuse me, we are on the guest list.'

'That way,' he replied gruffly, pointing towards a queue without looking at us.

Rach barged through a clipboard woman and waved wildly at a startled-looking dignitary.

'That's my husband, excuse me please,' said Rach, pulling me with her.

I breathed a sigh of relief to find us in a room in which most people were holding a glass in their hand. 'I don't believe you just did that, Rach.'

'Attitude and determination, Toots,' she said, glancing around. 'Oh my God, Toots. Don't look now.'

'What, who is it?'

'It's flaming whatsisface.'

'Who?'

'Michael.'

My heart stopped. 'Oh my God.' What was it he did to me? I'd forgotten how incredibly lovely Michael was in the flesh.

I glanced up and saw him: deep in earnest conversation with another man.

Rachel, ignoring my look of panic, was hijacking the waiter, and produced two plastic glasses of white wine.

A scarlet-dress woman sauntered over to where they were talking and was enthusiastically welcomed into the conversation by Michael. She responded with a demure giggle and moved a step closer.

'You know who that is he's talking to, don't you?' whispered Rach, who was absolutely, totally and utterly in her element now. 'Isn't she gorgeous? She's so petite, so feline.'

'Yes, like a cute little pussy cat,' I replied.

'No, don't worry about her Toots; I've seen him in the papers. He's dating that girl from the telly now, the sexy, witty, clever, funny presenter one. They're like London's cool young, gifted couple – it said so in the *Standard*.'

'I feel much better for that knowledge, Rachel.'

I felt a stab of jealousy at the thought of his status and a little naïve for not knowing it. I tried to rationalise. What business was it of mine? I'd been away, a confidante of Clay Allison no less. Politicians were all dubious, wasn't that right? I looked over again and decided I didn't care; dubious suited me fine. I should have gone with my heart, not let Roddy's involvement bother me.

'Mick Hucknall and some opera singer fella are on the bill too!' said Rach with a curious expression.

'Oh sweet Jesus Christ, this is going to be a long night.'

Rachel let out a small involuntary scream. 'Fucking brilliant, though, isn't it?'

I realised we had found ourselves standing in line a couple of places behind Michael Dawson as we waited to be seated. I attempted to hide.

But I could feel the creeping sensation of a sneeze gathering strength. Eventually I couldn't hold it in any longer and it came out as a great explosive unglamorous bellow. '*Aarrghhhchoooooo.*'

Everyone in the queue, including Michael, turned around simultaneously to look at me. His eyes lit up with recognition, and he produced a handkerchief from his pocket and handed it to me wordlessly.

'Thank you' was all I could manage in response.

'No problem. You can give it back to me another time.' Radiant smile.

We were led in different directions to our seats. I wanted to follow him, take his hand, stand there at the dawn of the Millennium. Michael Dawson (representing all that is just and good) and Me (representing all that is shiny, slutty and showbiz). But my ticket said otherwise. Me and Rach were on a stand to the right of the main stage; the dignitaries and truly important people were to our left, facing the main stage.

Tony Blair and his wife Cherie were ushered in and led to their seats. The eyes of everyone in the building were drawn towards them. Then moments later we were summoned to rise from our seats for the Queen, a vision in orange.

I found my eyes drawn to Michael again, sitting a few rows back from the Blairs. As the show went on, I couldn't help glancing over at him. Having his handkerchief in my pocket was nice. I felt proud of him standing there amongst the great and the good.

I put the fabric to my face and could vaguely smell something of him, locked away in my memory.

'Toots, look at the Queen and Tony Blair now. It's hilarious; she doesn't know how to do it, look!' laughed Rach.

The Queen was limply holding the prime minister's hand as though it might be diseased and, possibly because of some weird royal decorum, had refrained from actually crossing arms like most people do when singing the traditional anthem.

'Cherie's making up for it though, she's giving it large,' I replied.

When the strike of midnight finally arrived, the place erupted, I turned to Rach and we hugged each other. Tears in our eyes. 'Happy New Year Rach, who'd have thought, eh?!'

'This is all for us, you know,' I winked. I stood there for a moment thinking about what I'd normally be doing, getting wrecked at the White Swan.

'Pass me my bag, Toots, I want to see if anyone has called me to wish me Happy New Year,' said Rach within two seconds of the New Year. 'Shit, I can't even get a friggin' signal.'

I glanced over to where Michael was standing and saw him kissing a woman next to him tenderly. I was bombed back to earth.

9
Cannes

Five am. My phone bleeped in my pyjama pocket. I'd started to keep it on me even in bed, permanently on call. My heart leapt and I felt the fear.

'Miss Silver, you have just struck gold.' Roddy's voice came down the line.

As I struggled to regain consciousness, the *Going for Gold* theme tune started going round in my head and I pictured myself as a contestant – except instead of Henry Kelly, Roddy was the inanely grinning host.

'This has to be the sexiest ticket in the showbiz calendar and I want you there centre stage, on the red carpet. I'm sending you to Cannes. Don't let me down.'

'Well, if anyone can, I Cannes...' I answered immediately, like a total prick.

'Any more of that and I'll make you take that new features' bird with you.'

'Who? Marisa?'

'Yes, her – the soft one. Anyway, get yourself to a fax machine and Ange will send you the itinerary. I repeat: do not let me down. Do not fail me. Oh, and by the way, I'm seeing your friend Michael on Friday for drinks. I'll send your regards. Hey, maybe you can catch up with Clay Allison while you're out there, his film's on the list.'

The phone went dead. The rush of fear turned to adrenalin. I decided to ignore the bit about Michael. I didn't want to think of him any more. I couldn't imagine why Roddy and he would be meeting for lunch. Michael had given me the impression he didn't like Roddy, Roddy the same. So this meant one or both of them was being disingenuous. After seeing Michael at New Year I'd concluded that was the end.

So I would concentrate on the trip. On meeting Clay Allison again. The thought gave me a thrill. I was going to Cannes, the film capital of the world. The home of glamour. Brigitte Bardot, Madonna, Béatrice Dalle, now me, Toots Silver. A vision of myself standing on a beach in the Pucci bikini sprang into my head. I was exhausted from the long hours of putting the last issue together, but Roddy must have known that incentivising me with the trip would be rejuvenation enough, while keeping me working, of course.

The easyJet flight to Nice was packed with film types on their way to the festival. The guy next to me leaned over and introduced himself. He had floppy black hair, wacky thick-rimmed glasses and a T-shirt with a beautiful woman shaving her bearded face. 'Hi, I'm Neil, are you a journalist or a PR or a film-maker?

'Oh yeah, erm… right first time, I'm a journalist.'

'Great, here, take my card.'

He went into his pitch without stopping for breath.

'I've made a film about a single mother from Salford, whose everyday pattern of hopelessness is a poetic commentary on the futility of modern society, and her gifted daughter, who is the rollerskating champion of the North-West, gives the story a com-pelling sense of possibility and future.'

'Oh! What's it called?'

'It's called *Reach for the Skates*,' he said, pressing the small card into my hand.

'Er… Rollerskates, thanks… nice…'

'Don't worry, I've got hundreds.' Neil opened his bag a little to show me wad upon wad of cards. Clearly business cards were the currency in Cannes. He was rich.

Shame I hadn't got any.

By the time we touched down, my purse was brimming with similar cards from people whose mission was to finance their incredible, inspirational films.

It was early evening but I was too excited to settle, so I hit a bar just off the Croisette. People watchers. Regulars. Office workers, loosening up under sundown. I took a seat outside and mooched with a cold beer.

An old-fashioned telephone tinkled on top of the zinc-plated counter. The maître d' answered, spoke briefly then laid the receiver down. He walked around through the tables as though he was looking for someone. Then settling on me, eyeing me up and down suspiciously. I expected him to tell me there was a call for me. But he looked concerned, quickly darted back to the phone (which looked like it had last been used by the French Resistance), and said 'Oui', nodding furiously. Something about his posture, an air of deference maybe, suggested to me that the person on the other end was important. Calling the shots even.

Within moments the murmur of polite conversation and daydreams was sonic-boomed by an almighty roar. The collective horsepower of a battle tank sent shockwaves reverberating down the narrow, stone street. Motorbikes, and lots of them. A swarm of leather-clad Hell's Angels pummelled along the cobbles. One by one, parking up their snarling motors next to the al fresco parasols. Big, burly, bearded. Gutted, studded, grizzly beasts. Twenty-five of them, chaotic but moving as one. Tribesmen.

The spectacle went on for a few minutes, until a pillion passenger got off the back of a Harley Davidson. This man wasn't like the rest. Dressed casually but suave. The only one not in leather. Unshaven but slim, more lace than leather. Most incongruously of all, under his right arm he carried a handsome, well-groomed fox terrier.

I couldn't take my eyes off the mystery man as he headed into the bar, asking myself what someone like him could be doing with these primal beasts? But he looked calm. Strolling around, the dog at his feet now. Arms outstretched, embracing the maître d', quick conversation. Then a wolf whistle through his fingers, gesturing to the mob, while the maître d' instructed multiple tables to be cleared.

The Angels didn't stay for long, inhaled their beers and disappeared, sending the briefly reconciled peace of the street into chaos once more. One of the bikers, with a red-and-white New York patch on his back, held on for a moment to speak to the terrier man privately, before smacking him fondly on the shoulder, by way of farewell.

The man settled their bill and then the dog on his lap. An exotic cigarette was sparked up from a Zippo. Fascinated now, I was overwhelmed with a desire to talk to him. This was the man with the story. I needed to know who he was.

I decided to give it a go, ask him for a light, see where it took me. Nodding at my request, then wordlessly, as I leaned in, whacking up the flame full pelt. Trying to catching me off guard, defying me to come into his circle without setting my hair on fire.

'Bonjour, do you speak English?' I asked him, trying to look unfazed. 'Je m'appelle Toots.'

'Good God. Bloody idiot woman.' Directing his words to the dog, but I was pretty sure he was speaking to me. 'I know that awful, desperate look, the tragedy of it. For heaven's sake. What do you want?'

'OK,' I said, pretty flabbergasted. 'Well, I guess someone who knows how things work around here, an insider? You look like you might be able to point me in the right direction, if that's not too strange a presumption.'

Pausing, he brushed a hair from the dog's face.

'Nine thirty at Chez Astoux, you're paying. I'll book. *Un table pour trois. À tout à l'heure.*'

At that, he upped from the table and headed to the street, the dog trotting on beside him.

'Thank you so much,' I said, reaching for a serviette to write down the name of the place, 'I'll definitely see you in there. Sorry, I didn't catch your...'

The man glanced back over his shoulder and I saw he was smiling at his own wonderful vivaciousness. '*Simon, et le Desirée, Enchanté,*' he replied.

I found my way to the restaurant without too much trouble, one of the established seafood places situated right on the front, opposite the Old Port. Sure enough, Simon had booked a table for three.

Desirée the dog strutted her stuff like a catwalk model, her neat little ginger tail as pert as the butt that wagged it. All the waiters came rushing over at once. Clearly Desirée was a regular, and Simon too, as they were greeted with a flurry of three kisses on each cheek and a warm pat on Desirée's furry backside as Simon lifted her up to greet her public.

Every year Desirée presented her own version of the prestigious Cannes award known as the Palm Dog, only it was presented to winning performances by cultivated canines in a movie, not actors.

I found out later that Simon's job was to make sure they met plenty of celebrities and to get Desirée's picture taken with them, which wasn't as hard as it might sound, given that (a) Desirée and Simon were charming and (b) celebrities were always eager to show their humorous side. Either that or they were just bamboozled by the absurdity of it all. But this was just his day job. Simon seemed to have a passport to the more shadowy world of celebrities, one in which the beefcakes on bikes also played their part. So far, I just hadn't figured what or how.

'Drink?' I offered by way of introduction, instinctively avoiding any boring, unnecessary niceties. On cue, the waiter arrived with a bottle of something crisp and white that Simon said he always had at this establishment and went perfectly with oysters.

And we were having oysters. True to form, I'd never had oysters before and felt pretty damn sure the Welsh terrier on Simon's lap knew infinitely more about how to eat them than I did. Desirée looked at me, tongue hanging out, as if to confirm it.

Just as I was about to begin my patter about how I needed just a little bit of guidance, being an oik and that, Sebastian arrived. Sebastian was our dinner guest and Simon's surly French boyfriend, who he hooked up with in Cannes. Simon had a different lover in Paris, he informed me matter of factly.

They kissed and scowled at each other, a grumpy sexual passion of sorts, I guessed. Simon then began talking to Sebastian in English with a practised French accent, which was so pronounced it seemed to obscure the need to actually speak in the language. He was amazing. Or, as he would say in 'French', 'Eye eees amaazing.'

I stood up to offer Sebastian my chair. Desirée was already seated and I didn't have the nerve to shift her. Besides, I understood my role as the underdog.

This broke the ice at least, sending Simon and Sebastian into hysterics.

'Sit down you daft bitch,' Simon said, nudging Desirée to the ground gently. I assumed he was talking to me and seated myself humbly in the warmth of her seat.

A flurry of excitement ensued as the waiter produced platters of ice topped with what the waiter called '*une exquise assiette d'huitres*' wobbling around in their pearly-shelled glory. I was relieved to see they had been opened already and I wouldn't have to perform the tricky task of chiselling one. All I had to do was slurp it down with some pink vinegary stuff. But as I homed in on one, something moved.

'Simon, there is something crawling around in my oyster, like a little grub thing. Is that normal?'

Simon lunged over and peered at my oyster, laughing out loud gleefully. 'Theese means it eees sooo fresh, darling. Eat it. *Bon appétit.*'

It was a challenge rather than a command; failure to do so would also mean social rejection. And I figured, as they say in France, *le ridicule ne tue pas*. Either I rose to the occasion and proved to this incredible man that I was a woman with enough balls to swallow any critters that crossed my palate or I walked away now to face the music alone, like one of the lonesome hangers-on with autograph books and carrier bags who stood outside on the Boulevard de la Croisette waiting for celebrities.

Holding my breath, I raised the cold mass of living matter to my mouth and let it slip down my throat like a cold, thick blob of snot. I gulped and felt a rush to my head. Then I looked up to see Simon roaring in approval. We both laughed. From that moment on, we were partners in crime. Masters of the absurd.

Sebastian smoked. He did not eat. He did not laugh. Then he left. Desirée sipped an oyster under the table and wagged her tail on the floor in enthusiastic endorsement.

Outside, Simon made a flurry of phone calls, his expression serious, assuming another persona, which I wouldn't have expected. In control and firm – a glimpse of his dark side.

'C'mon, we're going on somewhere.'

Our taxi climbed the winding route that would take us to an exclusive party being held at a secret location in the steep hills beyond the town. Simon whooped with laughter as the taxi driver nearly killed us on a sharp bend.

'Now, darling, you will thank your uncle Simon for this, I know.'

When Simon spoke to me, he did so with his strongest Yorkshire accent, as if to underline the fact he was briefing a unsophisticated idiot. It was an affectionate distinction to demonstrate we were conspiring together as undercover common folk.

'Quite frankly, luv, you're unworthy of such an event. You being there can only be explained by the fact that you are with me. So please, my sweet, dearie, darling, don't do anything stupid. Just look pretty and stick to me like glue until I tell you otherwise. At which point, disappear pronto, because I might be talking to someone interesting.'

'What? More interesting than me, Simon?' I said.

'Precisely, which won't be hard. I am probably the only person there who will understand a single word you say in your thick Northern accent anyway. You have that in your favour. It may even mask your banality, a little.' Simon winked at me as he spoke. Every five minutes or so, he took a phone call, whispering down the line in French and huddling up in the corner of the seat as he spoke.

'At least mine's real. Better than your comedy French one, Simon. How long have we been in this cab anyway?' I smiled. I figured it was best not to ask him who he was talking to because I knew he wouldn't tell me anyway.

'Hush, we are approaching our destination. Now remember, breathe in, look serious and interesting, and sashay, don't slouch.'

The car stopped precariously at the edge of the mountainside; the magical view of Cannes lay beneath us, illuminated orange in the haze of the setting sun. Beckoning us into the chateau was a drawbridge lit with hundreds of tiny silver fairy lights. At either side, aquamarine silk scarves positioned as flags billowed in the warm night air.

In the courtyard, waiters milled around serving champagne and canapés to the guests, resplendent in their honed film-star Cannes catwalk perfection. On closer inspection I saw there was an edgier crowd too. This was the Cannes of a new generation where actors and dance DJs mingled with pop princesses, who'd come over from London to soak up the atmosphere.

There were also those odd celebrity hangers-on who seemed part and parcel of all such occasions, the yang to the yin. Sanjay and Debs, formerly from *EastEnders*, and squat-bodied Mick Hucknall yet again, surveying the room like a deadly spider. Lips wet with saliva, Hucknall dived on any strays straddling the party, plucking them into his web with his 'friends in high places and full wallet' mode of seduction.

I laughed to myself, remembering Rach at the millennium concert, piss-take dancing to him as he sang some ballad. She'd confessed how as a thirteen-year-old she'd gone to see Simply Red perform at Manchester Free Trade Hall, got so cidered up she'd attempted to get on stage with him, only to be lifted away by bouncers, as she warbled *Sad Old Rach*. She would have loved tonight, although she was much too sophisticated for Mick these days. I wondered what she was doing now. Eating cold cocktail sausages from the fridge?

Simon's crisp running commentary on the night's events made the whole spectacle even more entertaining.

'This guy has the power to lift these girls from strutting around in their pants on the catwalk to the Hollywood stratosphere where they really want to be. Watch him work them,' Simon said, pointing at a collective of Victoria's Secrets models. Crowded around the imposing frame of the film mogul, they looked like a row of box-fresh Barbie dolls, with beautiful hair and perfect breasts.

'How do they manage to laugh like that, without snorting or showing their teeth? When I laugh, I do this weird choking thing,' I whispered in Simon's ear.

'Yes, you do, sweetie, but they are not made from the same stuff as you or I. They are well-bred racing horses and you, my dear, are a pit pony. That is why.'

'A well-dressed pit pony?' I inquired.

'Last season,' Simon whispered, before clicking his tongue at me, as if telling a pony to 'trot on', whisking me down another seductive corridor of the chateau. After a few seconds Simon spotted a famous face he planned to ambush for a photo op with Desirée. He disappeared, leaving me alone in a corridor.

Suddenly, the party stopped being intriguing and beguiling and became strange and alien. I looked down at my outfit, which had looked passable when I put it on but now felt a little bit understated next to everyone else's full-on glamour. I was a sprat in a sea of exotic tropical fish. My instinct was to finish my champagne and go. But I wasn't quite sure how to hail a cab from the mountainside.

Conscious I needed to check in with Roddy the next day, I felt the pressure to do something, but what?

As I turned to look for an escape route, I felt arms slipping around my waist. Then a seductive voice murmured in my ear.

'Pocket Bardot?'

I turned and saw that face. That incredible face. Relief and joy. I smiled massively. Too massively.

'Hey, missed you,' he said flippantly.

'Me too,' I said.

And I suppose in a way I had, I just never meant to say it out loud. It must have been the relief talking, that something was going my way. His charm extended to everyone, I knew that, but it didn't stop it being enticing.

Clay smiled knowingly. Confirmation again of his firm and

entrenched belief in himself as an irresistible magnet to all womankind.

'I mean I missed our challenging conversations,' I corrected
myself, too late. I was eager to realign myself on the edge with
my cultivated image of a brainbox journalist. 'What better place to
continue our discussion about the transience of fame than Cannes?
The ultimate celebration of the fleeting moment of glory.'

'You looked like you were rather enjoying yourself from here,
going with the free flow?' he said coolly, gesturing to my empty
glass.

'Well, obviously one has to get into the spirit of things. Watching the celebrated congratulate themselves takes some inebriation.
The alcohol just sweetens the bitter taste it all leaves in my mouth.'

What the hell was I talking about now? I'd gone from one
extreme to the other, from seductive to destructive. It was like a
repeat of my feminist rant at the pool. Round Two. But why? We
had moved on from that in LA, we were friends, sort of, we'd had
dinner, hung out.

Clay motioned to one of his hangers-on for a drink, almost
imperceptibly. It was a gesture so practised as to appear he was
merely scratching a mild itch. But to the entourage surrounding
him, it was a signal potent enough to send them scurrying back
and forth like ants.

The minion appeared. I was aware of how amazing she was:
petite, fit, just short of perfect: they all looked like this. She fitted
in well with the crowd of celebrated folk, just a few percent short
of being one of them. She looked smug on delivery of the drink,
like a self-satisfied mother who had just brought a bottle of milk
to soften her child's cries. I pondered momentarily what it must
be like to be an adult in possession of that sort of immense power,
whose every pout and scream is responded to by those around
them with adoration and without question.

But wasn't I guilty too? Performing to the best of my abilities,
trying to titillate the star in my midst?

'Refreshing,' replied Clay, and for a moment I wasn't sure
whether he was talking about my hard-bitten honesty routine, or

the drink. 'Crystal-clear Cristal,' he continued, gazing affection-ately at the pale yellow liquid in the glass. I realised he was defi-nitely, 100 percent referring to the obscenely expensive brand of champagne he was drinking.

Tonight Clay was dressed as the superstar doing casually gor-geous, a rich man's version of understated style. Perfectly fitted jeans and a brown kid-leather jacket, which looked so soft and supple I wanted to stroke it. His hair thick and rich, like he had good blood running through his veins. And his face was as poster-boy perfect as any human being had the right to be. Damn him. It must have taken ages to look so undone.

'What are you doing here? Work or pleasure?'

'Yeah, it's all pleasure in my life, babe. I'm on a promo for a movie we shot last year, *The Tangible Lie*. Seventy-two hours here, then we go to Berlin or somewhere. Hey, Jen, where we go next?' he called over.

'Rome, sweetie,' minion Jen replied on cue.

'Wherever,' Clay shrugged. 'It's all the same shit. You, babe?'

'Oh, I'm here for the mag. Deciphering the atmospheric details for the purposes of providing wonderment and fulfillment for the masses, whose lives, in comparison, are frankly rather crap.'

'Like it. Funny,' he said, not actually breaking into a smile or anything. 'You still make me laugh, Toots.'

'Do you want to see a real Cannes party then? Strictly for your own wonder this time?' he asked, eyeing me suggestively.

I nodded dutifully, as many before me had, no doubt. And I was hand in hand with Clay, being led through the chateau to his wait-ing car.

Catching Simon's eye as we whisked past, I saw something pass between Clay and him. They knew each other? I wasn't sure. Then astonishment and even a touching note of concern passed across his face, as he saw me outperforming myself.

I supposed I probably looked a little bit smart arsed, walking out like that, tail in the air. Or maybe I looked like I'd taken leave of my senses. I probably had. I'd forgotten I barely knew him. Forgotten he had a girlfriend. His terrible reputation. I was just remembering the excitement of my time in LA with him. I got into his car. Never get in a car with a stranger, well never get in a car with a stranger unless it's got a chauffeur. It's all right then, isn't it? I suspended all reasonable doubts, Hollywood style. I was going with the fantasy.

But still, the look on Simon's face lingered in my mind.

As the car headed off down the mountain, Clay squeezed my hand, lying next to his on the seat, and a surge of delight passed through me and all else faded from my memory.

10
Starsucker

The yacht was berthed on the Cannes seafront, easily within walking distance of my apartment. The moment I set foot on board I felt like I'd entered a parallel universe.

Just the act of being suspended on water seemed to add to the feeling. It was done out like a harem, a posh pulling pad, with beautiful Moroccan fabrics, silk throws and antique Persian rugs. The ambience was sheer luxury, smelling divinely of the finest fragrant candles and the purest, sweetest essential oils, bergamot, sandalwood, ylang-ylang, which burned gently, making my brain soften like putty.

Lo-fi Indian beats grooved softly on the surround-sound music system, complementing the sound of the waves lolling up against the boat. They seemed like they were programmed to hit the same spot. The atmosphere was designed to say Karmic cool, or something mad like that. I had to hand it to him: it blew my mind.

'Where is everyone else?' I asked.

'It's not that kind of party,' Clay replied.

He put something small in my hand and popped something in his mouth. 'Ecstasy, that's all,' he shrugged, so I put a pill in my mouth as well.

We washed it down with champagne, straight from the bottle. Clay led me out onto the deck with one hand, holding the neck of the bottle in the other.

There was a massive, ostentatious white sunbed positioned invitingly in the middle of the deck. It was easily as big as mine and Rachel's living room. Clay beckoned me over so we could both lie down, heads back, looking at the millions of stars above our heads in the otherwise black expanse.

'Makes you feel kind of insignificant when you look at them, doesn't it? Like we're just one tiny little speck of light, burning among a million others, exactly the same as each other.'

'Yeah, I guess. Or maybe it's different for you, Clay? Do you feel like you burn a bit brighter than everyone else? Is that what the difference is? Are you that one?' I asked, pointing at a brightly flickering star in the distance.

'Yeah, that's me, for sure.' He actually laughed this time. 'Sometimes, I do. On a good day, that is. I know I've got something I can give people. Something bigger, that will get into their heads, I guess. Then, on another day, I'm maybe just that one.' He pointed at a smaller star. 'But everyone is expecting me to do the fireworks stuff, only this time a bit brighter and a bit longer. Then, you know, it's kind of hard to get to that place.'

I could feel the warmth of the Ecstasy coming up and it made me feel like I was glowing from the inside. Clay took my arms and held me down by the wrists, smiling at me, challenging me. I was charged with sexiness, suffused with a beautiful erotic glow, deliciously happy. The contact from his body felt electric, my sharpened instincts were like an animal's; my ears pricked up, my eyes were dancing, drinking him in. It was the drug most likely, not his star quality, but I was willing to give him the benefit of the doubt.

'More fireworks please,' I said. 'More fireworks.'

His eyes were amazing: wild and vivid. He kept them open and kissed me. I closed mine for a moment and felt the softness of his mouth against mine. 'Yes, I'm feeling them now, definitely feeling them.'

All my senses were on overload. Greed took over: he was too much, yet I wanted it all. And we merged into the universe, in a sea of strange fireworks. And yeah, if I'm honest, the earth moved. But then we were on a boat. Gravity was on his side. Even gravity was on his side. Mother Nature wanted to please this man; she knew he was a star.

'*Puppy Love* – you know, like the Donny Osmond song.'

I was looking at a bright pink canvas. It depicted a black dog humping *Star Wars*' R2-D2. Doggy style, I guess you'd call it.

It was the first thing I saw when I regained focus the next morning. The sight of it ensured the general feeling of whoreiness and earth-crashing comedown I was about to experience; it gave me a heads-up before my sorry head was even off the pillow. It was all I deserved. I felt vulnerable now, exposed and sober, out of my comfort zone. Last night had been dreamy and now it was real. I wasn't sure I was ready for this bit.

'Do you like it? It's a Bansky.'

Clay was standing at the far corner of the bedroom, holding a mobile phone out against his ear, looking at it like it was an alien object. He was wearing a silky Indian bathrobe, open at the front; he was naked underneath. Clay didn't look at me as he talked, but I assumed it was me he was addressing, as I was the only person here, to my knowledge.

'I collect art, don't I?' As if it was a given that he would, someone in his position. 'This guy Bansky's where it's at apparently. My investors are never wrong.'

'Yeah, um, it's erm, cryptic. Umm. Yeah. Hectic,' I offered by way of a response.

'What the fuck is wrong with this thing?' He hit the phone on the wall. It was just as well. I wasn't really up for discussing art right now and even if I had been I'd have preferred something a bit more friendly, like a nice landscape or something. Something that said romance, not animal sex. And if we were going to get clever about it, I suspected the message this particular piece of art conveyed was that Clay was the dog and I was the *Star Wars* robot getting hoofed.

He was going out. I gathered this from the conversation he was having with one of his assistants on the other line.

'OK, so car's five minutes, babe. Yeah. Why the fuck hasn't anyone done my packing? I'm so sick of this, Sarah. How many times? Where did we get her from? How the fuck am I expected to function? And why do you never answer your fucking phone...? I don't care where you are, you know the score, go take a piss later, you're on my time, you piss later, or piss your fucking pants. Piss-taker. Yeah whatever. Come over later and just make sure it's done. You can send the bags to me, all right? Later... Later... Later...' He snapped the device shut.

By this time, I'd managed to procure a towel from the floor, which I'd wrapped around myself modestly, before I began the humbling task of looking for my knickers. Which could have been, by all accounts, absolutely anywhere.

Clay had other ideas. 'Listen I've got to go, but find yourself a hat and a pair of sunnies before you leave, will ya? There's a stack in the wardrobe through there. Paparazzi, you know babe. Can't be seen leaving the boat. OK. Cool. See ya later, babe, call ya, arrange something. Good times.'

'Good times,' I replied, disturbed, in mild disarray.

And there it was. 'Good times.' Was that a reference to his enjoyment and gratification last night, or an 'of-the-moment' catchphrase? Hard to say. But that was it. That was our postcoital chat. Our intimate moment of reflection.

Nevertheless, I dutifully began my mission to leave undetected. I would keep his copybook clean, erase myself from the surroundings. Thanks to my Ecstasy hangover I was wildly, illogically paranoid that paps might be surrounding the whole yacht, lenses poised at the ready like I was Princess Di getting off Dodi's yacht or something. So I crawled out onto the deck commando-style, on my belly, shuffling on the towel to gather my clothes, fearing if I stood up the paps would pounce on me.

Having said that, a photograph of me like that, white backside in the air and shimmying onto the deck, would have been a whole lot better. Dynamite, probably. I looked like I'd been taken hostage for a night of debauchery and was trying to escape – which wouldn't have been that far from the truth, if I hadn't come so willingly.

My clothes were strewn next to the white star-gazing love machine. Looking at it now, I could see the sunbed routine in a whole new light. How many girls had lain there before me looking up at the night sky? A zillion? More? One for each star, up there…

Humbly, I began the task of disguising myself, getting ready to leave in one of the morning-after-the-night-before hat-and-glasses combos Clay had kindly laid on, ready for such eventualities. Teamed with a skimpy party dress, it was a bizarre look. I looked like a fool and felt even worse. Cheap. Who would have thought it was possible to feel so cheap after a night of passion on a multimillion-pound yacht?

Banksy's dog looked at me in his robot-fucking triumph.

'And you can fuck off 'n' all,' I said.

As it turned out, I passed by unnoticed. A couple of paps were stood at the quayside, but they carried on as normal, smoking cigarettes, enjoying a break thanks to the early-morning lull in activity. Other than that it was quiet except for a Hell's Angel sitting on his bike opposite the boat.

Weirdly, once I knew I'd got away anonymously, a different feeling crept in. What was it? A yearning? A longing? I didn't want to be photographed, but I didn't want to go back to normal either.

My phone went off in my bag. Was it him?

'Now, miss, I think you have some explaining to do, don't you?' said Simon on the other end.

'Oh my God, yes, yes. Sorry.' I felt terrible. I'd completely forgotten Simon.

'Do you realise how long it takes to walk from a mountainside at three o'clock in the morning in the pitch dark? All you can hear is the sea crashing below you like a wild animal. You can't know the despair of not knowing where the cliffs end. It's like walking on a knife's edge. Your toes cling to the ground. All you can do is cry out in the wilderness, 'elp, 'elp, hoping a kind French farmer might find you and guide you home.'

'Oh Christ, Simon, I'm so sorry. I had no idea I would end up leaving like that. It was just exceptional circumstances. When did you get back?'

'Back? I'm not back. I'm still walking, Toots, I may never be back…' His voice trailed off into a whisper. I stood there on the spot, dumbstruck for a few seconds, not knowing what to do. He was lost and it was all my fault.

Suddenly I heard a disgusting hoot of laughter behind me, and I turned to see Simon sat in the corner café opposite, on the phone. Desirée sat at his feet, head to one side, unimpressed.

'You bastard,' I mouthed at him as I walked over, shaking my head but smiling.

'Pot, kettle, madam,' said Simon. 'Now sit down and order me a croissant, you little harlot. You owe me breakfast. And out of interest, what the hell are you wearing? This is Cannes, luv, not Camberwell.'

I didn't have time to change my clothes, as it turned out, but I did ditch the stupid hat. Simon was keen we get to a film screening immediately after breakfast. And because I understood that this was what people did for work in Cannes, I was going along. I needed to do something to justify my existence here.

At that moment the ringtone went off in my bag again. Hoping it was Clay, I grabbed it immediately. It was Rach this time: I recognised the number. I so wanted to speak to her, to ground me, make light of things, help me rationalise, but Simon was whistling at me and I knew I had no option, so I let the call go.

And that was what we did for the next few days: go from film screening to party, to beach, to film party and so on. I picked up stories for the magazine. Roddy was satisfied. I was having an amazing time. But all the while in the back of my mind I was hoping I might bump into Clay again.

Even though I didn't explicitly tell Simon about what happened on the yacht, he certainly didn't need me to spell it out. Once the floodgates had been opened, I'd been on about it ever since. I hadn't told Rach, though; after not telling her immediately, it didn't seem right to slip it into the conversation later somehow. In our phone calls I'd stuck to the films, the parties and stuff. 'Having a blast, it's amazing here. The clothes are incredible too, the cars, the money, you wouldn't believe,' the peripheral stuff. So, Simon was getting it instead. I did this in the full knowledge he was as about as discreet as a Vivienne Westwood basque on a glamour model, but my stupidity and self-indulgence ruled.

'How do you return to normal when you've been bitten by the celebrity love bug? With an actual lovebite to prove it? When you've bedded one of the hottest people on the planet, according to America's very own *People* magazine, Simon? Do you just go back to being one of the "Not Hot One Hundred"? Or do you raise your game and stride forwards to claim your own piece of the celebrity pie?'

'Darling, shut up. I'm watching the film and it's been three days now you have been banging on about this. Can you purlease change the record *s'il vous* fuckin' *plaît*? Just be grateful you have been touched by the hand of celebrity, felt up by it, sweetie, that's more than most, and move on. And get yourself a good once-over by the doctor when you get back home. No one wants to wear a nasty virus as a badge of honour whether it's a celebrity-endorsed version or not. Believe me, there is no status involved in A-list VD.'

'Simon! Leave it out.'

'Listen, sweetie, wake up and smell the eight-euro-a-pop espresso. You are not the first starry-eyed honey to crank up another notch on his gold-leaf bedpost. I'm telling you this because I care. And, frankly, because I'm bored. So let's finish watching the film and get back to what we are good at. Having a good time.'

Simon kissed my hand to show his scorn was well intended, and I turned my attention back to the film screening. If anything, the film made me feel worse. It was *Nurse Betty* starring Renée Zellweger as the eponymous delusional nurse who, after suffering post-traumatic stress disorder, becomes obsessed with a soap-star idol.

'I haven't even got bereavement to blame for my malaise; Nurse Betty's husband died. Maybe I'm suffering post-traumatic sex disorder?' I whispered to Simon, but he pointedly ignored me.

By the time the film was over, I'd just about put Clay to the back of my mind. But when we left, the whole situation was made immeasurably more terrible by the fact that little reminders of Clay had suddenly popped up all over Cannes. Not so little actually: ten-foot-tall billboards of him advertising *The Tangible Lie*, coming soon to a cinema near you. It was like he was haunting me with his million-dollar smile.

I decided to try and remember personal things about my Clay in order to separate the experience we shared together as lovers from the man in the picture. The smell of him. The tattoo on his back, written in Cherokee Indian script, to commemorate his ancestral heritage. His mother's name, Lily Sue, in a little heart with a ribbon through it, tattooed on his bicep. (At least that's whose name he'd said it was.)

I remembered his explanation when I'd asked him what they all meant.

'My body is a journal, in a way. It's what sailors used to do, where every tattoo meant something, a specific time in your life. When you make a mark on yourself, you give it a permanent place.'

'Maybe that's what I should do,' I said to Simon. 'Have a tattoo, get the whole thing out of my system and confine it to history. A commemorative tattoo. Something nice. What would it say?'

'Starsucker?' offered Simon crisply.

Once it was clear I'd exhausted Simon's sympathy, I decided it was time to finally tell Rachel. But all she could offer me was awestruck enthusiasm, which just made my hunger even greater.

'Clay All-is-on. Oh my God. That is just sooo amazing, unbelievable, he is absolutely gorgeous... A yacht. An actual yacht. Jesus, Toots, did you get a picture? Did you get his autograph for me this time?'

'No, I did not get his autograph. What was I going to do? Stop him in the middle of everything and say, "By the way, my mate Rachel, she's a really big fan, do you think you could sign this for me?" Pull out a photo from my handbag?'

'OK get you. But what was he like? You know, what was it like? He is amazing, isn't he? Tell me it was amazing...'

'He was amazing.'

'I knew it. So are you going to see him again?'

'I don't know. He said his assistant would call.'

'Wow, cool, has she?'

'No. Not yet.'

Rachel sensed the disappointment seeping into my voice. 'She will, Toots, don't worry. Imagine how busy he must be. He is, like, the biggest star on the planet.'

Rach had confirmed what I knew in my heart: it was his assistant's fault. Sarah was just inefficient and not worthy of being Clay's PA. Poor Clay, he was right: you just couldn't get the staff nowadays.

'By the way, Toots, when are you coming home? The electricity bill's come and I'm short.'

'Tomorrow. Don't worry, I'll pay. Fill you in then. Got to go. Love you, Rach. Bye.'

'Bye... And Toots?'

'Yes?'

'Wow.'

11
Back to Life, Back to Grim Reality

A grey May morning. There was nothing spring-like about it. The clouds hung overhead like the low ceiling of a factory roof where you've just clocked on for an eight-hour shift. It wasn't raining as such, but there was a fine mist of drizzle in the air, enough to make everyone look lank and lacklustre. Unforgiving, unglamorous London.

The flat was freezing. The fact that it was the basement of an old Victorian terrace meant it was pretty much saturated with damp, and without the benefit of heaters 24/7 it smelled like a musty boot. I tried to plug in a heater, warm up a bit while I unpacked, but the thing wouldn't turn on. In fact, none of the lights seemed to be working. Neither was the toaster.

Pinned to the fridge was a note from Rachel saying 'Sorry ran out of cash!' in swirly pink 'forgive me, I'm a girl' script. I glanced from the note to the picture of Clay, then pulled them both down, screwed them up and threw them in the bin.

Opening the fridge door, it belched warm, rank breath back at me. There was no food and even if there were, it would not be fit for human consumption.

I thought of the last meal I'd eaten in Cannes: baguette au fromage, chewy and fresh, washed down with ice-cold sparkling water for my breakfast. Simple everyday luxury. Money wasn't an issue there. I'd planned to put everything I'd put on my credit card down as expenses. My mind was still in Cannes with the turquoise sea and the warm sunshine beating down. I thought of the rows of seafood restaurants up the hills behind the port. The beach parties, the fashion, the shops... Clay Allison.

Leaving my bag on the bedroom floor and shutting the door, I headed to the bar instead to wait for Rach.

It was hard to be angry when she breezed in. I'd missed her loads, for one thing, and besides, she was the most colourful thing I'd seen since I'd got back. Destiny's Child's *Independent Women* was blasting out triumphantly from the bar, and she did a little jiggle to the song, mouthed the chorus and threw her hands up in the air as the song commanded, strutting towards me, like it was a kind of victory march. The irony was completely lost on her. Draped in a lime-green pashmina tied in a Fulham knot, over washed-out jeans and a animal-print baguette handbag, she was easily the most stylish skint person I'd ever seen.

'Hi Rach. I've seen the fridge.'

'I know, I know. You're looking at my bag, thinking, "That's my electricity she's wearing," but Toots, without looking the part I'd lose my job. Know this. Also, it's really hard being surrounded by delicious stuff all day without getting to have just a teeny-weeny taste... So good to see you, Toots. I'm so, so very sorry.'

'I just don't get it, Rachel. They can't have cut off the leccy after just one late bill. I've been giving you way enough money to cover it. It just doesn't make sense. It's a mistake, that's all. Don't worry, babe, I'll speak to them, sort it out.'

'Yeah, erm, I know. You are technically right.' She paused. 'But it's not that straightforward. I've been meaning to tell you for weeks, actually. I had a problem. I had to take a little loan from the money you've been giving me and it kind of never made its way to Mister Electricitee. And I had to borrow some of it to get my uniform for work and stuff, and even with the discount they give us it's just massively expensive. So basically what I'm telling you is...'

'You spent it.'

Rachel looked at me teary-eyed and smiled, a sort of pathetic upside-down smile that confirmed her earlier comment. She was indeed wearing my heat, light and hot water.

At least it looked good. Not especially warm, mind.

Beyoncé and the girls carried on defiantly in the background to the declaration of female independence at the end.

We had let ourselves down. We had let Beyoncé down.

Although I was sure I had given Rach enough money to cover my bills and more, somewhere, in between my giving her my share and her paying it to the landlord, it had evaporated in her purse. So I rang my dad. To beg.

I spent the rest of the day alternating between phone calls to the electricity board, the landlord and my parents, who agreed, magnanimously, to lend us the money we needed to cover the bill.

I hated asking them, particularly as I hadn't so much as called them to say hello in weeks. Speaking to Mum and Dad reminded me of real life and it all felt slightly at odds with my new one. I'd convinced myself they wouldn't understand, although deep down I knew they'd just be proud. Maybe it was me who didn't feel particularly proud? When I spoke about this stuff to them, it all sounded, well, faintly ridiculous and shallow. Nevertheless, I wasn't due my next pay packet till the end of next week, so this time I had no choice but to call them. Rachel's mum was broke (like mother like daughter), so it was up to my mum and dad to bail us out.

It was made more humiliating when I had to have one of those breezy catch-up conversations. Somehow lately, I'd become anaethetised from hearing about mum's MS. The obstacles she faced, which had incensed me daily when I lived at home, seemed more detached from me now. These days it was easier, anyway; all we talked about was me. I perpetuated their image of me with the usual series of elaborate lies strung together with occasional facts, for the purpose of giving them the story they wanted to hear. I described how 'smashing' it was in France, omitting all details of the smashing 24-hour hedonism package and my smashing sex antics with a global superstar.

Instead I relied on details like, 'You'll never guess what I did: I tried oysters for the first time.'

To which they whooped and gasped, especially Mum. Then they went into a Monty Python-style whipped-up routine about the experience, which they did in these situations. Only I wasn't in the mood. It felt all wrong explaining that stuff to them, it was unnatural, and I felt the fairy dust losing its lustre with every line that came out of my mouth.

'Ooh, fancy that, oysters! D'ya hear that, John, she's tried oysters. Well I never, can you believe it? Our Toots tried oysters, fresh seafood at la med. We must be going up in the world,' said my mum down the phone, as though I'd been invited personally to take tea with the Queen at the palace. 'Hang on a minute, I'll just get your dad, he'll want to hear this for himself...'

Before I had the chance to make up an excuse, he was on the other end.

'What's this I've been hearing about oysters? Goodness me, what will it be next? Caviar most likely. When I was your age I didn't even know that sardines didn't always come in a can. That and Spam we had. Mind you, nothing wrong with that. Underrated, really.'

'Shut up dad, it wasn't the war!'

'And tongue.'

Oh for fuck's sake... I resisted the temptation to tell him I'd had my share of that in Cannes as well.

'And that was as a treat.' He was still going. 'Well, Toots, I've got to tell you I'm extremely proud of you. A young girl like you experiencing so many things.'

I tried to block the image of the wildly exotic things I had experienced in Cannes that immediately sprang to mind. Things that would boggle and befuddle my sweet father's mind.

'Thanks, Dad,' I muttered instead. 'It means a lot.'

Luckily, they were impressed enough not to be struck by the jarring discrepancy of it all. While I'd been slurping down the best of France's finest culinary delicacies, they'd been the ones footing the bill. It felt humiliating and childish to wait until the end of all this and then ask them for money. If I had earned the praise, then I wouldn't have been asking my parents to transfer money into my account for my electricity bill, would I? Their sweet-natured excitement and my cunning duplicity made me want to cry. If I'd taken the time to think about what was happening, I might have realised that the more absorbed I became in that world, the more it cost me – and them, for that matter. But I was too far gone for that.

The Cannes trip felt like a world away now. I wanted to go back to that heady, spirited world where the only electricity people thought about was the magic of the movies or the flash behind the eyes of the people in them. I thought about calling Simon, but listening to him glamming it up in Paris would be too much to bear. Then I thought of Clay again. Then I did cry. He was the one person who could restore the feeling, the only one in possession of the magic I was craving.

Rachel came into my room, sat down on the bed next to me, silently handed me a tissue and put her arm around my heaving shoulders. 'I know all this is a bit shit, Toots, it must be awful coming back to all this hassle especially after, you know, him. But it's just a blip. Thanks for asking your folks for the loan. You saved the day, and you know I'll pay it back.'

I looked at her and nodded. Maybe it would be all right. 'OK.'

'Still bloody freezing, isn't it?' said Rach.

I clicked into gear again. There was no way I was sitting here moping around, even if I was still annoyed. I decided to do something about it. 'Let's go to Blue Elephant, get some Thai food in our bellies, see where it takes us, eh?' I said, and instantly Rach's big toothy grin landed on her lovely face again.

Seventy-two hours later, we were back in the luxurious land of warm, electrically powered living. I was taking particular pleasure in the joy of a warm shower after two days of cold ones and copiously heaped crème brûlée sugar scrub onto my body. I felt good enough to eat and forgot the time. Stepping out of the bathroom, I could feel the knot forming in my stomach before my phone even rang, such was Roddy's power. Some kind of primal response. I knew instinctively it was him.

'Hi, Miss Silver,' Roddy purred, in frighteningly charming mode.

This meant he was about to hit me with something nasty, or was angry and pretending to be nice.

'Oh hi Roddy, I'm back. Well, I guess you knew that. Anyway, here I am, raring to go. Just on my way in actually. Any, erm, news? Anything to report?'

'Apart from the obvious, Toots?'

'Erm, that being?'

'Oh, you know, just the fact that the first editions of your maiden magazine have just landed on my desk and you're not even within spitting distance of them.'

'Oh fuck! Oh sorry! I mean, oh shit! Of course. I forgot. Well, of course I didn't forget exactly, not that, of course not that. I mean I forgot to tell you, that is, that I would be 15, sorry, 20 minutes late. The train, that is, not me. Wouldn't miss it for the world. So annoying. See you in a jiffy.'

The phone went dead. Roddy had hung up. I legged it to the Tube, panicked but excited nonetheless at the prospect of seeing the magazine, my new, revamped magazine.

The cover. Oh my God. It hit me like a tonne of bricks. What would Clay think when he saw it, saw us? What had I done? What on earth had I done? Like some sort of crazed bunny-boiler. That was what he'd think: that I was a lunatic living out my fantasy on the front of my magazine. That I was stalking him.

I breathed in slowly and tried to think. But I hadn't had sex with him when I'd decided on the cover, had I? I mean at that point I might have imagined it, but I didn't know it would actually happen. It must have been like a premonition or something. I hadn't known I would look like a mentalist at the time, had I? Convincing Clay of that might be a different matter, though.

The atmosphere in the office was euphoric already. The staff were all looking bright-eyed and bushy-tailed for about the first time in their working lives in anticipation of seeing the magazine in print.

'Hey, guys, great to see you. Ready for the grand unveiling?' I shouted across the room, trying to bravado it out.

'You bet,' Marisa answered, while a few of the others flicked me the thumbs up. Even Stephen looked happy.

I spotted Roddy sitting at his desk through the door to his office and walked over, knocking gently on the glass. I smiled optimistically. Grinning back, Roddy waved me in.

My eyes were drawn to a picture of him that I hadn't noticed before on the shelf next to his desk. It was the sort of self-consciously natural black-and-white shot people like Roddy have on hand, proving them to be a great dad, like in the movies. Successful in every field: work, home, fatherhood, the caption might say. He was lifting a young girl into the air and she was laughing spontaneously.

Even though I knew he was probably a rotten dad and husband, the picture nevertheless made me look at him in a new light. Parenthood was a world I had yet to understand.

'She's gorgeous. How old is she?' I asked him.

'Amber, she's three. Beautiful, isn't she? Just like her mother.' Roddy looked over to the picture and his poise softened a little bit. Then he snapped himself out of it. 'Mood swings like her mother too, come to that. Anyway, Toots, come here, say hello.' Roddy beckoned me over to him and kissed me once on both cheeks.

He patted a package on his desk, 'prepare to be amazed.'

'Can I look? Have you looked? Of course you have. What do you think? Roddy, is it OK? Does it hit the mark?'

'See for yourself. I think you will be pleased.'

Roddy waved the brown package in the air. He played with me a bit and made me snatch at it a few times, pulling it away from me at the last minute, before he finally gave in.

I pulled the magazine out from the package. My hand was shaking as I turned it over. Even though I was familiar with the image on the cover, seeing it like that was still a shock and I laughed out loud. Nervous excitement.

But it worked. Clay was a practised cover star and the shot was world class. I felt a sort of clandestine pleasure in the knowledge that the magic behind the photo was my little secret.

'Wow, Roddy, it's really bold. Are you happy?'

I looked up at Roddy to check his expression. He held my gaze, poker faced. I was filled with a sense of dread; didn't he like the magazine? Then an even more devastating thought hit me like a blow to the stomach: did he know about Clay? Had Simon told Roddy? I stood meekly waiting for an answer, mortified at the thought. Finally, after what seemed like a lifetime, he spoke.

'For sure, and especially because it's already generated so much interest,' he winked. 'You certainly seem to have captivated the minds of the media with your confident approach, Toots. *Incite* is going to be the most talked-about magazine out there.'

'Whaddya mean?' So did he know? I still wasn't sure.

Roddy pulled out a newspaper from his drawer and handed it to me. No wonder he looked pleased, and it was a happiness tinged with danger, his favourite kind. On the front cover of the newspaper's media section was a picture of me with the headline: 'I want to be more famous than my cover stars. I'm going to take on Planet Celebrity and win.'

Underneath, the journalist had written, *'Hot young editor Toots Silver (pictured on left in swimming pool) says celebrities are worthless and her new magazine is an attempt to ignite a* Bonfire of the Vanities *movement aimed at the showbusiness industry. Does she really want the fight? Or is she just another desperate, fame–hungry wannabe trying to elbow her way to success?'*

'Oh my God, Roddy, that's terrible,' I said. It hadn't yet dawned on me that only one person could have approved them using this sneak preview of the mag. I felt sick and my stomach lurched, although perhaps this was a result – and when I thought of what they could have written about me and Clay. Bad? Yes. Devastating? No. 'What are we going to do? How can people write those things?' Simultaneously for some reason the thought of Michael Dawson reading the article popped into my head. Any credibility I had with him was surely lost now. It was like he'd become my psychosomatic moral compass, whom I just couldn't shake, which was both plain annoying and unfathomable.

Roddy was thrilled. 'Toots, it's fantastic. It's just what we need. At least they're talking about you, talking about us. Don't you see it's a platform?'

'My God! I sound like a conceited megalomaniac who hates celebrities. I actually quite like some of them. Surely no one will want to appear in the mag after this?' In my head, the scenario was much worse. What would Clay think if he read this? On top of the cover, I was developing the psychological profile of a madwoman.

'Of course they will, Toots. It's just a case of choosing your targets carefully. There is such a thing as a celebrity hierarchy. Surely you know that? And fame is so damn common these days, everyone's at it. Even real people. It's going to be à la mode in the showbiz fraternity to distance oneself from fame, pretend you didn't want to be famous in the first place, like it was just an awful and embarrassing by-product of your unique gift. You know the stuff: "I was born to act/sing/dance/make people laugh, I just didn't want all the terrible attention that goes with it." The stars love that bullshit.'

I was neither convinced nor comforted by Roddy's words. I wasn't ready to take on board his critique just now. The mild relief I'd felt at not being found out, at least not yet, had been rapidly replaced by the new fear of my horrible minor-celebrity status. I needed grounding again. I needed Rach.

I met her for lunch. I suggested Beetroot, a wholefood café off Oxford Street, thinking: healthy eating equals nourishing thoughts. And, as usual, she put things into perspective for me. 'Firstly, Toots, I've not seen any of the newspaper articles you're on about, so by my reckoning neither has anyone else in here. Most people are busy, with lives,' she said, gesturing to the other people deep in conversation and root vegetables, 'and if anyone has, so what?'

'OK, Rach, even if that's true, what about the cover? Now you have to admit that is more serious shit I'm dealing with there: what happens if Clay sees it? What will he think of me?'

'Well, babe, chances are he will. But will he care? And more to the point, why should you be the one who has to worry so much about the consequences? Has he called you?'

'You know he hasn't, Rach.'

'Well then, that suggests to me he isn't sitting around in his Hollywood crib worrying about it too much.' Rach reached over the table to add some dried chilli flakes to her noodle salad.

'OK, so he might not care now, but when he sees it, then he'll care, and what if anyone else finds out?'

'Unlikely, Toots. The only person you've told is me, remember.'

I omitted to mention Simon, although he was the one I was worried about. I couldn't say this to Rachel, though, she would feel betrayed if I told her I'd confided in someone else. But Simon was in the background, ticking away like a time bomb. One I'd set off.

'You're right, Rach. Anyway, the cover decision was a professional one; what happened between Clay and me was something else.'

'Some. Thin'. Else!' laughed Rach.

'Yeah, and that. That was the real Clay Allison; this is the one he sells to the public. And that is my job, so it's the same thing, it's what I have to do, my responsibility.' I was firing myself up now. 'Yeah, and you're right, Rach, his assistant hasn't phoned, so why should I take the blues?'

'Exactamundo, Toots. But honey, now I'm going back to work.'

'But Rach, you've hardly eaten anything.'

'I know,' she said, stuffing a forkful in as she grabbed her bag, 'I've to be back before Mimi finishes her lunch. That bitch robbed my uniform. James had to practically pull us apart. She is virtually following him around these days. I get to work and there's Mimi strutting round the shop with the Preen trousers I ordered last week: she got in there first today, opened the mail and snatched them as her own. I said to James, "They don't fit her saggy ass, so how is any customer going to see them and want to buy them?" He agreed. So it's payback this afternoon, I'm afraid. I'm on her customers, I'm telling you, no more loyalty from me, no way.' It was a pity I hadn't taken the time to read between the lines of what Rachel was saying right then, I might have realised there was more at stake than a pair of trousers.

When I returned to the office, I had a more constructive conversation with Roddy and I felt calmer and clearer. A light switched on in my brain. Roddy was right, of course; the more I thought about it, the more it made sense. And maybe I needed to let go a little, learn to enjoy my own moment. After all, like Roddy said, at least they were talking about me.

12
Beef Calf

A row of shot glasses was lined up on the bar of the Cactus Nachos Mexicana Experience. It was Tex Mex-Spanish fusion night, and one by one Stephen, Sara, Anna, Vicky and the rest of the team threw them down their throats to rapturous cheers.

Marisa took a more unconventional route to the dizzy heights, pouring her shot over her head and climbing onto the bar to dance the Macarena, with tequila tears running down her face. Others followed like beef calves to the burrito hotplate.

We were at our unofficial launch party. The real one was the following day, when we would put our message out there. It was unlikely any of us would be able to speak or walk by then.

At the bar I checked the messages on my voicemail. There was one from my mum checking I'd got the money and one from Rach asking me to call her a couple of hours earlier. There was another message from a voice I didn't recognise.

'Hi, I'm Holly, calling from BBC's *Liquid News*. We would really like to talk to you about the possibility of appearing on our show tomorrow.'

I called the number and Holly answered. She did a little check-if-you're-sane-style chat with me on the phone and I managed to get my head together enough to sound credible.

'We feel like the attitude you and your magazine represent would be great for the show. Actually, it's the vibe we are looking for. Right up our mojo, if you get me. We love the idea that you are this young, opinionated female and want you to really give it loads in our discussion. Do you think you can do that, Toots?'

'Absolutely, Holly, I won't hold back,' I said, making a mental note to up the bellicosity.

It didn't occur to me I might feel differently without the bellyful of Tex Mex/Spanish/Dutch-infused courage.

I called Rach. 'You are going to love me, Toots. Am I not the most amazing friend a person could ever wish for?'

'Well, yeah, Rach, of course you are.'

'No wait, you don't know what I'm talking about yet, do you?'

'Huh?'

'I've only gone and secured you the once-in-a-lifetime opportunity to wear the most stylish, of-the-moment dress of your dreams for tomorrow night's launch party…'

Rach was trying to make up for the electricity debacle. Perhaps if I'd been just a little less self-absorbed, I might have realised this flourish of breathy excitement was suspect.

'One thing, Toots: you have to give it back the next day, sorry. But that's no biggie. You are going to look amazing.'

'Wow, Rach. Let it be said now, for the record, that you are absolutely the bestest, the most fantastic-ist friend in the world. And I love you. More than anything,' I garbled through my glass.

'When a woman is given the chance to shine, it's probably not the best idea that she goes on a 10-hour bender the day before. This is a positive lesson we have learned, am I right?'

'Yeuhh.'

Rach was holding my hair back out of my face while I vomited into the toilet bowl.

'OK. I'm going to look shit, and I have to be on telly at tea-time and that's before the big launch an hour later. I've fucked it. I don't deserve to live. I want to die. When can I die?'

'No, no you haven't. Pale skin, deep-set eyes and a concave stomach are all the rage. The dress will probably fit you better now. They are all made for the hungry.'

'But I just want to go to bed.'

'You get in the bath and your fairy godmother will do the rest.'

She'd filled it with strange floating salt stuff which resembled the head of a pint and made me want to be sick again. I sat at the end by the drain, letting the hot water run straight from the tap over my sorry body.

The dress of my dreams wasn't what I imagined. It was made of wispy sheer material in a tropical print of wild, acid-bright colours. Nothing if not bold. The sort of dress an actual, real-life, celebutante might wear, only after a month in boot camp.

It required what Rachel referred to as 'tit tape' to hold it onto my breasts. 'All the pros are using it,' she assured me, like that made sense.

'You will shine, Toots, don't worry. It's a real statement piece. Everyone in the room is going to be captivated by you. It's your magazine, your night. Toots, you'll knock 'em dead, promise.'

'But you won't be there.'

'Can't babe. James wants to go through some of the new season with me,' Rach replied.

I looked at my reflection in the mirror of my wardrobe. Barefaced, etiolated, drained of colour, the patterned material overwhelming my form, like a child playing dress-up.

Then I stopped, gave myself a menacing stare. The launch was going to be a success. I needed to start believing I was up to it. What was it Rach said? This was going to be my night. And the TV show was a platform too, right? Like Roddy said, I was doing it for the brand. It was nothing whatsoever to do with the seductive thought of seeing myself on the television, or of Clay Allison tuning in to see me on TV from his hotel bedroom somewhere to be reminded of my ravishing loveliness. I was luxuriating in my own ego trip, giving myself a mental big-up to get cerebrally shipshape, like a boxer going into the ring. Personal motives didn't come into it, did they?

A silver chauffeur-driven car picked me up from work, to take me to the BBC, with my name printed on a piece of paper in the passenger's window.

My bit would be a tongue-in-cheek discussion of the day's entertainment news and gossip. Proceeded by a feature with a tortoise called Mystic Mike, who was a celebrity psychic pet. He came out of his shell if a massive showbiz scandal was about to break.

When we got there, a young, gamine researcher called Daisy, wearing a headpiece and a Puffa gilet, rushed me through to make-up. A nozzle blew a cold, wet layer of foundation over my face. A thick layer of bronzer powder was applied on top. That made three layers in all (I'd caked myself in slap in the car), then some sheeny-shimmery eyeshadow. I looked like a festive citrus fruit. Unrecognisable in my own skin.

Daisy whisked the newly orange me back through to the green room. There was another guest too, who I vaguely recognised as a sneery 'serious' music journalist called Cat. She asked me, 'are you here with the tortoise?'

'Yes, I'm part of Mike's entourage, yes,' I said.

Fortuitously, Mystic Mike, who was sitting in a Perspex pet box in the corner of the room, made no sharp moves to say otherwise.

Cat looked a little surprised when they led us out to our places on set and realised she was sat next to me on the sofa, one down from the host. Christopher, the show's anchorman, was gracious and chatty, so when the credits to the show going live started, I was taken aback. I'd expected a warning.

The numbers on the cameraman's screen counted down to lift-off. Behind him, the producer in a headpiece was miming us in with his fingers.

Three, two, one, and…

And suddenly we were live. We had entered another dimension of human existence where our words were directed to the world outside.

Christopher transformed from merely charming to epic personality mode, blitzing his way through the autocue ebulliently.

But I was nervous. I needed to get a grip.

I tried negative self help.

This was BBC Choice, no one was watching.

Truthfully, it did feel cosseted in the studio, so it was easy to suspend disbelief that it was on the air. A little futuristic den in telly-land where all the furniture was from *Star Trek* and the control unit was a big screen with showbiz reports flashing up, controlled by Commander Christopher.

When it was time to speak I saw myself in the camera opposite. And watched as words began to come out of my mouth. Were they making sense? Possibly? I felt like the me on screen was somehow functioning outside of myself. I was a more animated, souped-up, shiny version of Toots Silver.

We watched a montage of the week's news events on the telly behind Christopher. I tried to walk the delicate path between mild ridicule and affectionate expertise I'd seen other commentators pull off. The crew laughed at my jokes. Cat looked peeved. Then an image of Michael Dawson and his TV presenter girlfriend flashed up on the screen.

The caption running across the bottom read *Lights Go Out on London Style Couple. Have Westminster Womaniser Michael Dawson and TV Presenter Marsha Laponi called Time on Relationship?*

Throat dry, I glanced at the camera again and saw that my reflection didn't register the shockwave of two realities colliding. My smile was fixed. I heard words coming out of my mouth and telly-Toots continued.

'If it's true, it's a shame. They were the perfect pairing who had it all. There were rumours that she wanted to be Britain's first lady but sadly it looks like it won't be going her way just now. Sorry honey.' Had I just said that? That was stupid and weird. Hopefully Michael Dawson wasn't watching.

The remaining 20 minutes flashed by, and when the Balearic house music started again to signal it was the end of the show, I wanted to carry on. I felt buoyant.

Afterwards, putting on the party dress in a BBC toilet cubicle outside the studio, a transformation in which I would become Superwoman, the nagging doubts began to creep in again. I wondered why, since the onset of my sparkling career, had I seemed to spend so much time in a state of undress in a loo?

I tried not to dwell on my noxious comment about Michael Dawson's ex, or the fact that the knowledge of their break-up had actually given me a massive thrill.

13
Night of a Thousand Stars

The Sanderson Hotel: one of London's chicest gathering places, monument to the times, custom-designed furnishing, lighting and textiles by Philippe Starck. It couldn't be more Right Here, Right Now. And Roddy, being Roddy, couldn't resist the allure. 'The perfect launchpad,' he'd called it.

The imposing glass building was reflected in the window of the taxi as we pulled up at Berners Street. Why couldn't he have chosen somewhere just a little more discreet? Paparazzi were positioned outside on the red carpet, lights flashing as guests preened to be photographed.

My hair was a disaster, so I'd scraped it back tightly from my face, attempting a truly sophisticated look that women with faces that matched their exotic names, like Sade, Yasmin or Bianca, could pull off with ease, due to their overwhelming beauty and finely chiselled features. My northern pug grid: a high-risk strategy.

The car stopped outside and the driver opened my door. It was time to do the walk.

'Who are you?' shouted one of the paps as I made my approach. It was hard to stride with the confidence I'd imagined in a dress that was as thin as a handkerchief without it blowing sideways off my body, so it was a perilous path to tread in the night breeze.

'Get out the way will ya, luv?' shouted a globular-faced, surly pap, as a well-known TV actress appeared behind me. She was dressed, I noted, in a simple, yet chic and understated, black cocktail dress.

'For God's sake. Mind ya fuckin' back, will ya?' said another photographer, scrambling in front of me and booting me sideways as he positioned himself for a better shot of the telly queen.

Suddenly someone I recognised moved forward in the pap line.

'Hey Toots, over here!' he called at me, removing the camera briefly from his face and giving me an encouraging look. I turned to the camera and flashed him a relieved smile, not because someone was taking my photo, but because it was Adam and he'd done it for me. The other paps followed suit, and for a couple of seconds it was my moment. I stood rooted to the spot, hand on hip, fixing my expression like a mask. Then one of them shouted, 'Looking sexy, Sadie. Over here darlin',' and like a swarm of locusts changing direction, their wave of energy was channelled somewhere else.

Roddy had secured the Long Bar for our party. The bar was the focal point of the hotel. Some 80 feet in length, its dramatic glowing onyx surface glared light like a radiation panel. And the fact that its bar stools were moulded to the floor along the entire length of the grandiose structure meant it was almost impossible to get through to the finish line to get a drink in my hand at the speed needed. Relief came in the form of a waitress carrying a tray of cocktails.

'Is that vodka?'

'It's our house special, 10oz Martini.'

I noticed the glasses carried the *Incite* brand on them.

'Would you like to try one?'

'Yes bloody please.' I gulped the drink back – it hit my throat like a capful of bleach – then chewed pensively on the soggy olive while I scanned the room for a familiar face. The *Incite* brand was everywhere: copies of the magazine were laid attractively on the spare surfaces and the cover shot had been projected across the clear white walls. My face and Clay's were universal.

I felt Roddy's hand on my backside before I saw his face. And I realised, to my horror, that I hadn't flinched. Stockholm Syndrome.

'Hey babe, you look bold.' He paused. 'And beautiful, of course. Quite a dress, Toots, something for the gentlemen I take it.'

'Oh God, Roddy, is it that bad? Does it look ridiculous?'

'Babe, I like it, I can see you are thinking big and in that I can be 100 percent confident that you are doing your bit for the brand.

Now go over there and strut your stuff. Those marketing execs need an eyeful to remind them they have warm blood running through their cold veins. Just what the doctor ordered.'

"Shut up, Roddy.'

'No, seriously, this is important. That's just warming-up stuff. Tonight I want you to be a friend of the stars. Have you seen who's already arrived, Toots? This is going to be the most talked-about event on the planet. See over there?'

I turned to look but was sidetracked by the back of Michael Dawson's head at the bar. A new level of anxiety passed through me on top of the existing nerves.

Roddy was still talking. 'We've got Sadie and Jude and Meg and Goldie, the rapper not the dead dog from *Blue Peter*, and yes, the rough end, but it's looking good for starters. Very good. But I want you working it, Toots, you got me?'

'Yes.'

'And Toots?'

'Yes, Rod?'

'You might want to, ahem, tuck yourself back in a bit. Not that I don't appreciate the gesture.'

I glanced down and saw a sliver of translucent tit tape trailing down my arm like an operation scar. As a recent innovation, the manufacturers clearly hadn't got the stick-to-your-body bit right, the most vital element. My left breast was almost fully exposed to the marketing team opposite. Captivating: wasn't that what Rach had said I would be? By the look on the face of the man in my eyeline, she was bang on the money.

At that moment, I saw Adam across the room talking to a scowling celebrity agent I recognised called Tamara. I dashed over, to her revulsion, pulling Adam outside to the garden so we could talk. It was a lush open-air oasis brimming with flowering trees. A welcome relief from the hubbub of the bar.

'Hey Toots, nice dress,' he winked.

'Don't you start. Please do not go there. I feel like an idiot. And Roddy made me feel like a chunk of prime meat hanging up at his exclusive butcher's.'

'Never mind. Listen, great turnout though, Toots. Just the right balance of B- and C-listers, with only a smattering of Zs – forgivable due to the presence of least three A-listers by my reckoning,' Adam said, gesturing to the celebrity royalty by the bar.

'For all I know, Roddy paid them to be here. But yeah, I think it's a success.'

'And a few hearts-and-minds bods too; intellectual types are always important.'

'What do you mean?'

'Listen, I know everyone, it's my job.'

Adam reeled off a list and I glanced at them one by one... 'Society editor from the *Standard*, Alan cockface at six o'clock, and Michael Dawson, hot New Labour MP, standing by the sofa.'

I glanced over as casually as I could manage to Michael Dawson. He was serious faced, gently brushing the outline of his lip with his finger as he listened to the man he was talking to. I melted. There was something about him, he consistently had this effect, made me go soft in the head. Go off my head. Shit.

'Who invited him?'

'What's the matter? Haven't you heard of that guy? He's good for the mix Toots. Blazed quite a trail. He was a barrister or something worthy, human rights, dead right on and all that, and now he's part of that whole New Labour flash pack thing.'

'What do you mean?' In the back of my mind I knew some of this but I wanted to hear it from someone else, someone credible like Adam, rather than Roddy who sort of soiled it. Why was everyone talking about this man?

'Michael Dawson. He's one of Blair's inner circle, one of them special advisors, got the ear of the PM. Really ambitious, one of the "one to watch" types. Word is Mandelson persuaded him to become an MP.'

Michael. I felt really strange knowing this was the man I'd woken up next to all those months ago in my bed, not knowing who he was at all. God, I was awestruck now, too, listening to his greatness CV.

'Oh Jesus. I do know him. Listen, shield me. I don't want him to see me, OK? Not dressed as a pina colada. Last time I met him was at New Year and that time my nose was the colour of a small stoned fruit. Now I'm dressed like a tropical cocktail. It's not good.'

But it was too late. He looked up and caught us gazing at him. His eyes fixed on mine, as though he was searching for something. Eventually, perhaps not getting what he was looking for, he dropped his gaze, nodded and smiled. I wanted him to look back again so I could tell him and show him I was actually OK, that I was a serious person, like him, not a pineapple enthusiast.

'Toots, are you OK?' asked Adam.

'Yes, sorry. Where the hell are the rest of the team though, Adam? I've not seen any of them since we got here.'

'They're hiding in the billiard room downstairs, all of them nursing hangovers.'

'I don't believe this. It's just typical. Leaving me to face the music alone.'

Adam put his arm round my shoulder and gave me an affectionate squeeze.

'Do you want me to get them, bring them up here?'

'Nah, it's fine, I'll go. It's not them. I'm just feeling a bit weary with all this, I think.

'Look around the room, Adam, these people are all so fickle. Give them a glass of champers and some free nibbles, they'd say they love anything.'

'Toots, listen to me. The dress looks beautiful and so do you, except for one thing.'

'What?'

'Well, seeing your smile would be better.'

I managed to contrive a smallish smile.

'And these people would not just turn up to the opening of an envelope. Believe me, I've covered enough of them in my time. They are here because they are interested in the magazine, your magazine. They want to know what the buzz is all about. Take no notice of people like Tamara; she's just pissed she's not you. Look, see over there.'

There was a flurry of excitement near the door, as a bunch of men in sharp white suits ushered a hip-looking black guy wearing an even whiter suit and exceptionally shiny sunglasses into the room. The whole party took a little gasp and stared as he arrived. Their gobsmacked images were reflected back in the glare of his lenses and he nodded in self-appreciation at their 'correct' response. Yes indeed, a star was in their midst.

'Oh my God. Is that—'

'Exactly. He's come here to your party. I rest my case. Now, are you going to stop moping and do what you're good at?'

'What's that then?'

'Work the room like Sharon Stone in *Casino*, that's what. Listen Toots, you love the magazine, don't you?'

I nodded.

'Now go get the guys and put some cement onto all that work you've been putting in, otherwise it's all been for nothing. OK?'

I saw the *Incite* PR, Henrietta, heading towards me with that possessed-by-enthusiasm face that said, 'You need to do your stuff for the brand, Toots.' Luckily one of our gorgeous work-experience girls, Alice, was walking past at just the right moment carrying a tray of drinks.

'Hey, Alice,' I said to the girl, 'you're doing a great job.' She swung her hair and beamed at me, a smile straight out of a toothpaste advert. 'Could I just take one of them?' I said, and I reached over and grabbed a drink before she went off. For a millisecond, I was left gazing into the space left by Alice's statuesque frame and I caught a fleeting glimpse of Roddy. He was talking to some suit over the other side of the room, but he was looking over their shoulder. At first I thought he was clocking me. But I was invisible to him. His eyes homed in on Alice's legs like he'd seen an apparition. And he ogled them as they strode over to another gaggle of partygoers. Bloody Roddy! He was old enough to be her dad – and some.

I squeezed Adam's hand. 'You are so great, you know, you always make me feel better. I do appreciate it, honestly I do.'

Henrietta turned to me before he had a chance to respond. 'Time to meet a megastar!'

'All in a day's work, babe,' I replied and we headed in the direction of the main man and his people.

For the next few hours, I was buzzing on a heady mix of vodka and stardust. It was contagious. I grew in confidence the more people I talked to. It was an unspoken pact: we were all in the room; we were all A-list tonight.

Just as I was on the lookout for the Martini girl for another drink, I saw Michael Dawson heading for the exit. Now I was more confident, I felt like I needed to grab him, to say something maybe to clear the air between us.

'Going already?'

'I've got to be up early in the morning, Toots, big day.'

'Thanks for coming. I thought maybe you would have mixed feelings.'

'I get invited to many of these things.'

'Because of your girlfriend.'

'Possibly.'

'But she's not here?'

'No.' He wasn't taking the bait about his romantic situation.

'Listen, I'm being genuine. It means a great deal to have someone like you here and you know, lend some gravitas to the occasion.'

'I'm not sure about that Toots,' Michael laughed drily. 'I'm off duty, I was curious to see the, what was it? "Hottest magazine I am ever likely to read," for myself.'

'Oh yeah that, well, maybe I embellished that a little.'

'I work at Westminster Toots. I understand. I wanted to wish you well and say congratulations. You should be proud. And it's no mean feat working with Roddy either. You're winning.'

'Am I?' I said and looked him straight in those lovely dark eyes. But Michael was going now. He leaned in and kissed me once, on either cheek, looked at me deeply, then said goodbye. Leaving the longing in the air.

14
What Not to Wear

The morning after the party I was still on a high. Even though I'd only grabbed a couple of hours' sleep, I was enlivened, jittery with energy.

Rach bounced into the kitchen, where I was sitting, and stuck the kettle on. 'How was it then?'

'It was brilliant, Rach, everyone was there.' I reeled off a list of celebrities, which Rach responded to with the appropriate 'oohs' and 'aahhs' until we got to Daniel Bedingfield, when we both let out a collective 'urgh'.

'What did you do, Rach?'

'Nothing quite so glamarama as you. Right. We've got no coffee. I'm going to grab a couple from over the road before I shoot off to work. Shall I get the papers as well, babe? The party's bound to be all over them, isn't it? How exciting is that? Well done you; I'm really proud of you, Toots.'

Rach made my jittery look like Bob Marley, she didn't stay in one place for a moment, jumped all over the kitchen. I wondered if she'd taken something the night before or something and was about to ask her what it was but she was out the door. I decided to put her distraction down to her being in a hurry. Poor Rach, stuck at work when I was out at one of the most glamorous parties of the year. She didn't even seem to care much, which was out of character, but then she was so wrapped up in her job. I knew how much she would have loved it though. I decided she was probably being magnanimous for my benefit, pretending not to care. It didn't occur to me she might have her own stuff going on.

While I waited for Rach, I checked the messages on my phone. Roddy had called, of course, hailing the night a winner; Henrietta had been on. And there was one from Stephen singing *Young Hearts Run Free* in falsetto, presumably in a taxi, because he stopped every couple of bars or so to offer a 'left' or a 'right here.' Which didn't ring true to the original.

Dumping down a stack of papers and a takeaway coffee, Rach gave me a kiss on the head.

'Right, I'm off. Don't mind if I grab the dress back do ya, Toots? Better get it back in one piece. Have a good day.'

'Sure, it's on the back of the door. See you later, and thanks for these.'

I didn't have time to read them. I'd have to save the moment and look at them in work. I got in the shower and sang my own rendition of *Young Hearts*.

Success is a funny one isn't it? One minute you're riding high, feeling on top of the world after hosting one of the most talked-about parties of the year. The next you're on your arse. The subject of humiliation, red-faced ridicule, splashed across the papers, hung, drawn and quartered.

'Frock Horror!' screamed one headline.

'Who's that girl? And where's her stylist?' asked another.

'Fashion faux pas,' declared another.

And it went on. And on.

A photograph of me arriving at the party was juxtaposed with one of Geri Halliwell and another of J.Lo, all in identical dresses, with the strapline: 'Freak Un-Unique.'

My mouth was hanging open, slightly slackjawed, and I realised that the moment the picture was taken, I had been asking one of the paps, should I move? YES. I wished he'd shoved me a bit harder out the way. I looked mildly deranged.

Each picture was dissected from head to toe. Feet: mine were 'pigeon-toed and in dire need of an emergency pedicure SOS' said the article. Limbs measured: mine were 'stumpy and milky'. Hairstyles critiqued: mine was a 'chav's facelift'. Right down to the 'exposed tit tape', mine, of course, not J.Lo's (tucked away neatly). Clearly she didn't get dressed in a public loo then.

Underneath, accompanying the fashion journalist's acutely

detailed piece about how I utterly failed to possess the fashion credentials necessary to look good in a dress of that calibre, was a piece in which the designer himself admitted he had not given permission for me to wear the dress and would almost certainly be consulting his lawyers in the morning.

Despite the sickening sense of shame I felt leafing through the papers, it was strangely compelling too. Rather like how I imagined watching video footage of yourself being shot at by snipers might feel: taking one bullet after the next, walking blindly onwards into the crossfire, to face another and another. Hypnotic, horrific. Poetic.

My only salvation was a thought piece, written by the slishy-sloshy society critic Alan (cockface) from the *Standard*, which claimed I was simply acting out the ethos of my magazine's anti-hero stance. Wearing the dress, he said, had been a shrewd and sharp critique of the perverse way in which celebrities and fashion designers work in cahoots, to manipulate the public into mass consumption. Crikey.

And there was me thinking I just looked shit.

Looking up from my desk, I felt I could feel everyone's eyes on me.

'Miss Silver,' came the shrill cry from Roddy's office. 'Here. Now.'

'Here comes that public flogging then,' I muttered to myself.

As I walked anxiously from my desk to Roddy's, I felt my team looking up at me furtively from their workstations. Only as I drew nearer did they suddenly glance down or reach for their phones frantically. Sara darted for the paper room. Marisa dived into her handbag under her desk. I felt like a dead woman walking.

Closing the office door as softly as possible, to draw as little attention from my colleagues as I could, I shuffled into the room. This was, of course, utterly pointless. Sure enough, I felt their gazes shifting to the door like lightning. Synchronised. Phones down. Ears pricked up.

Roddy stood with his back to me. He was holding a newspaper wide open on an article I recognised, a particularly venomous piece about my debacle. He paced up and down a little, like a tiger about to go in for the kill.

Roddy's bollockings were legendary, and possibly his favourite part of his job. Rumour had it someone once pretended to drop dead to escape a hit. He'd just stepped over the body and carried on.

'I know Roddy, I can explain. Thing is, it was Rachel, not me, she convinced me. I'm not a show pony, you know that, it was all just a horrible misunderstanding,' came my blathering explanation.

'Toots. Be quiet.'

'Yes, Roddy. Sorry, Roddy.'

'This... Well, I can't put it into words.'

'Yes, Roddy.'

This was terrible: the slick-lipped man of a million well-versed words, left tongue-tied, because of me.

'This is... it's... just... unprecedented.'

'Yes. I know. I can imagine.'

'A media storm Toots, it's... And you are...'

I knew what he was going to say. I'd brought shame on him. I'd let the magazine down and I'd shown appalling lack of judgment. In short, I was a total idiot.

He paused once more for dramatic effect. 'Fan. Fuckin'. Tastic. Pure friggin' genius.'

'You mean you think it's a good thing that the fashion police want me put behind bars?'

'Truly awesome. Now we just have to make sure we monop- olise on it, get you out there at every party, every It bar, every goddamned showcase there is. You need to be there in a knockout dress. From now on, that's 50 percent of your job. At least. Got it?'

I was stunned. Was he for real?

'Erm, what about the other stuff, Roddy? I'm confused. How am I supposed to edit the magazine if this is 50 percent of my job?

'Easy. You get the other 50 percent done faster and better than before, like those editors in Japan and Germany. Then at night you change into a hot get-up and go out there and give it some more.

If you want to harness this moment, Toots, you need to give it 150 percent – 50 plus 50 plus 50. After all, not everyone gets their moment at all; you can't just let it pass you by. You have to ride the wave, catch the breeze, grasp the metal…'

'Roll with the punches, Rod? I feel like I've just been beaten to a pulp by those bastards. Again. Is this what it feels like to be winning, Roddy? Deeply humiliating and embarrassing?'

'Don't be so soft, Toots, you need to toughen up and see this for what it is. An opportunity. Not just for you, for all of us. We can soon iron out those sartorial glitches; you are going to be the most talked-about fashion icon on the party circuit.'

'Yeah, Rod, one small problem there too. I really don't have a fashion icon's wardrobe. Or the budget to buy one either. Who's going to pay for all this?'

'Toots. I know people. People who can help. People who do this all day long. You think any of those actresses, popstars, wannabes actually own those rags? They all hire them for the night. Same as you're gonna do. Trick is, if there's a big party, let the fashion PRs know you're coming nice and early. Book your appointment and get a fitting before those lot have even woken up with sore heads and reached for their first espressofuckinchino. The early bird…'

'Catches a dress? Don't think I've heard that one, Rod.'

'That's it, Toots. And she's a better-looking bird for it.' Ignoring me, he said, 'Listen, leave that side of things to me. Ange will sort it out. Henrietta is on the case too. Didn't she call you? She wants a meet. Strategy planning for the brand. She's made up.'

Leaving Roddy's office, I didn't know whether to be happy or sad. I still had a job. That was good. But my punishment was the rather daunting prospect of spending the rest of my life as a 24-hour party person. What was the difference between what I was being asked to do and being told you had to dress up and wear a chicken suit all day and cluck about the merits of Nando's, or whatever? Not that much, really: just a better outfit, by my reckoning.

As I slumped at my desk weighing the whole thing up, I got a call from Rach. She was in tears.

'They've given me a written warning, Toots. Another one of them and I'm out. It's been terrible, just terrible. All morning Camille has been on the phone to Terry, that's the designer's press assistant, explaining what a terrible mistake I made, accidentally giving you the dress. It was meant for Kylie, for God's sake. The only person who's been nice is James, you know, Camille's husband, he's been so incredibly sweet, and that just made things worse. She exploded when she saw him being nice. I don't know what I'll do if I lose this job, I can't go back to my mum's. Thing is, it's not about the dress is it? She knows Toots, she knows. I'm sure she does and she's using it against me but he's stuck in the middle and I don't blame him. Not really, but I didn't think it would come to this.'

'Knows what Rach? I'm sorry, I don't follow.' Then suddenly, the penny dropped and I got it and it all slotted into place. 'Listen, calm down. Shh, don't worry, it will be OK. They haven't sacked you. It's a warning that's all.' I saw Roddy approaching again and lowered my voice, 'It will be OK.'

Suddenly, my designer chicken-costume fate didn't seem so bad. I was the one who'd got off lightly and left Rachel to face the music all by herself, when all she'd tried to do was help me out. I'd let her take a favour from James and a lot more besides, by the sounds of it. And the worst of it was, when I should have been feeling bad for my friend Rach, who'd risked it all for me, a small part of me was dead chuffed. Why? Because I'd got into a dress that was meant for Kylie Minogue.

I was out the rest of the day and didn't get back until most of the team had gone home. As I approached Roddy's office I could see he was still there, with the outline of another figure talking to him. This meant I would have to look busy for a while until Rach was here and we could make tracks. Then I noticed a missed call on my phone. One I didn't recognise. I pressed the button to call back. After a few seconds someone answered and on the other end I heard his voice. 'Hi.'

It was the first time I'd heard his voice since Cannes. The thrill stopped me in my tracks, pure exhilaration.

'It's me. Toots.' It was all I could say in a straight line.

'OK, babe. Listen, Pocket. I've arranged something. Two weeks' time. You can come?'

'Yeah,' I said, 'of course.' We didn't chat. I didn't care. I wanted to stand on my chair and jump for joy. He remembered me and still wanted me. In two weeks' time.

After about fifteen minutes of me sitting there taking in the thrill and staring at the magazine with Clay and me on the cover, I remembered I was meeting Rachel. Maybe she was still at work. I'd meet her there.

I shut down my computer, tidied my desk, threw out some rubbish, got my coat on. I'd debated whether to let Roddy know I was off, which could delay me as he was more than likely to suggest I go out to a party, but concluded it would be better to tell him rather than get a call back when I was halfway home.

Just as I was about to knock on the glass, the door opened and a warm fog of cigarette smoke escaped. I knew Roddy had a sneaky fag in there in the evenings but when he appeared I saw Rachel, fag in hand, following him in fits of laughter.

'Toots, I was keeping your lovely friend Rachel here company,' he was talking about Rach but looking at me, 'You've been hiding her dazzling charms from me, if that could be possible, so fortuitously I have taken the time to discover them for myself.'

I looked at Rach to see if she was as nauseated as I was but she was laughing along with Roddy conspiratorially. Finally, she caught my eye and I gave her what I hoped was a 'calm down and remember he's a bastard' look.

'Now you girls, I'm going to leave you to do whatever it is you girls do while I head home. Rachel, it's been a pleasure, and next time I hope we'll have a bit longer. Toots, enjoy.' He kissed her hand in the manner of an old-fashioned gentleman, which he was certainly not, but received a delighted giggle from Rach.

After he had gone I turned to Rach. 'What the...'

'Toots, don't get mad with me OK? Roddy was actually really funny. He cheered me up, you know. Hey, and have you noticed how good he smells? What is that? You know, have you ever thought that you might actually be exaggerating his weirdness?'

'No. Because I'm not. And, yes the smell thing, but it wears off. Anyway, you both stink of smoke. OK, shall we go home now?'

'Yeah, that would be cool.'

'I'll get a cab Rach, this one's on Roddy.'

We were midway through an Indian takeaway when Rach finally cracked and told me the whole story about her stockroom fling with James. First, I thought it was the spice because she'd ordered prawn madras. But her teary-eyed expression fast became great big hulking sobs between mouthfuls of curry.

'No, Toots. I think I'm in love, Toots. And it's horrible... Camille's husband, Toots. My married boss, like the biggest fool on the planet, and he says he feels the same way. Only he's stuck really, because, well it's complicated, but anyway, it's not a good time for the business. He's trapped in a loveless marriage, but he can't leave her, not at this "financial juncture."'

Rachel did that stupid thing with her fingers that people do when they make imaginary inverted commas in the air. I hated that, and felt it was out of character for her. Maybe it was 'his' influence.

'It's just I've never met anyone like him before and I know, I just know we are a perfect match. I mean, I love Dries, he loves Dries: if that's not destiny, then tell me what is?'

'What do you mean Rach, Dries? What's Dries, are they like healthy crisps?' It was the first thing I thought of.

'No. Dries Van Noten of course, Toots. Overlooked by the cynics, embraced by those with a real eye who love his work. It takes someone who understands beauty to appreciate his worth, Toots, and I've found that someone. Toots, I've even imagined it: we could have matching wedding suits... by Dries!'

'Yeah, I see. Like, Here Comes The Dries. Not a Dries Eye in the House!' I said before thinking.

I couldn't help myself. She looked at me, appalled.

'What, Toots? You're laughing. Why are you laughing?' Rachel was pretty furious now. 'Do you think this is a joke? Because it doesn't involve you, Toots? Because it's me? And I don't matter? Because I'm the one who flits through life and you, you're the one with issues? Well guess what, Toots, other people have problems too. Maybe if you talked to me once in a while you would realise that.'

'It's not you, Rach, it's us.' And I did the miming inverted commas thing straight back at her in an attempt to make her see the absurdity of it all. 'What are we like, us two? I mean, some pair we are. Think about it, Rach, look at us,' I said in between gasps for air, as I was now laughing pretty much uncontrollably. 'There's you shagging your boss's husband under her nose because, well, because he gives good suit, and oh yeah, you love him, obviously. And me, well, where do I start with me? Well, there's me thinking I'm a big shot because I had a fling with a Hollywood film star, being brought down to earth with a bang on the front of the papers. It's just, well, it's just a bit mad really, isn't it?'

And it was infectious. Despite herself, and not really knowing why, Rachel started to laugh too, in that way that sadness doesn't have anywhere else to go so it tips over into madness, and before I knew it we were both in fits of hysterics, tears running down our faces.

'How long has it been going on, Rach?'

'Just a few weeks, that's all. I feel so stupid now, I've risked my job, everything.'

'So do you really think she knows? Camille I mean?'

'I'm not sure. I think she suspects something. It's hard to be sure. For one thing, she's always a bitch, so it's not easy to tell if it's for a reason. Anyway, it's OK because I think it was an omen. It was just a few weeks and that's it. I've learned my lesson and I'm not going to let it happen again. We flew too close to the wind and nearly got blown.'

'Rach, I think you mean you sailed too close to the sun and nearly got burned.'

'Oh yeah, dunno where I got the blown bit from.'

'Erm…?'

'Oh yeah, oh no. Oh my God… Toots.'

At that we both broke out into another fit of hysterics that lasted about five minutes and seemed to have the magic effect of elevating Rach from her despairing condition.

'So that's it then. Only nice men from now on. Available ones and simple wholesome pursuits. M&S suits.'

'No, no way,' said Rach.

'OK. Nice men?'

'That'll do. That's a relief, I bought us a bottle of Smirnoff on the way home.'

'Yeay, a wholesome pick-me-up,' I said as Rach poured a shot into two kitchen mugs.

'So are you going to forget the whole Clay Allison stuff then Toots?'

'Well, I don't actually have any big decision to make there do I Rach? So that's a no-brainer,' I lied. I didn't want to tell her about the phone call right then. Also the stuff about her affair being ill-conceived was making me feel uneasy.

'What about the other guy, Michael?'

'I refer you to my first answer.'

'OK, so that's it, we are square. Back to where we started from. Young, Free, Single and Hopeful.'

'But Wiser.'

'Yeah that too.'

15
Friends: 'The One Where Adam and Toots... You Know...'

I needed to do a bit of skiving, have a night in, but I knew Roddy wouldn't like it. I wanted him to come up with the idea. When he approached my desk from the rear, hands prepared to bear down on my shoulders, I was ready for him. I eased southwards gracefully, letting the chair take the weight. He thought it was his natural power, flowing out from his grip, keeping me where he wanted me. But I was like an office ninja, using his strength against him – and he didn't even know it.

'So what's it tonight, Toots? Anything big on the social calendar?'

'No, not really, it's quiet,' I replied dead casual. Sure enough, within seconds I could sense his unease. Nervous energy started streaking out of his digits. Like a spin Svengali, Roddy wanted his people out there, partying for the cause, hoovering up stories 24 hours a day.

'I was thinking of popping into a gallery opening thing in the East End later, just to check it out. I'm not expecting much.'

'Excellent. I think you should go. That new arty crowd can always throw up a few surprises, can't they? Dead cow hoof in a jam jar, my student pit made into a million-quid exhibit, the contents of my handbag for sale. Still, it's all a good laugh. Sometimes you even get a few political types hanging around, you know, in the hope it might rub off on them, make them look a little less like dull bastards.'

'It's a smallish thing, Roddy, in one of those temporary galleries under an arch or something, I really don't think...'

'You don't know until you try, Toots.'

'I was thinking, if nothing comes of the party, maybe I should get back to mine and watch *Big Brother*.'

There you go: I'd said it. I'd revealed my true intentions. I looked at him to see if he'd clocked it. But his face was inscrutable.

'After all, it sounds like it's going to be the thing everyone's talking about. I mean, I don't really want to. But it's all over the papers already and it hasn't even started yet.'

Roddy's ears pricked up a little. He hated to think he was missing out on a zeitgeist moment. 'Yeah, yeah, *Big Brother* sounds great. Groundbreaking TV, is it? Yeah, like the sound of it,' he replied, stroking his chin.

Bingo! He was buying into it big time.

He stopped talking and started thinking. I could see his brain ticking over.

'But then again these TV types are always saying that, aren't they? They've got the next big thing – usually all bollocks. Can't some other donut from the office do *Big Brother*?' he said. 'Who's that fat girl who dresses all in black? Surely she can watch telly?'

'No, Roddy, you're not getting this. This is going to be massive. I need to watch it. So I can analyse it for myself.'

He thought for a minute. Was he taking the bait or wasn't he?

'All right then,' he sighed, finally, 'do both. Make sure you show your face at the gallery first, mind.'

'Yes!' I thought, already celebrating inside. My exterior remained perfectly calm. A partial win. I should have known something that easy would end up complicated.

'Night off. Make some food, watch something on the telly,' I told Rachel.

'*Friends* Season Three?' said Rach.

'Do we have to? You've seen it how many times?'

'It's still funny, though! Remember the bit in Episode 13 when Ross…'

'What about we watch *Big Brother*?'

'Sounds a bit boring to me, Toots. So we sit at home watching people in another house sitting at home. Erm, why? Can't we even choose what we want to watch on telly now? Roddy's like friggin''

Big Brother if you ask me; I'm surprised he hasn't asked you to be one of the contestants.'

'Listen, I just want to relax. Adam's coming over, said he'll cook, spag bol or something. Sound good?'

'All right, Toots, that's the plan,' Rach agreed.

When we got back to the flat, I settled down with Rach in front of the telly. Once our bums were on the futon, we weren't moving.

Adam, meanwhile, took to the kitchen. Good smells began to filter into the next room. It was the most relaxed I'd felt in months.

Rach nudged me, 'Hey, could get used to this.'

We ate in front of the telly, bottle of red at our feet, mouthfuls of pasta and tomato sauce, a hint of dried oregano, dead posh.

'Adam, where did you learn to cook like this?' Rach asked.

'I don't know really,' he replied. 'I just had to, there was never anyone home to cook, so I just taught myself.'

'Rach is impressed, Ads, she's the only girl I know who could burn a boiled egg.'

'Yeah but I make nice mojitos,' she replied.

'And that is a fact, Rach.'

'And what would you rather have?'

Adam was lying down on the floor on a cushion, but when Rach got up to go to the loo, he jumped in her seat next to me.

'Oi, that's my space,' she said.

'Yeah, but I made the food, so I've earned it. Anyway, I want to look at the paper to see if any of my pictures made it. I'm not watching *Friends*.'

He sat down the far end, horizontally to me, and put his legs over mine. The contact felt natural – having him lying there like that.

Adam stopped leafing through the paper for a moment and leaned over. 'Hey, isn't that the MP who was at the *Incite* launch, Toots? Looks like he split from his girlfriend. Another celebrity couple bites the dust.'

'Michael Dawson?' I said, peering over to look at the article. 'Yeah, he was going out with that *Popgirl* TV presenter, Marsha thingio, wasn't he?' I attempted to sound uninterested despite the buzz this gave me.

'Another celebrity couple bites the dust,' said Adam. 'I love it when they blame stuff like "conflicting schedules", which everyone knows is bollocks.'

'I meant to tell you Toots, she came in the shop,' said Rach. 'Size zero, honest to God, like a little doll. Wonder what happened there, eh?' Rach and I exchanged a look, but nothing Adam could pick up on. I gave her the cut-throat signal to shut up.

I was about to hand the paper back to Adam when I saw a full-page advert on the adjacent page for *Big Brother*. 'Oh shit, bollocks, bollocks. I was meant to be watching that.'

'Yeah, it's probably finished by now though, hasn't it?' said Rach. 'Besides, we're just getting to the bit when Ross sleeps with someone else behind Rachel's back. It's so mean.' I noticed as she was watching that my Rachel was actually mouthing the lines back to Ross in the scene on the telly. It really was quite astonishing; she knew them off by heart.

But *Big Brother* was still playing on my mind, and even with the story we had picked up earlier I knew Roddy would be expecting me to know my stuff.

'OK, fine. What about you two go and watch it in your bedroom and I'll watch this here then,' said Rach.

She was being cheeky, trying to manipulate a situation between us. I knew her comment about him becoming part of the furniture earlier was a nudge. She loved Adam, and loved being cooked for even more. Saying that, she had my best intentions at heart too. I still hadn't told her about my latest conversation with Clay, so she wasn't able to act as my moral compass just quite yet. 'All right,' I said, emptying what was left of the bottle into our three glasses. 'Enjoy!'

There was nowhere to sit in my bedroom except the bed. Adam crashed down on one of the pillows, arms crossed behind his neck, his long legs stretching in front of him. Lying on the other one, I felt fine. Sure enough, *Big Brother* was still going. The people on the TV were running around in the garden.

'That blonde looks rough,' said Adam.

'Nick has scary eyes,' I replied absently. 'This is really stupid, isn't it?'

'I can think of better things to do,' Adam replied.

'Oh yeah? Like what?'

Adam pulled his arm from behind his neck and reached out towards me. I moved into the warmth of his body. Put my hands on his shoulders and pulled his face down to kiss me. 'This better?' I asked.

'Bit more like it,' Adam replied.

From the other room we heard a cry of delight as Rachel exclaimed, 'I love this episode: *The One with the Morning After.*'

We looked at each other and laughed, 'Fancy that one?'

'Yeah, I like that one a lot actually,' Adam replied.

16

Nirvana: No Whatever Never Say Never

'Where are we going?'

'The Cliveden, babe, it's a cottage on the grounds. Spring Cottage. Very discreet. You'll buzz, it's cool. Quintessentially English.'

We were in the back of a blacked-out Bentley being driven at speed to our secret location. This was the trip Clay had been arranging when he called me that day in the office. Before what happened with Adam, which was not good. I tried to tell myself this was OK as it had been preordained. Besides, whenever I was with Clay, ordinary rules no longer applied. I could adopt the same attitude as he did, absolve myself of all responsibilities. Alcohol helped.

Clay had the Bolly in his hand and we were drinking it straight from the bottle, passing it back and forth between mouthfuls, like teenagers sharing a cheap can of lager.

'I come here to chill, it's cool. It's where some government minister, his name was Profumo or something, used to bring his mistress in the Sixties. Kinky, huh? And it's near to Heathrow if I want to make a sharp exit.'

'What, you mean Christine Keeler? Jesus.'

'Yeah, that's it. You can be her, Pocket, my sexy Sixties siren, if you want.' He pulled me closer and laughed.

'Oh, for God's sake, stop it, will you. If we did get caught it would be the Profumo Affair all over again, wouldn't it?'

'No one will find us here, Pocket, it's designed for people like me, who need to be discreet. That's what it was made for: illicit sex, babe.'

It was dark when we got there, but I could see the description 'cottage' was an understatement. It was bigger than the family home I'd grown up in, for a start, and looked like something from a classic British period film drama, tall, chimneyed, gabled up to death.

Nestled in secluded woodland and looking out onto the edge of the Thames, it was an adulterer's fantasy all right. When we got inside, I skipped from room to room to check it out while Clay, unfazed, crashed out on the bed. Opening the ginormous fridge in the kitchen confirmed my feelings – this place was enchanted. It was gloriously stocked with row upon row of gleaming bottles of vintage champagne, there must have been at least 20 in there, and punnets of the plumpest, juiciest strawberries, finest chocolates, caviar, colossal green olives, delicious cheeses: choice rich man's delicacies.

There was a fine dining lounge, three bedrooms, vast fireplaces in every space and even our own personal butler should we require anything whatsoever, like needing our socks ironed.

Clay appeared, stripped down to almost nothing. It must have been his stock mode of attire in hotel settings. I suppose he figured his body was just so perfect it must be revealed, admired and gazed at like a Florentine masterpiece or something.

It was a little unnerving just the same. Seeing him like that banged home the intimacy of the situation, which suddenly felt quite serious and beyond my control. Just the two of us, in the middle of nowhere.

'Hey, you hungry, babe? We got our own car on standby if you wanna have something to eat up at the main house, but I reckon we order-in tonight, get a takeout.'

'What, like a curry?' I said, aghast, more than a little disappointed at the prospect of Clay and I eating out of little foil containers, here of all places.

Clay ignored me, he wasn't listening. 'I say we have some Scottish scallops, lobster, salad. Anything else you want, just say so, tell me, it's yours.'

'OK, I'll have a scallop balti with a naan bread, Rusholme mile style,' I replied facetiously.

Clay shrugged at me. 'Seriously,' he said. 'Whatever.'

I had to admit I was ravenous. We'd been smoking some sort of weed all the way down and it had given me one hell of an appetite for something intensely sweet and sickly. I was just mulling over the idea of what that thing was.

Clay spotted the thought flickering above the surface and pressed me for an answer: 'You want something?'

'No. It's so stupid, it doesn't matter.'

'Just tell me, Pocket. What do you want, more than anything else in the world right now, babe? It's no problem. Say it.'

'OK, well, if you really want to know, if I could choose right now, this moment, it would be a great big slab of Christmas cake. Don't ask me why,' I said, embarrassed at the somewhat wonky, unconventional choice I'd made.

It was true, though. I had no idea why I'd suddenly thought of Christmas cake. I didn't even particularly like the stuff. It was just something that popped into my head. A self-edit mode had malfunctioned.

Clay looked at me dubiously and smirked.

'Listen, you asked,' I began. 'OK, I know it's June but that's it, that's what I'm thinking about all right, since you asked. Or maybe just the icing… or maybe just the marzipan.'

'Pocket, if that's what you want, then that's what I'll get you, with a big fat fucking Santa Claus riding his reindeer on top. Spring, summer or fall, makes no difference to me. I'll order.'

He grinned, and it struck me that possibly he was laughing at me.

But it was a lesson in Clay's approach to life. If you wanted something, you could have it, no matter what it was. Even if some poor bastard had to sweat blood and tears to get it for you. Ask for a rainbow, this man would make the sky weep and the sun come out until he got one. But to Clay, that sort of thing was someone else's problem.

'That's very kind,' I said, 'I appreciate the gesture, I really do, but give them a break, will you? I get who you are. I get this place, obviously it's incredible, so thanks for bringing me here, but you don't have to do that, OK? You're not Father Christmas. You're famous: that's different. Well, I guess he's famous too, but he's not real. Lobster will be perfect, more than perfect, but really anything would be lovely, and have you seen what's in the fridge? We're not exactly going to starve.'

Clay looked taken aback, a little pouty for a moment, not sure whether to take offence that someone had actually turned him down for once, even if it was just over a trifling matter of fruit cake. Or maybe it was because I'd told him he wasn't Santa. Maybe no one had dared tell him that before either. Then his expression changed into a smile.

'OK, babe, lobster. Let's eat.'

'OK,' I smiled back. I liked the way he said 'lobster' in his West Coast American accent: it sounded sexier, the emphasis on the 'lob', which was not a logical reason.

A phone call later we were in food heaven. The meal was amazing, utterly divine, served to us on an enormous table with a crisp white tablecloth, antique silver candelabra and cutlery so heavy it felt like stone. A huge vase stood in the middle of the table filled with pale pink peonies, deep green leaves and tiny white wild roses. It was like our own private restaurant, with our own personal staff, in the seclusion of our romantic getaway – simply beautiful.

We devoured every morsel between us, beginning with perfectly moist scallops and then the most meaty, juicy lobster, which Clay scooped out of its shell and fed to me piece by piece. It was pure carnal food lust.

Then straightforward carnal lust of the quintessentially English variety, right there in the dining room. Then some more in the bedroom.

Clay rolled over onto his side of the bed to face me and I could see his eyes were gleaming with some unknown sentiment, pure devilment perhaps. 'C'mon, Toots, let's go for a walk,' he said, passing me a tablet.

'OK,' I said, swallowing the pill without giving it much thought.

'I've got something to show you. Here, put this on.'

He passed me his leather jacket, the one I'd wanted to touch in Cannes, and he gestured to me to walk down the stairs and through the kitchen to the door, which led outside and into the dark summer night.

There was a warm breeze, and I wasn't sure if it was the heat of the evening or the drugs pumping through my body, but it felt invigorating, exhilarating, like I was buzzing inside. In the dark, everything seemed bigger, stranger, and the lines between what I thought I was seeing and what was real were blurred.

'Toots, this way.'

Clay took my hand and led me through the grass up a steep hill. We stumbled forwards towards a vague light, the coolness of the grass brushing my legs and feet. In the distance, I could see the imposing silhouette of Cliveden House and it felt like we were trespassing on the grounds of a royal estate, daring and adventurous. Thrill-seekers or anarchists or something.

After about 10 minutes we came to a halt.

'Stop. We're here.'

'We are?'

A high-walled square enclosure stood in front of us, with eerie, lacy shadows of flowers and climbing bushes cast upon it. I wasn't sure what I was looking at, and as Clay offered no explanation, I imagined it to be a secret garden.

'You know, sometimes I feel like the only parts of my life that are real are like this.'

'What do you mean?'

'Lived out in the dark.' He paused. 'Hidden away, stolen back when no one else is looking. It was easier when I was a kid; I could live in my imagination. No one asks much of you then, you're free to wander in your mind.'

'You can't do that any more? Surely that's you, that's your job. Don't you have to be free and imaginative to be creative? You're an actor: you feel for everyone,' I replied, fascinated.

'It's different. It started off that way, then it became something else. Something darker. It's not about speaking to people's souls, it's about manipulating them so that you can sell them something they think they need.'

'Like a stage, you mean, like you're on show?' I felt like he was beginning to reveal a little of himself to me...

'I can still reach inside myself sometimes, but I'm not sure it matters whether what I'm giving is the essence of my soul or the bottle of scent with my name on it, babe. It's all a show, kid, and so long as people are buying the ticket, who knows what part of it they bought into.'

At that moment Clay laughed outrageously and walked ahead of me. I realised he was no longer within my field of vision.

Edging forward, I saw the outline of a large wooden door. It groaned as Clay opened it and stepped inside, leaving me alone outside. A few moments later, I heard the unmistakable crack of something heavy hitting the surface of water. Tentatively I followed the noise and walked through the gate. Before me, a black shimmering pool reflected the moonlight on its smooth surface. I could make out Clay's long, lean form diving underwater, his body dispersing and disturbing the glossy light, agitating its uniform pattern to make dark, unruly ripples.

Around the edge of the ornate pool was a private courtyard. Shades of a decadent historical past. Stone statues stood provocatively, greeting their night-time guests as though it was nothing they weren't completely accustomed to. Their ancient marble forms gleamed seductively in the light and, before my brain had time to rationalise, I took off Clay's jacket, threw it to the ground and jumped in with him. I was bewitched.

The chilled water cast its spell on my naked body instantaneously. It was salty. Ecstasy and adrenalin mingled together, surging through my brain. Stretching my arms out wide in front of me, I made silent strokes through the water, enjoying the freedom of my movement and the icy-cold liquid surrounding me. My brain wandered into an almost transcendental daze, meditating slowly, turning random thoughts over in my head, taking in my beautiful surroundings. With every push and pull of my arms, I plunged deeper and deeper into a peaceful karmic stupor. I took a mouthful of the salty water and swallowed it, just for the sensation it gave me.

The only sounds were the soft strokes of our bodies through the water and the unwavering trickle from the fountain at one end, pouring the endless stream back into the pool. Occasionally, I had vague perceptions of the familiar rustles of night-time and the dim hum of cars in the distance, but they washed over me, melted away. Even though we were only 10 miles from London's busiest airport, I felt like I was in another world, a million miles away.

Clay pulled himself out from the water at the far end of the pool, drying himself briefly on the jacket. He walked towards me and offered a hand to lift me out. I was tempted to pull him back in again alongside me, but his grasp was firm, decisive, as if he'd read my mind. He was having none of it. He was the one in control.

I pulled the damp jacket around me and looked at Clay. We smiled at each other in mischievous complicity.

'Cold?'

'A bit.' My teeth were beginning to chatter, and the night air suddenly felt chilly and unwelcome.

'It's like the ultimate freedom, don't you think, Pocket?'

'Well, I've never really thought about it like that, but it definitely feels good, yeah.'

'I love this. Being able to breathe, to see, man.'

'It's lovely,' I agreed.

'When I was in Venice at the film premiere, I slipped off for a few minutes after the red carpet. The hysteria, you know, it got to me. I was standing alone in the empty lobby of the cinema and I looked out the window. Suddenly I realised there was a circus taking up the whole of the square outside and I hadn't even seen it! I'd just walked straight past it because I was consumed by my own world. A Venetian carnival. White-faced clowns, sad and grotesque. Baroque dancers wearing bauta masks. I could see the flames whooshing up from the fire-eaters as they were warming up, waiting for their curtain call from the ringmaster. Beautiful, man.'

'Cool.'

'You know it's like tunnel vision. Most of the time you can't see what's right there in front of you.'

He paused and looked at me as I was deciphering what he was saying, working out if he was asking me to feel sympathy for him or something, because he was famous.

'Then there are moments, I suppose,' he added with a roguish smile, 'when it all feels pretty wonderful.'

'Yeah, I guess. Most of the time it must feel like Christmas every day for you,' I laughed.

'I don't know any different, do I, Pocket? I was born this way. Come on, babe, let's get warm.'

And Clay was off. Running down the hill, laughing out loud, streaking like a man who'd lost his mind. I could see his impressive bottom in the distance, a beacon of seduction, so I had no option but to follow, screaming and laughing behind him.

When I caught up with him, we fell to the ground and lay down in the grass to catch our breath, panting like a pair of wild animals.

Clay looked at me casually, threw himself on top of me and licked the skin on my back, then he turned me over and rolled his tongue over my chest, 'to taste the salt,' he said.

Then, without explanation, he stood up, threw his arms in the air and started singing Oasis at the top of his voice.

I started laughing and joined in now, belting the song out to the moon like a total fucking certified loony, and it felt brilliant. I was dead happy. Deliriously so. The two of us naked, singing like a couple of angels gone wrong. Our souls slid away. Going to hell the pair of us, most likely.

17
Awake

When I woke up the next morning, I was eyeball to eyeball with a man with a little white fluffy beard and a red hat.

It was a small, perfectly crafted sculpture, but because it was directly in my eyeline, it was filling up my field of vision. My eyes, sore and gluey, were playing tricks on me: the hangover hallucinogens had turned the lenses into funhouse mirrors while I was coming round.

A faint aroma of sugar drifted across the pillow. The Father Christmas was made of icing and was sitting, somewhat unconventionally, astride a sugar reindeer pulling a sleigh, which was the centrepiece of the most magnificent cake I'd ever seen.

It came back to me: it was the Christmas cake I'd ordered last night. The ultimate festive *pièce de résistance* that I assumed the kitchen could never deliver.

But it had. A three-tiered cascade of snowy icing and marzipan, as smooth as the white sands of a coral beach. It was like something out of Marie Antoinette's pantry. Deep, dark vapours from the 200-year-old brandy hung in the air, mixed with the spices from the rich fruit, ingredients that had obviously been flown in fresh and prepared by a team of Michelin-starred chefs working through the night.

All for Clay.

I turned away and buried my head in the duvet. It was the comedown from hell. Why was it that every time after I'd had an amazing evening with this man, I was greeted by crashingly horrible images of reality colliding with the fantasy?

It was becoming a nightmarish pattern. The cake should have made me happy – a celebration. More than that – an indulgence beyond pleasure. But it was amazing how just looking at the thing evoked in me exactly the feeling I had on Christmas Day every year. I wasn't talking about the nostalgic, sentimental feelings to do with family and stuff, which you're meant to get. I was talking about that horrible, morbid feeling of emptiness. The bit when you realised the pile of crap you got for Christmas was just a pile of stuff you didn't care about or need, combined with that horrible loss of appetite when you were greeted with a mass of food you didn't want to eat either.

'What's that?' I said to Clay, who had his back to me and his eyes shut.

'That's breakfast,' Clay replied, coming round fast. He'd obviously got used to waking up in this state.

'Breakfast?' I stared at the cake, once again, incredulously.

'Yes. It's the fucking cake you asked for, Pocket, whaddya think it is?'

'And that?' I said, pointing my gaze towards the bottle next to it.

He opened one eye and smiled knowingly. 'That is ruinously expensive luxury, kid,' he yawned. 'Perrier-Jouet Belle Epoque, 1995 vintage, pure as the driven snow, honey. Oscar Wilde's champagne of choice, and the only one Coco Chanel ever digged. I only know that shit 'cos they sent me over a crate of the stuff. Chanel have been chasing Stella to get me on board for some campaign, which is cool, I guess. Just haven't got round to doing the deal yet, that's all. Wanted to mull it over, over a bottle, before she gets here. Want some?'

I would have settled for some tea and toast.

'Seriously? Now? We're going to drink that now?' I said to him.

'Well, you know what they say: "Too much of anything is bad, but too much champagne is just right." It's full of good chemicals, baby, makes your heart beat faster.' Clay passed me a glass and kissed me on the hand.

'OK,' I said, 'I guess.'

And so it was I came to experience the 24-hour magic of fizz, a champagne breakfast, the definition of decadence, the ultimate pick-me-up to the put-me-down. The only way to stay upright in Clay's world was to climb onto the merry-go-round and never get off. So on I got.

The day went on like that. We never got dressed. Necked the champagne, hopped in and out of bed. Ate a bit of the cake, then left it to rot, half-eaten like a spoilt masterpiece.

I didn't know what time it was, early afternoon maybe. I went for a pee. Clay was asleep again. Beautiful, even in sleep, no mouth hanging open, dribbling or snoring, just pure passive perfection. A man in harmony with the universe.

Climbed back into bed just to look at him. Could have looked at him forever. But then I heard something. My phone ringing, Roddy's number flashing up on the screen.

'Toots, I'm fuckin' furious. Wayne D?'

Wayne D was a new-kid-on-the-block wanker rapper who I'd interviewed in the current edition, giving him enough rope to hang himself out to dry.

'Yes, Wayne D,' I replied, 'The white kid from Walton-on-Thames who thinks he's from Compton.'

'I went to school with his brother actually and Wayne's a good friend of mine. So what's this about you going out of your way to piss him off? His manager's shitting a brick and that brick's gonna fly, Toots. You and I both know the rules – what goes on in the toilets stays in the toilets. Hell, darling, you got the shit on your T-shirt on that one. So what I want to know is what the fuck were you playing at the other night? And why am I having to call you up to ask you…? Takin' a fuckin' break, taking leave of your nulli-fied senses more like, why aren't you at your desk? Where the hell are you?'

Immediately my heart beat faster and I snapped out of my romantic stupor like a cartoon idiot, which is what I was, after all. And I didn't know. I couldn't think where I was or what I was doing here.

It was all I could do to reach onto the bedside table, lift up the glass on the table and pick up a coaster, which I flipped over to the right side. Embossed on it was 'Cliveden'. My brain was going, 'Where the fuck's the Cliveden?'

But instead I said, full of confidence, 'I'm at the Cliveden, I can explain, I've got a great story for you, Rods.' I don't know why I said it. It just popped out, the panic, the need to tell him something. I slipped quietly out of the bed and moved into the next room, shutting the door. It was the first time I'd thought about work in 24 hours, but my instinctive desire to turn everything into a story had reared its head. There was also an innate need to tell someone, to share this amazing experience, I suppose, but a few seconds later I regretted it. Why did I say it? 'A great one,' I repeated for suicidal measure.

As soon as Roddy hung up, Rach was on the line, which was more comforting but guilt-inducing too.

'Hi, you still coming back today? I thought we could go to that Thai café round the corner.'

I thought fast enough to agree and said, 'Yeah, the one that's a house in the day and a café at night, yeah? OK, we'll have to take some beers though, Rach, they haven't got a licence.'

'That's cool, I'll get some. Shall I invite Adam?'

'No, don't invite Adam, just us.' I knew I'd said that a little too fast.

Rach. I needed my Rach. Oh my God, and Adam, I thought of Adam, dear, kind, lovely Adam. And all of a sudden I wanted to get out of there, and fast. Back to who I was, back to my life before it all spiralled out of control. I felt sated, gorged on decadence. Admittedly, the thought of Stella arriving and seeing me there was another reason I wanted to leg it quickly. I hadn't seen her since the fateful interview in LA and I wasn't ready for that, at least not yet.

As it turned out, I needn't have worried. Clay was planning my exit faster than I was. Well, less 'planning', more 'had planned'.

'Pocket, is that you? Got a car coming for you in five, babe. Best you head back. I'm gonna chill here for a few more days. I'll get one of the girls to call you,' he shouted at me, insouciant, from the other bedroom. I felt like I was being dumped, and in a sense, I was, but with free transportation thrown in. Clay did this to people, to everyone, not just me. I knew that. He had his fun then threw you away. But instead of turning tail and telling him where to shove his car, I did something else. I did what everyone did in the presence of a celebrity doing something shitty to them. I thanked him.

Leaning over the bed to collect my things, as casually as possible so as not to alarm Clay, who was doing some sort of yogic pose on the bed with his eyes closed, I became puzzled as to whether he was aware I was still here.

'OK, so that is?' I said tersely, sitting tentatively on the ruffled cotton of the unmade bed.

It made me feel sullied to see the beautiful sheets like that. Clay grunted a little bit. This was the bit where he was meant to say 'yeah' at the very least, but he didn't, he just breathed out a sort of blowing sigh, rather like a labouring mother dealing with a very tiring contraction.

'Wwwrrrhhhhmmmm.'

'Bye then,' I said, loudly this time.

'Shhhhh.'

Had that jerk just told me to be quiet? The hurt spiked me in the stomach. Was that all he thought I was worth, a hushed good-bye and a taxi? Anger took over and I felt the sudden urge to push him off the bed and send his silly yogic-posing body flying. But I didn't have the nerve. Not quite.

'Motherfucker,' I mouthed at him, quietly enough for me to feel satisfied that I'd said it out loud but probably too softly for it to count as actual bona fide defiance. And I swear to God, I saw a flicker of a smile playing at the corners of Clay's mouth.

Then, just as I stood up from the bed to leave, finally and properly this time, he grabbed me, pulled me down backwards, bent my head round and kissed me fully on the mouth. Eyes wide open, twinkling dark pupils dancing in his gaze, loads of sexual swagger intent within them.

'Bye bye, my Pocket. Call ya. Shut the door on the way out, will ya?'

Then he snapped his eyelids shut again and returned to a Buddha position like a statue. The hint of amusement still etched on his face served as the only evidence of the real-life person beneath the stoic posture.

I walked out like I was walking on air, feeling the light summer breeze dancing in my hair. Because, by my count, if that wasn't a victory, then at least it was a draw. He had heard me tell him off and he'd liked it. No one had done that in a good while, and it had made him come back for more. For good measure, I left the door open by pushing a thick lump of bark lying invitingly on the step into the corner of the hinge. I tapped it into place with the point of my shoe to make sure it stayed that way. Then I stepped outside and into the comfort of the waiting car, which purred at my arrival, happy in the knowledge that sooner or later Clay would have to come downstairs to shut the door himself.

18
It Girl – Build Me a Woman

Four months, two nights of passion with the most famous man on the planet, 105 hangovers and 63 black cabs later, I was officially an It girl. Objective achieved. Roddy happy. Me tired.

'But I'm so knackered, Adam,' I groaned, leaning on his shoulder for comfort. 'I'm not even sure what day it is any more.'

Adam and I were sitting in Pizza Express in Greek Street, watching the theatregoers and Friday-nighters come and go. It was lovely to be doing something normal for once, eating a Sloppy Giuseppe, not worrying about calorie content or whether I had tomato sauce on my chin.

'Every book, film, launch, gallery and fashion event has my name on the list. You won't believe this, Adam, but I was waved to the front of the queue at Kabaret and Chinawhite last week. Remember when we all tried to get in there a few months back? Now they love me.'

'You're an It girl now, Toots.'

'How did this happen though, Ads? My head's wrecked. I know I wanted an interesting life, but I'm not sure I wanted this. It's just not how I envisaged it. I dunno. It's like, I wanted to be the one in control. This feels different, like I'm just another face, another body, moving from one event to the next. I guess I thought it would be more stimulating somehow.'

If he was bored of listening to me moan about my tediously glamorous life, Adam didn't show it. It dawned on me I was going on about myself again; this was meant to be a two-way conversation. I was vaguely aware I was turning into a classic narcissistic monster but seemed powerless to stop myself.

'How've you been, Ads? Sorry I let you down last week.'

'It's been fine, Toots, I've just been hanging out. Actually, I had to go home for a few days; my gran's been really ill.'

'Oh no, is she better?' I said. I knew Adam was close to his grandmother; lived with her when he was growing up.

'Thanks. No, not really, she's not too good.'

'What about work?' I replied, not really registering the serious nature of what he'd said, not because I didn't care exactly, just because I was so disconnected with real life that to try would be too hard.

'All this stuff with my gran being ill and everything, it's made me think. I didn't set out to stand around papping celebrities. I wanted to provoke an emotional response, you know? Not what I'm doing now, taking pictures that actually stop people thinking about the things that matter.'

'Celebrities. It's a freaky world, though, isn't it? My theory is simple: the problem with most of them is a case of starvation and a lack of oxygen getting to the brain.'

'What?' Adam looked at me, perplexed, possibly because I'd ignored the thrust of what he'd said and concentrated on the bit he said didn't matter to him.

'Well, take me for example, and I'm only on the lower rungs of famousness. I spend most of my life hungry, drunk or high, or all three. I subsist on a diet of gravlax, tepid mini hamburgers, slivers of asparagus and doggy-sized titbits. It's had the same transformative effect on my body as a gastric band might, which is, I suppose, a bonus, because if there's one thing I've realised it's this: if you want to be successful you have to be microscopically thin.'

'I don't know Toots, all I know is it doesn't interest me to photograph these people. Do you want another bottle of wine? We seem to have drunk this one."

'Yeah sure. Go on then.'

Truth was I'd drunk most of it, Adam was just too polite to say. As well as being hungry, I had forgotten what it was like not to be partially drunk at all times.

Suddenly I remembered we were meant to be meeting Rachel here too. It was just a given that whenever Adam and I went out, she came along too. Secretly, I was relieved, because Rach's being there meant Adam and I didn't have to talk about what had happened at my flat.

'There she is. Rach, over here!'

Rach waved with both hands and ran over to us, kissing me and Adam on our heads. Then she took my face in her hands and pretended to study it intently. 'Yes, it's you. It's actually you. It's been so long I didn't know if I would recognise you!'

'Shut up Rach, I stayed in last Thursday.'

'You were asleep.'

'OK, but I was there.'

'She's either out or she's half-cut, Adam.' She was right. 'Quite a dress you've got on there, girlfriend,' said Rach, eyeing me.

'Check the label,' I said, fishing down my neck to find it. 'I've got Claire to thank for it. I just send her to pick my outfits; I don't have time. It might look good, but you won't believe how grotty it is behind the scenes. All the up-and-coming celebrities get their stuff from these little warehouses full of designer gear. You borrow them for the evening, then a car comes to pick up the dress again the next day so someone else can.'

'Aw, yuck,' said Rach. 'Going from body to body like that?'

'No, it all gets dry-cleaned, doesn't it? This one I've got on, Alesha Dixon from Mis-Teeq had it on Monday at the *X-Men* premiere.'

'OK,' sighed Rach, 'I guess maybe it's not such a bad idea. At least you don't get any snooty customers breathing down your neck like in the shop, changing their minds over and over again... I hate them.'

'Exactly, Rach. You would love it: you get to style people how you want, no arguments, because basically they're there on the beg.'

'Hark at her, telling me about *my* industry,' said Rach, turning to Adam with a cheeky expression.

'Well, the point is, I'm not about to be traipsing off to some godforsaken north London industrial unit to trawl through rails of designer togs destined for the showbiz merry-go-round, am I?'

'Not when you have staff, darling!' said Rach. 'Babes, it is quite garish. Sure, I can see it on that girl from Mis-Teeq, but there's a reason they call that music "garage", isn't there?... garage sale, I'm thinking,' said Rach, with a smile, rolling back her shoulders to make her point rude-girl style.

'Yeah, what about the Hawaiian dress fiasco, Rach? I still haven't forgotten that. The point is, it's all make-a-statement stuff.'

'And the statement is?' Adam chipped in.

'"Here are my breasts, welcome,"' laughed Rach, looking at the low V neckline of my outfit.

I carried on imprudently, knowing I was just walking into a trap that contained more ridicule. 'I think Claire's done really well, one phone call and a taxi is pretty much all it takes to see me in a hot new outfit seven days of the week.'

'Hot to trot,' laughed Rach.

'Smokin',' said Adam.

'OK you guys. Hey Rach, you may be right. It is quite low,' I said, glancing down at my cleavage. 'Don't want to decorate my décolleté with Sloppy Giuseppe. Not tonight anyhow!'

'Slag,' said Rach crisply.

'Last slice coming 'atcha,' I said, handing her the plate.

Bringing up the dress fiasco had been a cheap shot, especially after the fallout Rach had endured on my behalf afterwards. To be honest, knowing Rach, she was probably more upset about the thought of someone else styling me than she was about any-thing else. But it was more than that. There were undercurrents of annoyance from both Adam and Rach, which I was choosing to avoid.

'OK, so seriously no. It's been unbelievably slow in the shop. Everything's marked down, so you get all sorts coming in, y'know, looking for a designer bargain. People you never usually see. Honestly, none of our regulars come near the sale. It's all the riff-raff, bridge-and-tunnel folk from out of London. "Trough dwellers," James says. Can't wait for the new stock to arrive; I can't look at the dreggy summer stuff any longer. Tell me the highlights of your week, Toots, I need some gossip.'

I mentally clocked the mention of James' name and the swift change of subject.

'I think Adam's probably had enough of me wittering on about my job by now, haven't you, Adam?'

'I don't mind,' said Adam courageously, smiling.

'He has,' added Rach, 'but he's too nice to say.'

'But I'm ordering more food,' he added, wandering off to bag a waiter. 'The usual, Rach?'

'Yes please, babe, Fiorentina,' said Rach breezily, but when she turned in my direction her expression changed. She scrunched up her mouth and looked at me with big eyes and a loaded question. She was asking, what was I playing at taking Adam for granted? And being such a prick in general? She was imploring me to see sense. I knew she was right. It was getting complicated and it had to stop. I knew it. But I wasn't sure how to deal with it all or how to unravel what I'd started. So I decided on a reliable course of action I knew would work. Drink it away.

'Get another bottle of red too, Adam,' I shouted over.

I gave her a look back and she shrugged.

'So? How's things?'

'Toots, what would you know about my life?'

'Well. I have an idea Rach.'

'No, actually Toots, you don't have an idea. You have no idea because your head is so far up your arse that you forgot what you were up there looking for.'

I'm stung, but that doesn't stop me correcting her English.

'That doesn't make sense Rach. Listen, if you're still hung up about James, that's not my fault.'

'From where I am it makes perfect sense. And if you think this is about me then you really are too far gone to help.' Her expression changed into a smile as Adam approached, for his benefit not mine, but not before she snarled at me, 'And sort this out. He's a good guy.'

19
The Secret

'*Voulez-vous coucher avec moi ce soir?*'

Only Clay could come out with a line like that and have any hope of actually getting away with it. Anyone else would sound like a knob, a handbag-in-the-balls job for sure. Not Clay: from him it provoked a giggle of nervous excitement, weakness at the knees, hearts-a-flutter and more often than not a willing shag. So far, from me, it had produced a weak smile. 'You?' I said, attempting a dry response. My resolve was strong. I hadn't forgiven him for his harsh goodbye at Cliveden either.

'Pocket Bardot, baby, you make me sing, you know that. I've missed you,' he whispered down the receiver.

'You have?' I answered incredulously.

'For sure I have. Hold on a minute... Just order the duck and frites will ya, salad on the side, no dressing, why are you even asking me that? I don't care if it's not on the "in-room dining menu", tell the fucking chef.'

Mentally I'd registered the harsh switch from the 'heart singing and missing me' routine to chip and duck dinner. Then I smiled. I couldn't help it; he was cheeky as hell.

Clay came back to the phone. 'Yeah, baby, it took my girls ages to track you down, just forever. So you gonna come over then?'

'What? Where are you? What time is it? Shit, it's one-thirty in the morning.' The sensible part of me told me I should go home, but then I thought, 'We've got unfinished business, haven't we?'

'I suppose I am in town already. OK, yeah, I guess I'm coming, yeah. Where am I coming to?' Now I'd said it.

'The penthouse suite somewhere or fuckin' other. Listen, I'll pass you over to Jules, she'll give you the deets.'

'Jules? What happened to Sarah, and Jen, was it, the other one?'

But he was gone. Minion Jules was on the line, so I took down 'the deets'. Already I felt peeved by the offload. I was willing to bet his room service had just arrived. I was getting to know him well.

I'd known Clay was in town on the UK leg of his movie tour: the invite to the premiere party for his film had been sitting in my desk drawer for a week but it was purely business. I'd risen above, moved on. Now I was ready to tell him.

In the cab on the way over, I examined my motivations for going. Closure. I would set him straight: I'd turn up and say it, then I'd leave. Nothing he could do could faze me.

The penthouse was the first thing to faze me. Actually, the private lift to the penthouse was the first. Stepping out the entrance into a world of consummate luxury, I was no longer thrown, I was seduced. The place took mood enhancement to new heights. There was a private dining area lit by an enormous opaque white chandelier. There were no interior walls; instead, the bathroom and dressing room were encased in a glowing floor-to-ceiling glass box wrapped in layers of curtains. It was like the biggest and best brains in the world of architecture and design had come together to sketch the perfect picture of modern style, complete with a sublime vista over London.

'Like the view, Pocket?' Clay appeared bathed in a spectrum of reflected light, wearing a pair of skin-tight undies and a white sheepskin rug on his shoulders. He was Mick Jagger in *Performance* for the year 2000. The sight of him, his sheer elegance, made me laugh out loud.

'What is it with you and looking at the sky? Don't you remember I've heard that one before? The night sky, waves lapping, starry eyes?'

'Well, it worked, didn't it, honey?'

I was pissed off now. This wasn't endearing or funny; it was just cruel. He was laughing at me.

I flipped. 'What about if I tell you it worked for me too. Maybe I just wanted to shag a star. Isn't that what it's all about these days? It's not really about you, is it? It's about the fantasy. You don't know me, I don't know you, neither of us cares. Isn't that right? Who gives a fuck?'

Clay ignored me, but he was pissed off. I could see it.

'I just like free stuff,' I said, provoking him a bit more.

'Babe, you didn't even get near to the good stuff,' he answered glibly.

'Oh fuck you,' I said. 'I wouldn't want it anyway. What is it they say… no such thing as a free fuck. It all gets paid for one way or another, right?'

'You sure, Pocket? I think you liked it.'

I stopped. He was right. I couldn't deny that, could I? The truth was, I hadn't stopped thinking about him, not really. He'd always been there at the back of my mind. This just infuriated me more.

But he was angry now too. I thought maybe I'd pushed him too far. I saw his face change. 'So who the fuck do you think you are then? Do you think I'm stupid? I've seen it all before, Toots. Doe-eyed journalists, I've seen every doe-eyed female of the species in one capacity or another, you all want the same thing. Thing is, I thought maybe you had something unusual about you. Now you want to fuck me over? Join the queue, sweetheart.'

Suddenly he threw the heavy-bottomed glass he was holding at the wall. It cracked against the surface and shattered into hundreds of pieces. The crystal fragments flew all over the floor. Clay raised his hands out wide to the air. 'Everything is disposable, see? Want a piece of me, Pocket, help yourself.'

I was alarmed, unsure of myself. I stood rooted to the spot. I hadn't thought that much about what I was saying. After all, he was right: I'd seemed happy enough when we'd been together; it had been beautiful and I'd taken everything he'd offered without question. And what had he done that had been so bad? Not called me, been offhand. I realised I'd gone further than I'd meant to.

'I'm sorry,' I said, breaking the silence. 'I didn't mean that, I never really wanted anything from you. I got it into my head you thought I was disposable, I suppose, like that glass. It pissed me off, especially as I thought we had a real connection. I'm going to go, it was a mistake to come.'

Clay stepped in front of me and looked me straight in the eyes. I could smell his rich, exotic odour and feel the warmth coming from his body. It was exhilarating just standing near to him. The violence had gone, and there was something else. Desire? He drew me in, the self-righteousness in me turning so easily into passion. In my brain the red lights were flashing and a voice was saying, 'Here we go again.'

Clay tossed the sheepskin rug over the broken glass, and I was vaguely aware of its softness against my bare skin as we moved over to the bed.

Afterwards I felt too high to sleep; I felt hyper-real. Clay was enlivened too. He poured some whisky for me and I drank it down. He grinned at me curiously.

'Come here, Pocket, I want to show you something.'

I pulled the sheet around my shoulders for warmth. I didn't want to leave the comfort of the bed.

'What is it?'

'Closer,' he said, gesturing to me. I went over to the window and he put his arm around me and pointed to a building in the distance. 'See that tower block over there?' He pointed and moved my head with both his hands to direct my line of vision to the right spot. 'That's where I was born.'

'But that's Tower Hamlets, isn't it?' I said, looking at the oppressive blot on the London skyline.

'Yeah, Tower Hamlets, that's it.' It sounded funny, incongruous, as he spoke the words in his accent.

'But wait, just hang on, you're joking, right? That's not right. I mean, I've interviewed you, remember, read the press cuttings. You're an American. "The All-American Boy done good."'

'Don't believe everything you read in the paper, honey, hasn't life taught you anything? No, that's where I'm from. The 11th floor, too quick for the doctors, that's me, so I was born on a towel in the kitchen apparently. Come a long way, haven't I, sweetheart?'

I imagined something like a nativity scene: Clay, as the baby Jesus, glowing in holy light. And perhaps I should have been sceptical, but I couldn't be: his face was absolutely the face of an icon, it was awesome. I didn't know what it was, but it had that quality, the shape of it, the space between his nose and his forehead and his eyebrows. He was just too much. He was a different animal, too much for the real world, almost too much for the screen to contain. He could say or do anything and it would be taken as gospel.

'But I don't get it,' I said.

'Well, it was no accident I ended up here babe. I was kind of born to do this job. Maybe you'd call it showbiz aristocracy, my heritage meant this was my destiny. That much is true, but my journey sure was a strange trip,' he said drily.

'So what happened to you? Exactly how did you get from there to America?'

'It's a long story, but my old girl, her name's Lily Sue, was beautiful. Too damn beautiful for her own good: green eyes, dark hair, longest legs you've ever seen.' Clay seemed like he was in full flow.

'Who was Lily? Your mother? What did she do?' I asked.

'Let's say she was a performance artist.' He smiled with some tenderness as he said it. 'But she had me when she was a girl. Real young, it was hard. She had no money, got in trouble, drugs, debt, dangerous men – you know the story. The circumstances were not her fault. So arrangements were made. A guy who looked after her made a few things happen. Got me a passport, a ticket and hooked me up with some nice folks in America. It was complicated.' He paused, 'I left her when I was three.'

None of this had ever been mentioned in the newspapers before, I was sure. I'd been through his cuttings dozens of times. This was a shocking revelation. Three. As he was speaking, I couldn't believe what I was hearing. The way he was saying it, so matter of fact, casual almost, it was incredible. 'What? Wow, three years old. That must have been heartbreaking. How on earth did you cope?' I asked, astonished.

'Babe, that's life. Look at me. I guess you could say I coped,' he smirked, but behind his eyes I could sense something else. I could see bitter-sweetness in his smile. Admittedly, I was flattered that Clay was talking to me like this, letting me in, showing me what lay beneath the surface. Simultaneously, my professional instincts were fired up like I'd just got three oranges flashing up on the fruit machine.

'But why are you telling me this? Me of all people? You know what I do: I'm a journalist,' I said.

'I'm telling you this because you remind me of who I am, what's underneath, what I might have been. You're an everyday person, y'know, normal, aren't you? And it's kind of refreshing. Me? Well, you can't process me with a regular brain.'

I felt like I'd been stung. 'Normal, that's it, is it?'

'Well, it's a compliment. You take it how you like, honey. I meant to say you're straight-talking, that's all. It's nice to talk to someone who doesn't bullshit me and, of course, to someone who's pretty well formed on the outside too. It's a rare thing. Foxy and smart, that's why I like you,' he laughed.

Clay wandered over to the kitchen area of the suite and pulled out a bottle of whisky and some soda water, then poured it into two glasses and came back, handing me one of them.

I leaned back in the settee and pulled the sheet around me, but I couldn't quite compute what I was hearing.

'But if what you are saying is true, how could your mother just let you go like that? How did she cope? I mean, you were so little.'

'She had to. She was in a bad way. Lily was in trouble with all sorts of mad, bad people. She owed money at the nightclub where she worked and was getting leaned on by heavies. Her career was dubious, I guess you'd say, and after she had me she couldn't work like she used to. She was on her own, you see, no family to take care of her, nothing. Seventeen with a baby to take care of, social workers on her back. By then she was developing a nice little relationship with the bottle; she took it up where my dad left off. The way things were, she was going to end up losing me. The social services were going to take me so she looked for another way out. She found another solution. She did it for me.'

Clay became agitated, dismissive, he gestured to the bleak silhouette of buildings in the distance. His tone turned to disdain, 'Look at that place: do you think I would be here now, if I'd stayed? Anyway, like I said, it was complicated. It was my destiny to do this, she knew that. I was too much like my father, even then.'

'I don't understand.'

'My dad was an American, you see, he made sure she was taken care of when he died. They were only together a short time, six months or something on and off, but they were in love. What they had was innocent. He remembered she had helped him out once, when he was on his knees. She came through, sorted him out, took him in, he was able to hide away with her. Get his head together. It became like their thing, way she tells it. Whenever he needed to escape, he'd turn up on her doorstep and she'd take him in again, for the night, whatever, no questions asked. He never forgot, even after things faded.'

'What do you mean, he was a GI or something?'

'No, he was a performer. He was legendary, just about as famous as you can get. He was going through a bad time in his life. He'd come to Europe to get away from all the craziness back in the States, and then one cold night, when he was down on his luck, my Lily found him slumped in a doorway outside one of the clubs she worked at. He'd gone real fat, grown a beard, looked more like a tramp at that point, she said, you know this was the Sixties, they all looked like that back then. She took him in, cleaned him up and they fell in love.' He laughed deeply. 'She loved a stray, Lily did, was always attracted to them, and she couldn't resist this one, could she? He was irresistible to everyone.'

'So they fell in love?'

'Yeah, I guess you could say that. Love of her life. Never got over him. Picture of him on the refrigerator, she loves him to this day.' I detected rawness in Clay's voice, but he changed mid-flow, became more insouciant again. 'But it would never have worked. He had to go back to Paris, he had a wife, a crazy redheaded girl over there, he was locked in. He loved his wife; he loved Lily too.'

'Fuck.' The story sounded like something from one of Clay's movies, but even more epic. So his dad was famous. In my mind I flipped through a stream of Sixties celebrities to see if I could get a match, but no. Honestly, coming from anyone else I wouldn't have believed it, but from him it was perfectly plausible. Everything about him was 'beyond'.

'OK, so what happened to your dad then? Where did he end up in all of this?'

Clay sighed. 'There were complications. Like I told you, he was famous, very, more than famous than I will ever be. It was fucked. Eventually he died of a drug overdose in Paris – as they did in those days. Didn't have rehab holidays in the sun then, babe.'

'That's so sad. Did he know? Did she tell him she had you, that she was pregnant? Did you ever meet your father?' I asked.

'No, we never met. But he could never have been a father to me, not in the state he was in. He was nurturing a serious heroin habit and that pretty much took over as the love of his life. I told you, he was a legend – egocentric, selfish, not exactly great dad material, from what I've seen and read,' Clay said with a shrug, conceding that he himself was guilty of this description. 'All around him were demons: the people, the drugs, his own twisted genius and everyone wanting a piece of him. Record companies, A&R men, businessmen: they drank his wine, spent his money – that kind of shit. In the end it got too much. Too much drugs, too much everything. He killed himself. Found dead in the bath.'

'Oh my God, that's tragic. And your mum?'

'Lily said she read about his death in a newspaper. She hadn't heard from him in a couple of months. It wasn't even that much of a shock, more an inevitable fact, the way she tells it.'

The heartbreaking nature of what he said was compelling. I was desperate to ask what his father's name was but to ask would be to expose myself, make me look like I was interested in the commodity rather than his feelings. And it meant more to me not to hurt him. I felt sorry for him. Despite all his success, it was such a sad story, especially for his mother, left like a victim on the roadside. What ever happened to her?

As though he'd sensed my regret, Clay smiled at me and answered my thoughts.

'That was a long time ago. She's OK now; I sorted her out babe, set her up in a place in Brooklyn a couple of years ago. She won't live in LA, says it doesn't feel right. I guess that's because she's a London girl, she likes to hear the city at night, crazy lady, crazy Lily Sue.'

Clay walked over to the expansive white leather sofa where I was sitting and threw himself down on it, stretching out like a pussycat. As though he had satisfied his own desire to tell the story. He betrayed nothing of how hard it must have been to recount the story. As a skilful actor, he hid it well, I supposed.

'Want a drink?' he asked, this time pouring neat whisky into our two glasses and gesturing to me to curl up beside him.

'Thanks.'

'So that was the end. Lily, God bless her, managed to save enough money to go to the funeral, although the whole thing had taken on a life of its own by then. It was a world event. Stars from all over the world flew in to be there: Lennon, McCartney, Dylan, the Stones, Jackie O. He was a big puller, even in death. Lily went along, paid her respects and all the time she was carrying me inside her. No one knew.'

'Wow,' I said, awestruck by the starry roll call.

'Well, almost no one. But when she was there, that guy, the one I told you about, took her to one side.'

'He threatened her?' I asked.

'Told her. Told her in terms she knew she had to listen to. He said she'd be looked after, I'd be looked after, if she stayed discreet, did a deal if you like.'

'He blackmailed your mum? What? I don't understand. What did he want her to do exactly?'

'It wasn't blackmail, babe; it's more subtle, more complicated than that. See, Lily knew she had to keep me safe, wanted that more than anything, I believe that. She knew that, on top of having a baby inside her, she was carrying the weight of knowing who my father was. It was more complex, especially as someone else knew. Lily was wise enough to know the impact of a secret like that. The guy had given her an option, you see, an opportunity that would allow me to be safe if ever it got to a point where she couldn't cope any more. He told her that, if she wanted, things would be taken care of. They would be keeping a close eye on her. She gave him her address scribbled on a piece of paper. So that was it. The deal that sealed and secured my fate was made there and then, at my father's funeral. She forgot all about it and went back to London to have her baby.'

'And that baby was you?' I said.

'Yeah, man. And for a while that was it: life was normal, not that I remember much of it. Then one afternoon, three and a half years later, some roadie turned up on her doorstep. He had a piece of paper with my name and address, the same one Lily had given to the guy, and she knew what it meant, the significance, if you like. Those guys' networks go all over the world and they had been keeping a close eye on her. Saw when it was all too much. He was a guardian angel – he *was* an angel for godsakes. That freakin' guy smuggled me back to the States, can you believe it?' Clay said this with a sense of amusement, like he was showing off a bit after all, like it was a great story and he knew it. 'Back then, that's what it was like – those guys did all the dirty work for the big labels. Lily handed me over. There wasn't any corporate stuff then. By then my mum was in a bad way, her drug addiction spiralled into oblivion and she couldn't look after me any more.'

'Fuck, that's awful.'

'It was as if he knew, my dad, like he'd looked down on me, like a rock and roll custodian on a motorbike. He'd taken care of me.' He laughed out loud again. 'She'd told him she was having his baby and he'd made sure I would be all right.'

'And how did he know? Your father, I mean?'

'She'd written him a letter telling him, but she didn't have his address, so she'd sent it to the guy he hung around with, his manager. She never knew if he'd got the letter. Never heard back. But he must have, because the guy at the funeral knew. He was looking out for her that day, so I guess he told him.'

My brain was working overtime trying to make sense of what I'd heard. All I could really think about was the little boy being taken away from his mother at such a young age. Every three-year-old needs their mother, don't they, no matter who they are?

For the first time I saw past Clay Allison and saw the child inside – he should have been protected.

'Do you think you should be telling me this? I mean, why are you telling me of all people? I just don't get it,' I asked him for a second time.

Clay paused and fixed his magnetic stare on me.

'I'm telling you this, Toots, because I trust you. Because I know you're not going to tell anyone.'

Then he kissed me. In each other's arms we fell asleep, with the silhouette of the city through the window shaping its own shadows on our weird dreams and our fucked-up lives.

With Clay asleep in the sprawling bed, I got dressed and left the hotel room at a discreet hour, as the sun was still rising above the London skyline.

Certainly he wasn't likely to wake up any time soon. A bottle of Ambien tablets lay next to him, which I guessed he'd washed down with the remaining whisky by his bedside.

As I was about to leave, I hesitated. I walked back over to where Clay was sleeping. His face was docile, a lost child. I leaned down and kissed him.

Glancing out the hotel window one more time, I saw Tower Hamlets, visible in the morning light. It looked as hopeful as it was ever going to, in the white glow of a new dawn. It was a grim and greying sight. Sixties tower blocks and blackened pre-war tenements don't scream Hollywood glamour.

Mornings usually brought some clarity and optimism to my thoughts but as I recalled Clay's revelations, I was only filled with questions. It was easier to think of him like before, in simple terms: a Hollywood star. I could be infatuated with him. Now I'd seen what lay beneath, I was edgy. He'd told me his secrets, let me in – did that mean his feelings were more serious? Is that what I was yearning for, or maybe a venal desire, was it the story that exhilarated me?

Deathly cold, but I needed to walk. Instead of getting a cab, I began the journey through sleeping central London, taking me back through the streets of Knightsbridge, then on towards Fulham. Topped off with a sneaky detour through Kensington Gardens. I wanted trees, green stuff, natural surroundings. No one around. Realising what I really missed was walking in the countryside. Where I was from, a quarter-of-an-hour in either direction and you were in the middle of vast spaces. Dank, mist-filled fields and murky, ominous hills around Manchester that always sorted my head out. Only here, in London, there were no gaps between the buildings, no room to see, no natural beauty to give you perspective on what was made up and what was real. No space to think. It was a poor substitute. How could anyone think?

Suddenly my thoughts were pierced by a ringtone.

'Toots, where've you been? I haven't seen you for three days now. I really need to speak to you.'

It's Rachel on the phone.

'I'm on my way back, hon. What the hell are you doing up? It's six o'clock in the morning or something.'

'Yeah, well, I've got something on my mind, haven't I? A bit of a situation. I think I might need your help.'

Her voice was flat. Depressed enough to trigger alarm bells.

'Yeah, but aren't you going to work, what time you in?'

'I'm not going in. Will you call in sick for me, please Toots, I just can't face it today.'

'OK no sweat – what shall I say?'

'I dunno, anything, just tell 'em I'm ill. OK? James will cover for me.'

'OK, Rach. I'm coming home.'

The phone call was like a shot of adrenalin. Firmly putting the surreal night with Clay behind me. Rachel needed me now.

When I got back to the flat, she was sitting on the futon, still in her pyjamas, unwashed hair, the lot. When Rach was undone on the outside, you knew she was undone on the inside. too.

'Hey, what's up, glamourpuss? What's with the student chic? You having a grunge moment?' I said, trying to lighten the situation.

164

'I had an abortion yesterday,' Rach replied, matter of factly.

I didn't know what to say.

'Rach,' I put my arms around her thin shoulders. 'Oh Rach.' Feeling the rhythm of her silent sobs.

'Had to, didn't I?'

Silence, which she couldn't stand. Rushing to fill it with an explanation, justification.

'Wasn't about to end up like my mum, was I? No way. No hope, no money, no father. It's done.'

She blows her nose and looks at me with resolve. 'Done. Gone. Dead.'

'What…? Don't say that…'

Clear pebbles of tears form in the apex of her eyes.

'Binned like a dead plant.'

'Rach…'

I put my arms around her.

'I wish you'd told me Rach, I would have come with you. I'm so sorry.'

'That's OK,' she says. 'James came with me. He even fronted the 500 quid.'

'But I should have been there, Rach.'

Her complexion was white now, drained and puffy. I knew there was worse to come.

'Irony is though, it wasn't his.'

'D'you mean James? It wasn't James'. But I thought you were…'

The pebbles, fat now and barely contained within their surface tension, rolled down her cheeks like shale gently pulled under the tide.

'I had a bit of a thing… a fling.'

'What?' I asked. 'Who? What do you mean?'

Rachel started laughing, bitterly.

'It was only fucking Roddy.'

I haven't had many proper shocks in my life. The ones where people say they take your breath away. Suppose that comes from being an observer, a reporter, hearing the misery of human adventure everyday. But this was a real head-wrecker.

'Can you believe it?' Rach stared at me. 'Roddy? A one-night stand, and hey presto, game over.'

'Oh my God Rach! No, Jesus, not Roddy. When did you? I mean, how?'

'One of the nights I was meant to be meeting you. I turned up at your office and Roddy said he'd sent you out somewhere or other.'

I remembered the exact night they'd met. Roddy being a bit shifty. The fleeting memory of Rach appearing from his office came back to me.

'We got talking and next thing it was "did I fancy going out with him instead?" Go for a meal somewhere nice? You know the script.'

Yes, I did know the script. Off by heart. Roddy the fucking lech.

'But it wasn't just him. I was confused around then, that time. Things with James were over and I was feeling lonely, hungry. You know me Toots. I'm always starving. Always up for a quick Chinese.'

'Your eyes were always bigger than your tummy,' I said, drawing a tearful smile from her.

'Suprisingly, Roddy turned out to be funny and kind of charming. Not like you'd described him at all. We had a nice meal, got wasted. I knew it was a mistake, I just thought it was a little one. Turns out it was a car crash.'

20
Christmas

'All passengers for the 9.43 to Manchester Piccadilly please come to Platform 13.'

'That's us, Rach. That's us, Adam.'

'I'll just grab some chewy and see you in a sec,' said Rach, breathing into the palm of her hand to check her breath, as if to emphasise the point, and heading in the direction of the newsagent on the other side of Euston Station.

'I think she's trying to be discreet, bless her. Give us a chance to say goodbye.'

'It's only a week.'

'Yeah. I still wish I was staying down here, though. It's so maddeningly dull at my parents', I feel like a little girl again, sitting there nicely for meals, bumming around, everything is so slow.'

'Toots, at least you have folks to go back to, who want to see you. Now my gran's gone, all I've got is my brother in Southampton and his crazy girlfriend, and he doesn't want to see me. Listen: relax and enjoy. It's Christmas.'

'Shit, Adam, now I feel guilty that you aren't coming. You are welcome, you know that, right? It's just my family would read a lot into it, and listen, I wouldn't wish that on you.'

'Hey, don't worry about it, beautiful, I'm cool,' Adam smiled, revealing the gap between his two front teeth that gave his handsome features a quirky boyishness.

I reached up and kissed Adam on the lips, tasting the familiarity of his unshaven loveliness. Then I nuzzled my head in his biker jacket that smelled of a million musty nights out. Its stink warm and consoling.

'Bye Adam. Call me.'

'Toots, take this. Open it on Christmas Day, OK? It's just something small.'

Adam handed me a flat, heavy package wrapped in thick, gold paper.

'But... I didn't get you anything. I've been so busy, oh shit, sorry. Thank you, Adam.'

'No worries. Please, just go, OK, you're going to miss your train.'

He squeezed my hand.

'Adam.'

'Yeah?'

'Happy Christmas.'

Turning to join the mass of people stampeding north to see their families for the big day, with plastic bags stuffed with cans of strong lager and suitcases on wheels rattling behind them. One bashed me in the ankle as a woman bustled past.

I glanced back for Adam and caught him looking towards me. Rach bounded up to me ebulliently. She was going up to her crazy mother's house for Christmas, but we decided to go up together. She seemed happier at the moment, mostly because things seemed to be 'on' again with James. I didn't question the rationale of this, how could I? I wasn't in a position to advise. I was just worried about her. On the surface, she seemed to have put what had happened behind her but I wasn't so sure. Occasionally, when she thought I wasn't looking, the joyful face slipped and in its place was a new sadness I didn't recognise. She was mourning. I felt like my neglecting her had been partly to blame. I didn't want to say goodbye. She had caught the exchange between me and Adam.

'Toots, be careful, he's lovely, you know,' she said.

'I know,' I said, but at the same time I wished she hadn't said it out loud, the thing we both knew. I'd already clumsily played with his feelings, treated them with disregard. It would all have been OK, if it weren't for Clay. Adam would have been perfect, things would have been perfect then, wouldn't they? Why did Clay have to come along and spoil things? Why couldn't it all be that simple?

Noddy Holder interrupted my thoughts, screaming: 'It's Chrissssssssmas.' He was being blasted out to the helpless shoppers in WHSmith, who had only come in to buy a pen to do their crossword, or a newspaper for the journey. His enforced brand of seasonal merriment blitzing tired, work-worn brains.

A pissed-off teenage shop assistant with regulation tinsel around her neck smiled weakly with a latent sense of apology, even though it was her who'd had to listen to Christmas hits on a loop every day from mid-September. I gave her what I hoped was a consolatory smile and glanced down at the *Standard* in my hand.

I registered the image of a man I recognised and it shook me back to full awareness. 'Michael Dawson rejects offer to stand for Mayor', said the headline. I remembered the Christmas card that had come into the office from him for me last week and that Claire had remarked how swish it was to get a card from a politician signed 'Always, Michael.' I'd played down the buzz. He remembered me. Funny to watch our fates played out across the papers in parallel, in this crazy city full of opportunity, for those who wanted to take it, that is.

'Oooh, Slade, I love this one, really gets me in the mood!' Rach grinned. 'You ready, Toots? We better leg it.'

And we ran breathlessly for our train, ready for as many more blasts of Noddy as we could endure, not knowing how many there would be, or from where they would come from, in Noddy's native midlands territory.

My first proper boyfriend I actually loved, or thought I loved, Cam Walsh, was standing at the bar of our local pub, the White Swan, like he'd been waiting there for me ever since I'd left him.

'Oh my God. Hello Cam. Wow, how are you? I mean, how've you been?'

The Pixies' *Here Comes Your Man* came on the jukebox almost on cue, as it probably had every day since I was 16, and I felt like I was in some bizarre timewarp, as if I'd never been away. It wasn't just the songs that were the same, everything was: the old fellas at the bar nursing their brown and mild, Edith the pub quiz team genius perched on her honorary stool. Jesus, even Margi 'No Neck' the barmaid was there pulling pints.

'Remember we used to dance to this?'

'Well, I danced and you just perved off me. If I remember correctly.'

'Yeah, then later all those thoughts came to fruition in the back of my brother's Mini.'

'OK, times have changed. I'm so much more sophisticated now! How is your brother?' I smirked.

'What, so now I'd have to buy you a bottle, not just a couple of glasses? Al's fine, got rid of the car though, sorry.'

'Yeah, and the car would have to be a limo, at the very least these days, Cam.'

He ran his hand through his hair, which I noticed was thinning slightly at the hairline where once it had been glossy, gleaming and gorgeous to my teenage gaze. He caught my eye as I watched him, looking slightly apologetic for his diminished condition.

'That seems like a long time ago now, Toots. Dunno what happened there really.'

'Well, I guess things took over. Life?'

'You did all right, hey Toots? My mum always sees you on the TV. She even videos you sometimes, and I've seen you in the papers at those showbiz parties. You've really hit the big time, girl, everyone knows who you are, but then I always knew you would be famous.'

'Shut up, Cam, I'm not famous. I just write about famous people.'

'You are, Toots, didn't you notice half the pub staring at you as you came in? Even Margi smiled when you bought your drink: that's a miracle, that is. She hasn't smiled in a decade.'

I felt a bit self-conscious suddenly, and a quick glance around the pub confirmed Cam's observation. I was getting some weird looks, like I was an exotic bird in a cage or something.

I spotted familiar faces I couldn't quite place, probably from school, as well as the faces I remembered. They were parked in their favoured seats that they'd rightfully earned from services to drinking beer. There were some younger ones too I didn't recognise, a new generation.

It seemed that way anyway. I'd been in London, what, 18 months? And I felt like I'd aged 10 years. A pretty teenage girl and her mate, who couldn't be more than 16, were laughing nonchalantly. Pretending to ignore the lads eyeing them up at the bar, while they drank their pints of snakebite and black. It all seemed so juvenile somehow, but five minutes ago that could have been me.

'I never figured out why you never moved to London, or into Manchester or something. You were so full of ambition, big ideas and that. You still could.'

Cam shrugged a little, tightening the shoulders of his navy Henri Lloyd polo shirt. It was his standard Friday night pulling attire, a look he'd been sticking to since his teens and probably would well into his forties, moving through the decades, size by size, year by year, looking at the fellas around us.

'Circumstances, I dunno. Amy got pregnant – you know I was seeing her? I wanted to stick around, try and make a go of things. Not everyone wants the same things, I guess. Here, d'you want to see a picture?' he said, pulling something small out of his wallet. 'This is Sean. He's a bit bigger now, walking and that, cheeky as anything. Little bugger, he is!'

He handed me a passport-sized photo of a fat-faced baby dressed in a mini polo shirt and Adidas trainers. So I said, as I was meant to say, obviously, because of the 'aren't I just like my dad' uniform, 'He looks like you, he's really lovely.' And Cam looked dead proud and puffed up a bit, pigeon-chested in his shirt. But if I was honest, I was unmoved by the picture and a little disappointed for Cam that he'd never done the stuff he'd meant to, like becoming a chef in a big city hotel. Baby or no baby. Then I thought of Rach and the choice she'd made and I wondered if choice was the right word.

We chatted a bit longer, then I told him I was leaving and I went to kiss him goodbye.

'Is that all I get?'

'What do you mean, Cam?'

Cam went in to kiss me again, eyes like a sick dog, full of longing, and tried to stick his tongue down my throat.

'Get off, will you!'

'What's the matter with you, Toots? Not good enough for you any more, is that it?'

'Cam, you've got a kid and a girlfriend, and that was a long time ago.'

'You always were up your own arse,' he snapped, in a huff now.

In my mind, I turned over what had happened as I walked home. I didn't feel angry with Cam, it was me I was annoyed with. He'd shown me up for who I was. I walked in there as the big-shot local celebrity and his knees went weak. Pathetic, yes, but wasn't that exactly the same sin as I'd committed with Clay? Somehow, coming home, being around people I'd known all my life, made me more uncertain. It was impossible to hide from myself here. I wasn't sure I liked what I saw. What happened with Cam unsettled me deeply, not just because it was crude and embarrassing but because it was weirdly humbling too. I felt conflicted, ashamed. Who was I to castigate Cam for not fulfilling his dreams anyway? At least he had something he was proud of in his little boy. I could barely remember what it was I'd set out to do, and what did I have to show for it? And if I had achieved it, then why did I feel like this?

When I got back to my parents' house, my dad was still up, lying on the couch, comfortably pissed, watching telly. A film depicting northerners as soft-in-the-head sentimental idiots who loved brass bands and male strippers. Dad was having another drink and polishing off the last of the cake Mum had made. Mum was asleep already. Knackered, most probably.

'Well, someone's got to eat it, haven't they?' he said with a grin.

'Yeah, and it's always you.'

My mum had made a Christmas cake for us every year, for as far back as I could remember. She wasn't one of those superdomesticated women; it was something else. Driven still, but her physicality meant most of her aspiration was contained in small domestic wins. At Christmas, she went into this sort of self-imposed competition, where the only contender was herself. Yet she still couldn't win. How could she ever win? No woman could, least of all her.

It was pathetic really, ridiculous I supposed. Her condition made it agonising to watch at times, but I admired her for it too.

The MS diagnosis came when I was 13. The signs were probably there before then, the only thing was, you don't see them. Not unless you know what to look for. First, we thought the symptoms had something to do with her eyesight, tiredness maybe. Perhaps, it was better when we didn't know. Life before fear. Fear that she would end up in a wheelchair, that every time she got a cold that she was going to get really ill. All the time, gnawing away at us.

Looking over at my dad, lying out like that, shirt unbuttoned to the belly, he'd put on a few pounds since the last time I'd seen him. But, in a way, he was in good shape for his age. Sixty-four, a good few years older than Mum. She'd always been the active one, not him. Before, it was her dragging him round. Dad just ignored her fads and crazy ideas and stuff, dutifully wearing the fashionable shirts she bought him. He never said as much, but I knew it killed him to see her vulnerability.

'You can watch what you like now,' he said, throwing me the remote control.

I flicked through a few channels and settled on one of those review of the year shows. I knew it was a mistake because it would be accompanied by one of Dad's running commentaries, but I left it on anyway.

'Princess Di, now there's a face I'm sick of seeing. But every Christmas we have to relive her death. What's all that about? How long's she been dead now?'

'Four years, I dunno?'

'And that hard-faced tart Madonna, marrying that young fella.'

'Guy Ritchie?'

'Yeah, him. I mean, how long's that going to last, eh?'

It kind of brought me down to earth hearing Dad talk like that. All that energy we piled into writing about these people, and to most people it was meaningless. They didn't care.

We turned the channel over to a topical news quiz. I was about to flick onto the next one but caught a familiar face on the screen.

'Shall we watch this, Dad?' I said as the camera zoned in on the smiling face of Michael Dawson.

'Yeah luv,' but I'd stopped listening, even though the sound was turned down low. I was watching the words come out of Michael Dawson's mouth like he was talking to me, and me alone. It felt surreal, especially after tonight, like he was the ghost of Christmas past and all that.

My trance was interrupted by an earthy belch from somewhere deep in my dad's gut. Dad had the same frame as my brother, Marc. I'd have told him that if he'd been there, but he wasn't. Marc was spending Christmas with his wife and daughter in Germany where he was stationed now, as part of the the 1st Armoured division. My brother was eight years older than me. I was what Mum called a 'pleasant afterthought'. They hadn't contemplated more than one child after they'd had Marc; he was such a shock to the system but at least she hadn't been ill then. Most of my teenage life I felt a desperate sense of guilt for everything my mum had to endure as a result of me, part of me wondered was it having a baby later in life that caused her to get ill? This was stupid, not based on any medical fact I'd read, but I couldn't shake the idea.

There were advantages too. I think it made them much more relaxed parents second time round, and almost 10 years down the line, it meant I could do what I wanted most of the time when I was growing up.

'Hey, Dad, you've put on a bit of weight you know; 'ere, better give me some of that cake,' I said.

'Cheeky.'

He pulled a bit off and handed it to me. I bit into the thick black lump and the sensation was overwhelming. I thought of Clay. The amazing night. The passion. Then I thought of Mum. The time she probably spent making this cake no one really wanted to eat. And I felt a bit strange. A bit disingenuous.

'It takes a lot of work, the humble Christmas cake. For the humble chef,' I said to Dad. 'We should tell her how nice it is, right?'

'Yeah, I don't know why she bothers really, gives me indigestion,' said Dad.

'Well, you'd miss it if she didn't. What would you wash your beer down with then, eh?'

'That's true. I'll tell her it makes a good lining for the stomach, shall I?'

'Something like that. I'm going to bed. Night Dad.'

'Night love.'

Later, lying in my childhood bed, staring at the Laura Ashley sweet pea floral border weaving round the wall, unable to sleep, I suddenly remembered the gift Adam had given me. I rummaged in my bag and pulled out the gold package. He'd made a label out of the same paper on which he'd written, 'Dear Toots, Thought you might like the original, fond memories and all that. Adam X.' His handwriting was really lovely, and you could tell he was an artist just by looking at it somehow. I slid my hand inside and pulled off the paper. It was the cover picture of Clay and me that Adam had taken. Framed and everything.

And I felt cold, panicked. A wave of guilt. Was Adam telling me he had known about Clay all along? If he was, did he care? Or worse still, much worse, he was just being kind. He cared, I knew that much about Adam, lovely genuine kind Adam.

Suddenly, I felt as though I was going to be sick. I ran to the bathroom and retched. The hideous feeling purged my guilt-ridden body.

I hear my dad outside the bathroom. 'Bloody cake,' he muttered as I flushed the loo.

21
Natural Highs

Back in London and Christmas was just a distant memory. I'd driven back in my dad's old Renault Clio, a gift to me because he'd bought a new automatic for himself and Mum to make things a bit easier. Mostly the car stayed parked across the road from the flat, at great expense.

A light bulb had gone on in my head – how I was going to be a better person, a better friend to Rach. How good Adam could be for me. Work harder so I could make some money, make a difference to Mum's life myself. My to-do list of worthy and replenishing New Year's resolutions. But just as I was about to put them into action, Adam called time on things. Served me right.

I remembered his words when he called me.

'I have other things in my life Toots. I'm not hanging around waiting for you any more. You're not ready. No hard feelings but I want to do other things too.' He couldn't have been more fair. I hadn't even cried even though it hurt.

I buried it somewhere, tried not to think about what letting things rot like I had with Adam meant. Although I hadn't been the one to break things off, it would have been more honourable if I had. But that wasn't it. The nub of it was, I'd stopped taking responsibility, that was what had happened. Things were out of control and I was both excited and sickened by it, but powerless to change. I was hooked on the mystery of Clay and the image of myself mixed up in it all. Not that it left any sense of lasting happiness, it was like stepping in and out of passion on his whim. With Adam I was in control.

Rach said it was my own fault. I'd lost the plot. That I couldn't see what was under my nose. Also, she said when she'd seen Clay up close in a film over Christmas at her mum's, he was 'too tannery', which I think was a way of saying tanned and leathery at the same time. I loved the way Rach did that, mixed up shallow reasoning with hard logic in a way that gave both equal weight. So I preferred to cling onto the bad tan as her reason for her degrading the whole thing, rather than the fact she was telling me I was being utterly stupid and lying to myself. Thing was, I was clinging onto the intrigue and possibilities of the story as much as I was the romance. It was still unfinished business in my mind.

Then, just when I'd given up hope, Clay called me again out of the blue. Not his assistant, not his PA: it was him on the end of my phone.

'Babe.'

'Hello, you, how are you?' I tried to sound calm.

'I'm in London.'

'How long this time?'

'Two days.'

'Right.'

'I want to lie low. What about you come out for the day with me?'

Adrenalin rushed through me. I was in my slob-out gear, planned to do nothing much, put some loud music on, maybe take some whizz and attack the mess in the flat.

'OK,' I said.

'I just want to be anonymous for the day. You know, get high on an ordinary buzz for a change.'

This annoyed me, probably more than it should have. Like that was my tag or something, the ordinary bird. Talking to him in this outfit didn't help.

'Am I supposed to give you that? Is that my purpose? Go to bloody Tesco's if you want ordinary. I'd planned to do some light hoovering at mine, carpet not cocaine, then go down to Argos – the catalogue shop, not the imaginary planet – to buy a new kettle 'cos Rach has fucked ours. That sort of normal any good?'

No response.

'Thought not.'

Still no response. He was really not taking the bait here, or listening even. Instead he made his offer again, this time with a vague sense of commitment.

'Pocket, babe, I'm serious. I'm down for whatever, you decide. It's the stuff I pay money for, privacy, it's a precious commodity. I'm not allowed to be normal, so I buy it. I need some head space.'

'OK…'

Pause.

'But I'm not sitting in a cafe drinking builders' tea for the benefit of yourself. Anonymity is possible, that's not hard. Wear a disguise. But why not go one better?'

'Told you, babe, I'm down for whatever.' Ignoring the speech.

Pause. Fuck it.

'OK, where are you? I'll pick you up, but first I need to change,' I said.

We headed to the south coast. Cuckmere Haven, in my Clio: I was in control, it was my music playing on the car stereo. Feeling as though I was carrying precious goods, or like I'd kidnapped him. Driving more carefully than usual to begin with, keeping my eyes fixed to the road. He was buzzing, unfazed, smoking cigarettes out of the window, one after another.

'Hey, what music's this?'

'Os Mutantes.'

'It's cool.'

'The unearthed voices of Brazilian folk genius.'

I began to relax more, to drive a bit harder. It started to feel natural having him sat by my side like this.

We parked in the little car park in the woods, then walked for half an hour down the winding path. It was the only way down to the beach, by foot. Chalk cliffs stretched out before us. The deep green of the grass on top of the high, steep cliff face and the expansive black of the sea made the whiteness of the rocks look celestial. We sat on the shingle, cold pebbles underneath us. I dug the toes of my trainers deep down to hear the crunch. My feet felt the cold wet seep through. We said nothing, just looked at the sea and heard its roar, the most humanising, powerful force in all of nature.

'Everyone is equal before the sea.' I said it out loud, although it was only really a vague thought. 'What I mean is, we are all the same. It's just this place: it's dark and brooding – it puts perspective on things.'

Clay said nothing, but reached out his hand to touch mine. I took it and moved in closer to him. It was arousing, the relentless smash of the waves, the brutality of it all enveloping us.

'Sometimes I wonder what it would have been like just to be the other me, the one my mum, Lily, gave birth to,' Clay said to me. It made sense to me now. He wanted to do this because he was exploring what it might have been like; to have grown up here, have a conventional existence.

'What do you mean?' I asked him quietly.

'I imagine just being there with her in the flat, her putting me to bed, that sort of thing. Crazy, huh?'

'Not crazy, no. Normal,' I said, looking up into his eyes, encouraging him.

'You know like just sitting together, Lily with her arm round me, making food for me, washing my face, putting me to bed, regular stuff.'

I looked at him and smiled; I wanted him to open up and tell me this stuff. I felt like I was in control, like the tables had been turned, like he needed me for the first time. As though I was the gatekeeper to his life that could have been.

He continued, 'I can't say that to her. Not now.'

'Why? Because it would upset her too much?'

'Yeah, that, and too much has happened. She's old, fragile. That moment passed. I just like sitting there with her sometimes, letting her talk, imagining who I would have been if I had stayed.'

It was strange to think that somewhere in this gargantuan figure of a man, this hero to millions, was an abandoned kid, still longing for a normal childhood, the simplicity of his mother's lost love. Lily and Clay, what they had lost, what it was worth.

'So you still see her, your mum?' I asked.

'Lily, yeah, we try. I never lost touch with her. That was part of the deal. She used to come and stay at the house, maybe once or twice a year. I didn't register much, there were always people coming and going. She was just another person in that sense, I didn't really see her as my mom, more like a familiar face but a curiosity too. She intrigued me, as a child. More than the other guests, I guess. I knew she was a little bit different.'

I was fascinated by the peculiar family set-up Clay described. What kind of unorthodox, bohemian household must it have been? 'Did you know she was your mother?' I asked.

'I suppose I knew, kinda. I mean, yeah. I must have, because deep down I knew.'

'I don't understand.'

'Like a bond, I guess. She used to stay downstairs, a guest room, different part of the house, private. I used to creep downstairs and watch her sleep sometimes. I liked sitting there watching her. She was like this little creature. Sounds kind of freaked out, but it was good, calming. Maybe because she was a piece of me.'

The story unnerved me, because the two of them seemed almost like prisoners in the drama. It was eerie to envisage the scene he described. But the Clay I knew wasn't a victim exactly. I had to remind myself that was just one part of the story. One facet of Clay.

'But I guess it was good that you kept a connection, even if it was a distant one,' I said.

'Yeah. That's true, although I always felt like I was waiting for her to come back.'

It was almost as if he pulled himself back then, regained a little of the Clay Allison persona: the man who called the shots.

'But I see her now,' he said flippantly. 'I bought her a place. I got her back.'

Clay stopped talking, picked up a stone, turned it over in his hand and was silent for a moment. It wasn't uncomfortable for me, but I sensed he was a little unnerved by the exposition he had given me.

'Here,' I said, 'made you a buttie!'

'What?'

'A sandwich, you'll like it. Eat.'

As we walked back along the path that led us back to the car park, the light was beginning to fade. Flocks of birds flew across the low, melancholy salt marshes in long diving swoops.

'Hey, Toots, this is kind of not what I imagined the British seaside experience to be. Where's the donkeys and the old pier babe?'

The car park was deserted now. The few remaining birdwatchers and walkers had gone home long before us. Clay smiled mischievously, and I knew what he was thinking. I was thinking it too. We got into the car, stripped off our damp clothes hurriedly and scrambled onto the back seat. I laughed as Clay got his foot stuck on the gear box and dragged him back into the front of the car, levelling the front seat so it lay flat.

'That better?' I asked.

'Come here, Pocket,' he said, grabbing me and pulling me on top of him. 'Better,' he said.

Afterwards we sat in the dark for a few minutes. Hunger crept deep into my belly, and I started getting my clothes back on, ready to get off. I picked up my phone from the floor, where it had landed in the scramble to get undressed. I saw I'd missed two calls from home. I pushed away the thought that something might have happened to Mum. Couldn't be arsed to think about that now.

'You know, cramped sex in a car, that there was one aspect of British seaside tradition you just experienced I reckon, but perhaps you're right.'

'Huh?'

'Greasy food. Newspapers,' I said, starting the car. 'Let's get some.'

'Well I'm liking the traditions so far.'

'OK, if that's what you want,' I said as I started the car. 'We have time. If you like, we can drive down to Eastbourne, get some fish and chips.'

The cheery lights of Eastbourne were a welcoming sight after the isolation of the South Downs. I drove to the front and pulled up outside the first chippy we saw. Cod Almighty. Clay raised a quizzical eyebrow. 'They're all like that,' I said. 'The Cod Father.

Schindler's Chips... I know, desperate. It's our British sense of humour.'

The chip shop was quiet except for a couple of teenagers on their way back from a night swigging cans of lager on the beach. The lad had his hand down the back of the girl's jeans and she squealed with mock indignation as he did it. 'Battered sausage and chips with curry,' he said to the woman behind the counter, who processed the order robotically, without a word.

The girl caught me looking at her and stared at us menacingly. I expected her to clock Clay and realise she was in the presence of a superstar, but she looked away.

Clay turned to me in horror. 'What the hell is a battered sausage, Toots? I'm guessing my nutritionist won't have heard of that one.'

I pressed my finger against the warm glass of the cabinet display. 'It's that one,' I said, pointing to a crust-covered sausage.

'That's not good,' he said, shaking his head. 'OK, so fish and chips then.'

'Two times,' said the robot chip lady, digging deep with her chip trowel. 'Mushy peas?'

Clay looked confused.

'Those,' I said, pointing to the large metal container.

'What the fuck?' said Clay, looking into the pale green gloop.

'Just the fish and chips please,' I said quickly.

The woman wrapped the chips into a parcel as if on autopilot and Clay went to give me some cash. 'My treat,' I said. 'Normal day, remember, my turn.'

Robot lady looked up briefly to hand me the bag. All of a sudden her face changed, and colour rose right up to her blue plastic head protector. She'd recognised Clay.

Clay noticed, but rather than hurrying us out of the shop, he stopped, smiled his most enigmatic Hollywood smile and leaned in to the lady. 'Thanks, beautiful,' he said. 'Now you have a nice evening, won't you.' She dropped her chip trowel in the gravy.

'She probably thinks she dreamed it,' I laughed. We were sitting on the beach, eating our chips in the moonlight. They tasted good.

We washed them down with a shared can of lager, the clean alcohol cutting nicely through the greasy, salty warmth of the chips.

'How are your chips, Clay?'

'Pretty damn fine actually, Pocket.' He kissed me on the lips and it tasted like vinegar.

'You even taste normal now,' I said. 'You're lovely.'

'You're lovely too, Pocket…' He paused for a minute. I thought he was going to tell me something more, and I nearly said it out loud too, but almost as though we had read each other's thoughts, we stopped ourselves.

'It's those stars again,' I said to him, pointing up at the sky. 'Doing strange things to your head.'

22
Rachel

'It's over, it's done. I've left him, I've left Lowndes. I'm movin' on, movin' up.'

'All right, Mrs Heather Flippin' Small, you gonna tell me what's goin' on?'

The Rachel I was talking to was virtually unrecognisable as my Rach. Her hair was extreme, cropped close and dyed pillar-box red. A tiny fitted black blazer and and tapered trousers clung to her, sharp and tight around her slender frame. She'd lost weight. Technicolor dominatrix style, she was digging her red-painted nails into the burning candle on our table with the artful strokes of a murderess.

Sclera clear, no more red eye, focused. An air of gravitas gave her the appearance of strength, hardness even. A good thing I guessed but I felt nostalgic for the old Rach, with her seat-of-the-pants approach to life. Not that it was a complete mutation: she still left the flat in a state. These days I made more time, was a better freind. The irony was she didn't need me as much as she did before.

Part of me had been tempted to confide in Rach about Clay, tell her his story. Perhaps if I told someone else it would be a gauge of how fantastical it sounded. When he'd told me, I'd accepted it but in the voids in between meeting him and being alone thinking about things, the whole thing just seemed too weird. Thing was I did believe him, no matter how stupid it sounded. Other things convinced me too, little clues. The Hell's Angels in Cannes. I wondered did Simon know? Had Clay sent him to find me? All these thoughts swam around in my head with no one to share them with.

Even as she was talking, my mind wandered. I couldn't help it; I couldn't stop thinking about him. I'd seen him on TV in a late-night movie; then another time, an interview with him on the set of his new one, on location in Russia, where he'd grown a rugged crop of facial hair; spoken on the phone, once. But we hadn't met since the beach. I couldn't get my head around it: it had been such a perfect day, then nothing. I'd felt like finally we were going somewhere. Now I was annoyed.

Maybe he had withdrawn. I'd got the feeling we'd got as close as he was prepared to go. Was he waiting to see what I'd do next? No, that was wishful thinking on my part. The fact was he'd just done what he'd always done, only this time I'd allowed myself to invest too much hope. What was I thinking? Because we'd had a day doing 'ordinary' things, suddenly we were going to become an ordinary couple? Ridiculous. To him, it was like a day at the theme park: enjoyable, amusing, not something you'd want to do every day. The truth was, I did; real life was groundhog day for little old me. But that was *my* problem: I wanted him to turn into something he could never be. For him, it was easy. He'd dropped the bombshell, opened up to me and got high on normality. Now he'd pulled back to the familiar territory of his own superior A-list highs.

Maybe I was being stupid anyway. If I was being truthful, my own life left no room for relationships with him or even with myself. Work had taken over. My private life had been put away in a box to be rediscovered some day when I was free to open it up again. Bills were multiplying faster than the mould on our walls, the flat was a mess, the credit card company was on the phone and, if I needed clean clothes, I bought them instead of washing them. A vicious circle.

Rach looked at me sharply for a moment, I smiled and she carried on, something about how she'd got a client list together while she'd been working at the shop.

I'd been looking into the story Clay had told me about his mother. Curiosity mostly, but also I wanted to know more about who she was, what had happened to her. I needed to know if what he'd told me was the absolute truth. The enormity of the story if true had the capacity to turn my world around. I knew it was horrible but I couldn't help fantasising about what it could mean. It could secure my career indefinitely; no doubt a story like that could also change my family's life. I could really help them. From the digging around I'd done, unbelievably it was half stacking up. In so much as the woman he told me about, Lily Sue existed. I'd traced his mum's family name to East London. It was a head-wrecker, and all the more so because I'd had to keep the information to myself for so long. Somehow, though, the story had that feeling about it some stories just have, it was pure gold dust, even better 'cos it was sprinkled with glittery hundreds and thousands. Not that I was planning to use it. I was just investigating, wasn't I? It was all so crazy and ridiculous: famous icons, drug overdoses, children being taken by men on motorbikes. Then a thought occurred to me. Simon: I had to call him.

'Are you even listening to me, Toots?' Rachel's voice snapped me back into the moment.

'I was just thinking, sorry, but carry on, yes, what did he do?'

'I told you, it's what I did, not him. I left him, Toots. Are you proud of me?'

'Of course I am, Rach, that's great news, isn't it? I'm not being funny though but I have kind of lost track of you two. How many times have you ended things?'

'Four and a half.'

'How did he take it this time?'

'Said he loves me, always will. But Camille is fragile at the moment, just "give him more time", all the usual stuff. Then he asks me, "have I told her?" When I say "no," he looks relieved and tells me I can choose whatever I want from the shop.'

'He never? What a shit. I hope you took something!'

'Waiter, a bottle of Merlot, please. Pronto Presto,' said Rach, ignoring me. 'James is history.' Her expression shifted slightly at the utterance of his name, but she composed herself and carried on. 'From now on, it's all about me.'

'All right, Rach. Darlin', you are right, you don't need him or his shit. But what's with the body transmutation and the get-up?

You look a bit frightening, to be honest, hon. Where's my friend Rach?'

'It's an Eighties-inspired jacket with a twist, duh! Don't worry, I haven't gone mad, I'm heralding a mini-revival. Tomorrow, something else. It's vital I project a strong look.'

There was more to it than that, though, She'd broken off with James before, but the radical haircut marked a sea change. An image metamorphosis of this magnitude was serious, especially in a woman like Rach. And she wasn't really eating much either, which was a sure sign she was resolute and focused. It happened rarely, so when it did, it made you sit up and notice. She was stabbing the piece of garlic bread with a fork and pushing the black olives round the plate; they were swimming in a sea of orange peel and oil like survivors in a diseased sea.

'What you gonna do then Rach, for work, I mean?'

'I have a plan. Toots: I. Am. Going. To. Be. A. Stylist. I haven't been wasting my time in that bloody shop standing around looking pretty all day, oh no. One by one I've been picking off the choice clients.'

'Wow, Rach. I'm impressed. You will be brilliant. One thing, though.'

'What?'

'Will you be my wardrobe mistress again?'

I knew asking this would pull at Rach's heartstrings more than anything else. The tough bitch act slipped and Rach's composure softened. It was as if I'd proposed marriage; her eyebrows did that thing and the sweet, vulnerable version I knew was back. Her eyes welled up a little and her mouth curled into a smile.

'Of course I will, you know I will.'

It was nice to escape the darkness of the Italian restaurant and get out into the fresh air. I'd forgotten it was the middle of the day.

We took our time going back to the flat and walked along the river by the Chelsea Embankment, arm in arm. It was one of those spring afternoons when you got a sense of hope that summer was coming.

'Have we changed, Rach, I mean since we came here?'

'Better dressed. Wiser maybe?'

The light had returned to her eyes again. My lovely Rach, the one who filled my life with optimism, laughter and possibilities. Yet I didn't feel that excited sense of fulfilment that we both needed from our lives. *Incite* made me feel trapped.

A couple holding hands walked towards us along the path. There was only room for two people, so we sized them up for a moment to suss out who was going to stand aside and let the others past.

When the girl saw me, she smiled excitedly and whispered something in her boyfriend's ear. His mouth opened to form a perfect O.

'After you,' he said, then added with a smile: 'Thanks... Toots.' They walked off, sniggering.

'Oh yeah, I forgot you were an 'It girl' now.'

'More like a tit head. They were laughing at me, Rach. Not congratulating me.'

'You know what they say, Toots. Be careful what you wish for!'

We carried on walking and didn't look back.

23
Second Coming

The dozen or so TVs situated above our heads streamed the news channel into the office: live coverage from last night's second Labour landslide in a general election.

Phenomenally, Marisa, our jobbing features writer (or walking donut, as Roddy called her), had suddenly and unusually been gripped by election fever.

'That dig, that's what won it, isn't it? Did anyone see the left hook on that fat one? When he chinned that protester 'cos he frew an egg at him.'

'Do you mean John Prescott, the deputy prime minister?'

'The one who looks like a fat norvern comedian?'

'Prezza does not look like Les Dawson,' Stephen piped up.

'Bernard Manning?' I offered.

'Nah, he looks like Jabba the Hut.'

There was no hope whatsoever of me finishing the flat plan now. A celebrity-lookalike conversation could grind the entire office to a standstill.

But I'd stopped listening; my attention had suddenly shifted back to the TV screen and I felt a thrill of excitement. I was scrutinising the figure of a man in a pale pink shirt. He was talking in someone's ear just behind the newly appointed Home Secretary. There was Michael Dawson.

At that point Roddy strode into the office, shoulders back like a prizewinning bullfighter. The team shuffled off to their seats. Every time I saw Roddy now, I was consumed by rage. I thought of Rachel's face that day, tearful and broken.

He gestured to me with a flamenco flick of his hand in the air and I followed him into the office at his heels. I sensed he was about to land something on me.

'Sit down, Toots,' he commanded. Obediently I sat myself on

the edge of the big sofa. I couldn't lean back or the whole thing would swallow me up.

He paced a little more, got ready to fire, cleared his throat and then shot.

'We're going global, babe! I want to expand the brand. I want to take *Incite* worldwide. By that I mean global media. Internet, television, radio: we need to be out there, and you, Toots, you need to be part of that. Like a rocket.'

Roddy grabbed my chin in his hand and made me nod in agreement, then for good measure brushed a stray hair from my eyes as if to emphasise the fact he thought I was his self-assembly robot.

'Rocket, yes Rod. Vroom,' I echoed in a mechanical voice, pressing my hands together to make the shape of a rocket.

He threw his jacket onto the chair, sending a waft of Roddy-scented aftershave and cigarettes my way, like a hormonally charged predator.

'No more jokes, Toots. We need stories, not just on the printed page, in every friggin' form of media we have at our disposal.'

'I agree, Roddy,' I chipped in, sensing an opportunity. 'In fact, I'm working on a big idea right now, it's a bit erm, political, I mean sensitive…'

I was thinking about Clay's story. I knew what I needed to do: I needed to get to his mother. I wanted to meet her face to face so I could put it to bed in my mind.

'A big politics story, eh?' said Roddy, getting the wrong end of the stick. 'Toots, that reminds me, have you seen our friend Michael recently? Hey, hey! Saw him on the TV last night, he's soaring through the ranks, that canny bastard,' he laughed. 'No, Toots. Politicians are boring as shit unless they're getting their kit off. I know you agree with that one, dontcha, Toots.' He winked suggestively.

Why on earth did he continue with this morbid fascination with Michael Dawson? Idiot.

'What about getting your mate Michael to do a "Torso of the Week" for us, eh? Get that six-pack out. That's the only fuckin' way I want to do politicians – turn them into celebrities. Mark my words, soon they'll all be at it.'

'OK, Roddy, I get it.' I nodded, but my undercurrent of anger made me more audacious than normal. 'But what is your beef, Roddy? Why him?'

Roddy paused for breath, for a millisecond, then turned his mouth up. 'Him. I'll tell you if you like. Reminds me what a lucky escape I had, Toots. I was going to go into the same thing, would you believe? Went to the same fucking Top of the Pops university, same bullshit degree course. All that crap you think when you're too wet behind the ears to know how the world works.'

So that was it. Jealousy. Michael got there first, beat him to the job he wanted. And the difference was people loved him. He had integrity.

A thought wandered into my mind: maybe I should call Michael Dawson, call Roddy's bluff, pay him back?

'And I want less of "the world doesn't understand me" interview shit and more pictures of celebrities looking shit, like real people. You know the stuff – fat bums, yellow teeth, surgical marks and, most of all, cellulite – readers love that stuff. That's what the other celeb mags are doing; we need to ride that wave. Do it better, do it worse, if you get me. Needs a name too: Celebrity Disgrace, Oh My Bod, or the Frocky Horror Show, something like that.'

'I see where you're coming from, Roddy. It's going to piss them off, though, isn't it, attacking them gratuitously like that?'

'Choose your targets carefully, babe, it's all about surgical strikes.' He grinned repugnantly and patted me on his target, my arse. 'Right, I'm off, got a one o'clock at Nobu. You on that *Kulcha Vulcha* show later?'

'Yup.'

'Good. Remember you are the brand. You are the brand. Stare down the camera and hypnotise.'

'I am the brand,' I raised a meek eyebrow. 'I've got it, Rod. You're spot on with all the big-hitting stuff, makes sense for sure, but I think it's going to take more than that.'

Then I did it. I said it. 'What's more, Rod, I know I've got just the magic ingredient we need to do it.'

'What you on about?' said Roddy tersely.

'I'm working on what could be the most explosive story in showbiz in a generation. It's got the potential to take the *Incite* brand global, do all the things you talked about, Roddy.'

Suddenly his breathing changed, like a cat who'd spotted the movement of a bird in the bushes. 'Only thing is it's going to need some work... I'm going to need to go to New York.'

I'd been yearning to say this thing out loud. He'd be chomping at the bit, but maybe that was also why I'd done it: to back myself into a corner, to find out what I really wanted to do. Roddy, the pressure, the perpetual fear he drove through me every fucking day, it all had to stop. A beast who would never be satisfied. The beast who hurt my best friend.

But maybe it wasn't just Roddy? It was me driving this: that was the reality. And even as I was saying it, planning the betrayal of Clay, the man I loved, knowing what I was about to do had the potential to ruin lives, hurt vulnerable people, I was still craving the story. I wanted to finish the jigsaw. If I could only do that, then what happened next could be something I'd decide later. At least it would be under my control.

24
New York

The foyer of the hotel felt pure New York. Male modelesque receptionists head to toe in black, funereal Armani. Floating from switchboard to front of house with faultless Manhattan ease.

This was the first time I'd spent time with Adam since we split. When I'd seen him sidling towards me in the lobby, apprehension melted away. I was just glad to see him. Happy it was him I was in New York with. Maybe this trip could be an opportunity to mend things, be friends again.

I was about to talk to him when suddenly I heard the ear-piercing squeal that could only belong to one of the Coquettes.

To be fair, Jess Coquette was cute, like a girl band member should be: plucked, tanned, polished, primed and made up. Her tiny waist peeped out of her jeans, revealing a line of flat, brown belly. An updated version of an old man's flat cap, perched just so, the quintessential jaunty pop princess.

'Jess, this is Toots from *Incite*. Have you two met before? You have, haven't you?' Dan the PR introduced me.

'Yes,' I said.

'No,' replied Jess, her eyes wandering already, bored.

'We met at the launch party for something or other and I interviewed you.'

'Nah. Dunno. Can't remember,' replied Jess, a broad Liverpudlian accent making her extra surly.

Squirming as he watched his property diss me, Dan tried to hammer home the purpose of our visit, in the vain hope of sparking up some professional decorum.

'But Dan, we don't read *Incite*,' barked Jess. 'It's just a rag. Very, very sly, isn't it, that magazine?'

Wagging her finger in my direction, Jess added, 'Imagine if we do a shoot with Red, you're just gonna take the piss, aren't ya?'

The atmosphere was taut now. She looked like she might punch me.

'No, of course not,' I said desperately.

But that was the cue for them to come out on strike.

'No way. I'm not doing anything for *Incite*, Dan, no fuckin' way. I remember her. She's the editor who wrote the article saying Sam's got a big fat arse.'

Jess directed her death stare straight at me now. 'That was so mean.' She shook her head slowly and angrily. 'She was gutted over that picture, Sam was. You flown out here to apologise, have ya?'

'I think you've got this wrong. I'm sure we didn't do that, did we?' I said, turning to look for Adam for support. But he'd managed to extricate himself and was deep in conversation with a porter who was loading our bags onto a trolley. Maybe we had, on Roddy's cursed *Oh My Bod* page, the content of which was left to Stephen. Now it had come back to haunt me.

'Erm, Dan, I am sure that story wasn't *Incite*.' I was thinking on my feet now, hoping to God it was one of the other magazines, not us, who'd done the number on Sam's bottom.

For the next three hours I was running between the phone in my room, the Coquettes in the bar and the fax machine trying to prove that Arsegate wasn't *Incite*'s doing.

Just as I was giving up hope, Marisa called me back.

'I'm in a bar,' she shouted. 'It's Sara's birthday. Hold on a minute, Toots… No, don't do the cake. Wait for me. Having a good time?'

'No Marisa, I am not. I'm having a shit time as it goes, and I need some help. Is Stephen there? I need to speak to him pronto, right now.'

'Sorry, Toots, what was that?'

A great cheer went off in the background, followed by wolf whistles.

'I can't really hear you, Toots, it's mayhem here.'

'Stephen, I need Stephen.'

'Did you say Stephen, Toots? It's just he's busy, he's about to do the Happy Birthday song, but he's dressed up like Marilyn Monroe, blonde wig, the lot, you know, he looks amaaazing, Toots, you should see him.'

'Well, tell Marilyn when she's finished her performance to phone me, otherwise she'll be dead, and it won't be suicide.'

Fifteen minutes later, a breathy Stephen called, obviously buoyed up on the drama and adrenalin of the performance. 'Whatssit, Toots?' he breathed.

'Well, I hope you have a bloody good memory for bottoms, Stephen, because I'm literally up shit creek here and I need you to help me.' I explained the situation to him.

Thirty-five minutes later there was another knock on my door as an envelope containing a photocopied print of Sam's bottom was delivered to me in all its monumental glory. On the top was Stephen's handwritten scrawl: '*Scorch* mag – would you believe it? Tell them where to stick it!!!! HA HA HA!!! Love Stephen x.'

Arsegate behind me, and with the girls' venom now directed at another unsuspecting magazine editor, I sensed an opportunity to finally make the call – the one that I'd come all this way to make. Falling back on the bed, so I could think. But the idea of it was, somehow, more unnerving than what had gone before.

The thing was the lure of the story wasn't it at all, it was the possibilities it contained which were becoming more and more alluring. I knew if I broke the story that it had the potential to make a lot of money. God knows Clay had shown me what that type of money could do. Other things would follow. It would secure something I'd been dreaming of doing that could make a monumental difference to my mum. And why shouldn't she have what she needed just once?

For the past year, Mum had become hooked on the idea that if she could get a particular sort of treatment, she would be able to get better. It was an obsession, which was nothing new, sure she'd always had them, but this time it was something she believed could genuinely change her life. She sent me articles she'd found in medical journals every week. It was all she talked about now in our phone conversations. Only thing was it cost a lot of money. More than Dad could muster. It was driving her and everyone around her insane. And her condition wasn't getting any better, her body kept doing weird things to her: rashes; one morning she'd woken up unable to see properly; her immune system was shot to bits. I would do anything to make that stuff go away, give her back the independence she craved. It had made sense when I thought about it at home. But really now I just couldn't imagine doing this to Clay. Maybe I could just go through the motions with the story, check it out and leave it right there. Untouched.

There was of course another problem to contend with too, one that brought me down to earth with a crash. Roddy. It wasn't a simple choice any more. I'd already had a call asking for 'any updates', and I knew by his tone he wasn't talking about the cover shoot. He was getting on the suspicious side of curious already, and he wasn't going to let me forget it. So far I'd avoided his calls or having the big conversation, and my only way out of that was a fait accompli. Everything else, the photo shoot, the magazine, it was as though it was all peripheral. The story was the only thing that mattered now. It was like there were no forks in the road any more. No options. Everything else was a dark umbra and this was the light drawing me in. I was compelled to go in this direction.

Rummaging in my suitcase, I found the notebook with Lily's address in it. I traced my handwriting with my finger. Would she be there, and what would she say if she was?

25
Unhappy Girl

I had traced Lily Sue back to an address in Brooklyn. Clay must have bought her the apartment, because when I'd searched the address it had come back with Fast and Fearless Licensed Entertainment Holdings, which I'd assumed was him. A catchphrase I'd vaguely remembered hearing him use: 'Hey man, you know me, fast and fearless.'

By the look of it, Brooklyn was an up-and-coming district, but I figured it might have suited Lily Sue, given her background in the less than salubrious East London tower blocks. Brooklyn fitted; gentrified New York wouldn't have been her.

I'd decided not to phone before I went to visit in case it set off alarm bells and triggered a reaction from Clay or his pitbulls. My plan was simple: find the address and knock on the door. Foolproof, time-honoured doorstepping.

Nevertheless, when the cab driver pulled up, I was reluctant to step outside and into the unknown. Part of me thought about aborting the mission and telling him to drive on.

The driver's voice forced my hand. 'Hey lady, you getting out? This is the address you wanted, right?'

'Yeah, sure, sorry,' I handed him some money. 'Keep the change.'

Strangely, he needn't have told me; something about the building seemed familiar. I would have known this was Lily's block even if he hadn't stopped here. From the outside, the apartment block resembled a disused factory. The shallow entrance was grey and dark, and on the wall there were four or five names written alongside each buzzer. Some just had numbers. None of them matched the surname I'd been given by the private detective. It was a guessing game really.

By a process of rapid elimination, I figured her apartment was either 5A or 7B. I tried 5A first, and a woman answered in Spanish, speaking briskly. 'Erm, excuse me, does a Mrs O'Connell live here please? Lily Sue? Lily?'

'No.' The line went dead.

7B gave no reply. I rang one last long buzz of the intercom. The low-pitched growl grated but I kept my finger on the buzzer, to vent my frustration more than in any hope that someone might answer. But still no joy.

The street was quiet apart from a group of lads dressed in North Face jackets standing around, chatting and cussing with each other. An old man picking up litter, inspecting it and stuffing choice pieces into his carrier bag meandered down the pavement past them. They stood aside, one of them nodding in salutation to this strange litter-picker, who must have been a familiar figure in the neighbourhood.

On the corner opposite was a bar with wide smoked windows and a faded red-and-white striped awning: it looked like a good place to sit it out and wait for my luck to change.

Sweating uncomfortably, as I passed by the gang I felt exposed. My too-clean jeans, dandy quilted jacket and pumps, which back home had seemed shrewd and streetwise, suddenly seemed to mark me out as an English tourist with the wrong sartorial guidebook.

I took a seat in the window with a vantage point from which I could see both the entrance to the building and the street's approach. The bar smelled like fried sugar. A middle-aged waitress with a jaunty schoolgirl's ponytail, whose uniform was a brighter version of the canopy's red-and-white stripe, came to take my order.

'What can I help you with today?' she drawled in pure Brooklyn, beaming widely, with her eyes fixed somewhere behind me.

'Just a Coke, thanks.'

'Regular, Medium or Supreme?'

'Regular.'

'Ice?'

'Yes, thanks.'

'Anything else I can help you with today?'

I half thought of giving her a list of the multitude of tasks I should have been performing for the magazine shoot but wasn't. Or maybe she could advise on the enormous moral maze I was about to take one step further into. Instead, I just smiled politely, reminding myself this was how she was programmed to respond.

Making the Coke last as long as I could, I fixated on every random passer-by in the hope they might give a clue as to Lily's whereabouts. About 20 minutes passed. Then, just as I was about to give up and pay the bill, I spotted the figure of a woman from the corner of my eye. Something about the way she moved, smooth and dainty like a dancer, looked familiar. An echo of dramatic expression in her body as she walked up the street that was imprinted in my soul.

Shoving a 10 dollar note down next to my empty glass, I darted for the door.

Catching her at the entrance to her building, I spoke. 'Excuse me. Mrs O'Connell. Mrs O'Connell, do you think I could talk to you for just a moment? I'm a friend of your son's.'

The lady stopped dead in her tracks and dropped the two bags of shopping she'd been carrying. Regarding me with suspicion, she frowned and her posture changed from the free-flowing, bird-like creature I'd seen a few seconds ago to a brittle, defensive stance. A tin from one of the bags rolled onto the floor, so I stooped to pick it up and held it out to her in my hand, in what I hoped was a pacifying gesture.

'I don't know what you're talking about. I don't have a son. You must have the wrong person.'

'Clay. Your son, Clay.'

The woman's deep eyes fixed on mine in an instant.

'You can step inside with me, but you have 15 minutes, no more. I have a date.'

The silence in the lift on the way up to her apartment was oppressive. I could tell she was nervous by the way she was breathing irregularly, in little rasps.

Her face was little and neatly formed with delicately pronounced bones; it spoke of the great beauty she must have been when she was young. Around her forehead and mouth, deep lines had developed, telling something further of the despair and heartache in her earlier life.

I'd expected her to be taller somehow, what with Clay's description of her amazing legs, but she wasn't much more than five-foot five or so. A little taller than me, perhaps. Incredibly slim, though, eating-disorder thin. I realised how fragile she was. In her baggy jeans, it wasn't really possible to say if she had world-class pins but I could see her clothes hung off her body in an unhealthy manner.

When we stopped at the fifth floor, a small, plump, dark-haired lady answered and took the shopping bags from Lily. She whispered in a Spanish accent, glancing up at me as Lily explained to her who I was. I realised she must have been the Spanish voice who had answered the intercom earlier.

The sound of yapping followed her, and two West Highland terriers bounded to the door and jumped at Lily's legs. 'Babies, my babies, Miami, get down, Cincinnati, Mummy's home. Good doggies.' Her expression softened a little. 'Come in, please, sit down.

'Nama, can we have some tea please?' she asked the Spanish woman. 'Tea?'

'Yes please, that would be lovely,' I answered in time-honoured fashion. A well-worn ruse to keep my foot in the door. Only a wet-around-the-ears journalist would refuse a hot drink, which gave the potential to stretch out a reluctant invitation into a good long sit-down.

The apartment was a converted loft: on trend and in style. An expansive space, with wide wooden flooring and exposed beams, it was divided into a living space and kitchen, with a side door presumably leading to the bedroom. Despite its fashionable shell, Lily had decked it out in traditional English style with a three-piece suite and floral chintz. Little tasselled tapestry lamps sat on mahogany furniture and watercolours of English landscapes hung on the walls in brassy frames. The table had a pretty floral cloth covering it and, bizarrely, a sheet of clear plastic covered the cloth. The whole place was immaculately clean, sterile and dust free.

On the trestle table in the living room was a small bowl filled with multicoloured sweets, M&Ms or something; there were others in the hallway and the kitchen. I wondered if these were all she ate: appetite suppressants perhaps? Or treats for the doggies?

I sat down on one of the armchairs. Lily Sue sat opposite me with a dog on each knee. She eyed me uncertainly.

'Why are you here? Have you come for money? Because I don't have any. Or have you come to upset me? You're one of his girlfriends, aren't you? I'm afraid I can't help you; my son's his own man, he does what he pleases. Always has done. Can't offer you anything.'

Her rambling voice was deeper than her small body suggested and had retained a dense East London accent.

'No, Mrs O'Connell. Anyway, that's not why I'm here. My name's Toots. I've come all the way from London. I just want to have a chat with you. Clay told me your story; I'm his friend, and I wanted to meet you. To talk to you.'

I could see that if I wanted her to confess what had happened when Clay was a baby, I was going to have to calm her down, coax her a little bit, get her to trust me. I patted my knee and gestured to the dogs. One of them jumped off her lap and ran over to my feet.

She looked a little shocked. 'Well, that's a first, Miami doesn't normally like strangers, it's Cincinnati who's the flirt, she must like you darlin'.' Sure enough, the dog jumped up and sat on my knee, its black eyes pleading for affection, imploring me not to betray her owner. I tried not to look back at her, swallowed the horrible feeling.

'They're Clayton's, the dogs, I look after them for him. His girlfriend didn't like them. Doesn't like people much either, she doesn't, unless they are giving her something but then he should never have bought them. They need stability, the babies, and Daddy's never home, is he? Daddy travels.' Cincinnati looked into her eyes adoringly. 'It's like everything else with him; he does it on a whim. So I took them, told him I'd have them, to help him. They're happy here, and we look after each other now, don't we?'

As she spoke, the dogs seemed to know she was talking to them, tongues hanging out, mouths open, following her every word. My mind was racing, knowing I'd endeared myself to her a little, ingratiated myself, that she was starting to open up, the hostility ebbing away. I kept my hand on the warm fur of the dog's back and it felt comforting, steady.

'Do you see him much now, Clayton?' I asked her. 'Is it good to be closer to him after all those years apart? That must have been difficult for you.'

I was trying to create a sense of complicity; letting her know that I understood that she had given Clay away when he was a baby, in the hope she wouldn't question why Clay had come to tell me this, his most intimate of all secrets. Pretending I was comfortable in the knowledge, so why shouldn't she be? Even though, in truth, I wasn't sure how many years in the wilderness they'd spent, or how they'd got back together.

'Now and again. I told you, he travels. It's hard for him too. I mean, it's hard to see me, I think. One day he wants to talk to me, he feels like I'm part of him. The next he's ashamed, wants to forget he has anything to do with me. I can see it. I can't blame him. He was my dirty secret. Now I'm his.

'Maybe it's justice. He's angry with me, but he's mixed up, isn't he? On the whole he's happy with the way things turned out, why wouldn't he be? He knows I did the best thing for him. He knows he's living the life he wanted, he just can't get over the fact I let him go.'

She stopped for a moment and fixed me with a stare. 'Gave him away, I mean.'

I took a sharp intake of breath and tried to stop myself from demonstrating any outward signs of euphoria. The adrenalin had kicked in and my trained emotional response was to channel this into a passionate push for the story, but curiously I felt uneasy too. As much as I was willing her to tell me, I was also willing her not to. Wouldn't it have been better if it wasn't true after all, if it was all an elaborate lie, a figment of Clay's overactive imagination? I almost wanted to stop her in her tracks, to tell her, 'Keep this to yourself: you don't need to tell me this.' The words formed in my mouth but they didn't come out. I sat in silence and let her run headlong into my trap. I had it. The confession. The story of my career. A bittersweet feeling crept through me. A black high.

Often the stories that seemed like they might be impossible to tell, with such hurtful consequences, came spilling out like this, so much easier than you would have expected. It was as though the secrets people kept close to them and never discussed with families, best friends even, for fear their whole lives might unravel, were just there, hanging in the air, waiting to be told. And all it took was for some lousy journalist to come along and ask the question nobody else had dared to.

And in customary form, Lily Sue couldn't stop herself now she'd begun. 'Sometimes he calls me up angry. Spouting abuse. Hurtful stuff. Nothing I don't deserve. Other times he's so sweet and kind, my boy, buying me things, jewellery, watches, beautiful clothes. Things I don't need, things I do, this apartment. Then he hates me again, cuts me dead. He can't help it.'

I was tempted to tell her that Clay did that to everyone, to soften the blow, but I saw that would make things worse; it would make her feel like the anger he directed at her was impersonal. At least that way it felt special. I didn't have the heart to say I thought Clay's was the anger of a spoilt brat.

'Maybe it's not how you think. Perhaps it's, you know, the fame thing. You shouldn't beat yourself up about it. I'm sure that's not how he would want you to feel. He talks about you with affection, not antipathy,' I said instead.

'Darlin', you don't need to tell me. I understand. Fame, I mean; I could write a book. Let me tell you what I know. I understand exactly how it works, what it does to people. I am an expert, a world-class authority when it comes to fame. Clay's father taught me everything I know. Not his fault: it makes you into something else, turns you selfish; disgusting and irresistible all at the same time. But people will love you no matter what you do, won't they?

'Thing is, once you do the deal, let it take you over, you can't go back then, can you? It's a deal with the devil, isn't it? My son was destined to be that way. Just like his father was before him. If I'd stopped him, I would have been standing in his way.'

She stared at me from underneath her fringe with those eyes, those sad but beautiful dark-green eyes that Clay had first described. She was willing me to understand her complicated, impassioned argument. And I did, I thought, understand what she was saying. In many ways it made total sense, gelling with the thoughts and perceptions I'd had already, and it awakened a part of me I hadn't expected. I was beginning to see just what it was to be caught up in the dark heart of it. How, really, she'd had no choice but to hand over her son and give him back to the family who would enable him to follow his destiny.

Still though, the other part of me, the journalist, was just hungry and excited, particularly as she'd just mentioned Clay's dad. I could see that the prize was in sight, so I was looking at her thoughtfully, kindly, open-faced, hoping if I remained that way she would just keep on talking.

'But you see, I did a deal with the devil too, didn't I? I had to; that was my son's providence. I had to let go of him. He would have been taken into care, I know that. Where I was living was a bad place, I had no money, I was in trouble, bad people after me and I knew that at least he would be safe, looked after. More than that: he would be set for the rest of his life. Given a life I could never offer him.'

As she spoke she fiddled with a delicate gold bracelet on her thin wrist. I noticed a tattoo inscribed along the inside of her arm. Quod Me Nutrit Me Destruit. The line stirred some vague memory inside me. Probably one of the numerous quotes I'd seen on Clay's catalogue of body art somewhere; I couldn't be sure.

'It corrupted me too, and in a sense it's defined my life. I fell in love with the wrong man and I've lived with the consequences ever since. It was out of my control.'

The conversation seemed to tire her, and Nama, the maid, gestured to me that it was time to go. I drew it out, taking my cup to the kitchen to put it in the sink. As I placed the cup down I noticed a breathtakingly handsome face I recognised in a picture stuck to the refrigerator door. I smiled at the continuity, thinking of the photo I'd stuck of Clay on ours in our flat back home, the circularity of it all. The man in the picture had the classic looks of a Sixties godhead. An icon. Even in this shot, a personal photograph in relaxed circumstances, turning to the lens with a smile, the camera loved him. A large, thick-lipped, sensual mouth, a cleft in his chin. Strong cheekbones and jaw, and that thick, dark, dirty-looking tousled hair to his shoulders that only a man confident in his supreme sexuality could wear with ease. But there was something else in the face that elevated him: something behind his stare, a light shining behind it, like a playful wisdom. His beauty was so extreme it should have been a cliché, but it was only then that I realised that could never be true. His was the face that began the cliché: he was the leader of the cult, the man who drew the image.

It was then that it dawned on me who it is I was looking at. It was Clay's father, Lily's pin-up, the man she adored. His picture stuck to the fridge, just as his son said it was. And even though it was the man I suspected it would be, had hoped it would be, still I was blown away by the hard fact, especially when I saw the truth spelled out in front of me like that in a black-and-white image.

I was half-tempted to grab the picture and take it with me, but I didn't, of course I didn't. I glanced over at Lily sitting in the chair and a throb of culpability hit me at the realisation of what I'd just imagined doing to her. Taking away the small thing she probably looked at every day that made her feel happy. Her eternal poster boy. The person she had loved and lost. What was I thinking?

And I realised that she was right: fame took no prisoners. It had left her in this piteous condition, susceptible, damaged, part of a story more his than it would ever be hers. Her own life stood still, paralysed.

'Thank you for speaking with me, Lily, I appreciate your time, it's been lovely to meet you. Maybe I can come back in a few days, speak with you again.'

But she wasn't really listening, I could see that, and it was Nama who spoke as she led me to the door. 'Mrs O'Connell is a good lady. She is a kind person.'

'Yes,' I said, 'I can see that. Please tell her thank you.'

Nama opened the door and turned her eyes towards it, gesturing for me to go.

'Goodbye,' I said, but she'd shut the door already.

As I moved down the floors, heading down in the lift, alone this time, I reached down into the inside pocket of my jacket and pulled out my tape recorder. The red lights blared at me, showing it was still on, recording. I switched it off and rewound it a little, then pressed the play button.

'Let me tell you what I know about fame,' said a woman's voice. I switched it off and my heart soared. I'd got it, bang to rights. Now I had to work out what I was going to do. I'd needed to hear the story for myself, for my peace of mind as well as for anything else I might do with it. There was also the excitement and a sense of relief that now I had the picture straight in my head. But now I'd met her, let her open her heart to me, I was beginning to understand a different story than the one I'd thought I would find at the heart of it all. This poor unhappy girl.

I thought of her and Clay, then of my own mother, her vulnerability. What she might have thought. She wouldn't have wanted me to hurt this woman. Would she have understood something of how it might have felt? How that bond between mother and child was rooted inside, what it meant to pull them away from one another? All mothers understand what it is to sacrifice something – in my mother's case it was her time, her own money, sleep, her health – but for Lily Sue it was the cold, hard shock of loss. Her sacrifice wept like an open wound.

Yes. I had come here to find out for myself what kind of woman Clay's mother was. It was curiosity and the desire to understand more about Clay. Only by knowing both of them and the events that shaped them could I understand them.

26
The Beginning of the End

Dan had booked a 'hot, hot, hot' restaurant a few blocks from our hotel. The two bands (boy and girl), Dan, Jo, Adam, me and a few people I didn't recognise were all seated round one enormous table. The Coquette girls were all waxy smiles and big hellos.

I was distracted, excited about Lily's story, nervous. I found it hard to summon up the charm and enthusiasm expected of me. I called Rachel a couple of times. Maybe by talking to her I would feel less guilty about Lily but the phone rang out. When eventually she did pick up she told me there had been a phone call at the house for me from Clay's PA. 'Something about were you going to be in New York. Like he knew. Did you tell him?'

'No.'

'That's strange because by the way she was talking it was like he knew. Maybe I got it wrong.'

'That's weird. How would he know? Why did he call home?'

I thought for a moment then remembered the conversation with Simon. Had Simon told him? Maybe I was just being paranoid, maybe it was jet lag.

Just as Rach started to tell me about what she'd been up to I got a wolf whistle from the restaurant to come back inside. The Red boys were jumping up and down: it was a signal some food had arrived.

They'd made it their business to court my attention, and the magazine's, for months before their first record release: popping into the office impromptu, buttering up Marisa, making juniors blush with kisses and neck massages – generally whipping the office into a hot froth.

Now they'd hit the big time and they were heady with restless delirium. Four young boys with the world at their feet and enough young pop junkies ready to jump into bed with them, to keep them going for as long as they had the energy, with which they were bountifully blessed.

Kayne was officially the tallest and best-looking member of the band – according to, like, God. (He'd scooped a 'best-looking male' award for the sake of legality.) He'd put his arms round my waist, kissing me on both cheeks. Then there was Mikey the dancer, Cam the cheeky one and Ben the small, cute one favoured by the tween fans.

'Babe, how's it goin', you look sexy,' Kayne smiled, undressing me roughly with his eyes, by no means an exclusive greeting. Lily's interview was the only thing I could think about; I was tense, not erotic. Now I had it in my grasp, I was worried something would go wrong. Perhaps she'd tell someone, raise the alarm. I needed to stay focused and act normal.

'I'm fine, thanks, Kayne,' I said gently, removing his arms from my waist and stepping away an inch. 'Excellent, cool. So glad you boys are here; I guess you know the girls already.'

'Oh yeah, we know them.' He grinned, showing a mouthful of shiny, whitened teeth.

I looked over to see Shelley, the quieter Coquette, sitting on Cam's knee, giggling. He was gesticulating with a bread stick, feeding her little pieces, which appeared to be unlocking Shelley's gaudier side. She was laughing like a clogged drain.

Adam had gone off and scouted for the shoot without me. I noticed he was drinking beers at a more alarming rate than usual, sitting at the end of the table not talking to anyone. His eyes dull and glazed over.

I smiled meekly, 'Hey, Ads, sorry about earlier, how did you get on?'

He blinked rapidly, mocking surprise. Did I really care how he'd got on?

'OK, I know you think I've let you down, but I've been working on something and I can't really talk about it yet, that's all. You're not pissed off with me, are you? It's just too contentious, too prickly. A sensitive project, you know. A Roddy special. You understand, don't you, Ads?' As the words came out I was aware of how weak they sounded.

'Sure Toots, I understand. Another secret, one I'm not supposed to be aware of. You just tell me when you're ready to discuss ideas about where to do the shoot, OK. That's what we're supposed to be here for, isn't it?'

'Yeah, brilliant,' I ploughed on, refusing to acknowledge his indignation. His behaviour was more than I'd bargained for. 'We could do that later if you like, when we get back to the hotel?'

'I'm tired. I think I might go back to the hotel early. This lot want to go a club or something after, but I'm really not in the mood. Hey, but you'd better go. More your kind of thing anyway.'

I snapped: he'd pissed me off. The story had got me fired up, and the shitty bit of me rose to the surface.

'What are you talking about, Adam? I wish you'd just say what you mean and cheer up. I've only been off for an afternoon working, that's all. It's not like I've committed a mortal sin is it?'

'I dunno. Is it?' Adam gave me a sideways glance that was meant to look menacing, but actually he just looked sad. 'Toots, I'm going back. Tell this lot I'll see them tomorrow, OK?'

We didn't head for a club. Instead we went over to the Four Seasons, where the boys were also staying, to hang out at the bar with Nick and put some drinks on his gold card. The bar was all 'New York does postmodern colonial glamour'.

'They've got friggin' trees in their bar, all we've got is palm tree plants at ours. This place is just showing off,' said Dan as he plonked himself down next to me.

'Know what you mean. But hey, let's enjoy: better trees, better drinks, right? Where are the girls? And the boys for that matter?'

'The boys headed upstairs to chill out with the Coquettes, so they can smoke and do stuff, hang out and that, they said.'

The combination of alcohol, jet lag, the strain of forced conversation and the meeting with Lily culminated and took its toll on my body and mind. My vision was becoming wobbly. I wanted to go.

Suddenly, Dan stopped talking and sat bolt upright in his chair, craning his neck like a hungry predator.

'Oh my God! You will not believe who has just walked into the bar.'

We all turned round on cue to see who he was talking about. And although from where we were sitting I could only see the back of a man's head and the slender figure of a blonde woman, I knew instantly it was Clay. I gasped for air. I'd explored this scenario in my mind, of course, only now, with his flesh in the same room as my own, my reaction was physical. Logic clocked off. The tiredness subsided and I was wide awake again. It had to be him, it had to be that night.

And her. I knew about her, at least I'd read about them. But somehow reading about it in a magazine or a newspaper didn't seem real. I suppose I'd decided it was a fictitious romance, something for the mutual benefit of their careers. The shot of betrayal I felt seeing them for real was horrible. It passed through my body like a sharp knife and stayed there like a vile infection. Her, the cow who'd got rid of the dogs. I felt a pang of guilt.

'That must be his girlfriend, Kirsten Kemal. She is a goddess. She just did the shoot for Loewe bags, you know, and she appeared on that video. God, if only we could persuade her to do something with the boys, can you imagine? Do you think I should talk to her? I'm going to; this is a once-in-a-lifetime thing, isn't it, Jo?'

'Well, it could be for her too, Dan. You've got garlic breath and smell like a strawberry daiquiri. I'm betting it's been a long time since she experienced that particular combination at close range,' replied Jo.

'I'm going in, commando-stylee,' said Dan, unperturbed, staggering out of his seat in the direction of the bar.

'I bet they call security. I have to see this.'

'Yeah, me too,' I murmured, but my heart was beating so fast I felt like I was going to keel over. I topped up my glass from the wine bottle on the table.

We were squirming as if someone was about to get hit; me for different reasons to the others, but then, against all expectations, Dan seemed to be delivering. Clay's beautiful partner was gracious and charming as this unknown stranger bounded up. She even threw her head back and laughed. At something he said? With him? Or at him? We weren't sure.

'He's only fucking well got in there, the bastard, hasn't he? She is actually being nice to him. I do not believe what I am seeing. Full marks, Danny Boy,' said Jo, beating a fist in the air.

Dan turned to us and waved a flamboyant hello, and Clay and his girlfriend turned in our direction. Clay and I looked at each other. I couldn't smile. I couldn't breathe. I felt tears prickling in my eyes. My body seized.

Clay cocked his head to one side, folded his arms casually and nodded. He betrayed nothing but ease and affirmation. It was like watching him in a movie. *The Intangible Truth* sprang to mind, his disastrous follow-up to the considerably more successful film he'd been premiering when we met that time in Cannes. It was the last film I'd seen him in.

He continued to look at me for a moment, then he turned back to Dan, swept his arm around him like an old friend and gestured for him to lead him over to where we were sitting.

Now I was glued to the spot. He was leading his girlfriend over to talk to us. I was about to meet the woman whose man I'd slept with. Or was it the other way round? Did a man like him belong to any of us? Kirsten Kemal glided, floated, like a swan on water.

'She isn't human,' whispered Jo.

Even Nick was moved to speak. 'Her body must have been made in a laboratory: it has perfect physical proportions.'

'Yes,' I agreed. 'It does.'

'Wow,' said the hanger-on, finishing Nick's drink for him.

Staring at her honeyed legs for a very long time as she walked I decided they looked like the smooth waxy surface of a newly dipped candle. How it would feel to stroke them?

The atmosphere in our group had changed from subdued conversation to heightened activity and audible, borderline hysteria in some cases. Dan had cranked up his life-and-soul routine to the maximum. He contorted his body into grand gesticulations to exaggerate the party-loving personality he wanted us to buy into.

Nothing Kirsten Kemal would not have witnessed before. Women like her inspired people to perform to their best. Entertain me, she asked, without even opening her mouth.

'And this is Toots,' said Dan.

'Hi,' said Kirsten. 'Pleased to meet you.'

A muted 'hello' was all I could manage, and I glanced away quickly, convinced just looking at her might betray who I was in some way.

Clay had been drawing attention in his own right. On the short journey across from the bar he had already been stopped and pulled aside tactfully by two gorgeous, well-dressed women, who whispered plaudits and purred congratulations into his ears. Clearly he wasn't remotely fazed by the prospect of a meeting between Kirsten and myself.

When he eventually joined our party to sit down, he artfully placed himself next to me, a short distance away from his girlfriend and our fawning crew, who had formed a semi-circle around her.

'Hey, Pocket, an unexpected surprise, just when I was getting bored. Jesus. She. Is. Dull.'

'Astounding,' I said.

'She's good to look at, Pocket, sure, but if you had to spend the whole evening with her, well, there ain't many laughs, that's for sure. Plus she's pissed with me all the goddamned time. I don't give her enough attention. Fuck her, she's never happy.'

'Hey, be quiet, she'll hear you. Jesus, Clay.'

'Nah, she's too far gone to hear me. Prozac, cosmopolitans and Jack Daniel's, she's on Mars. She'll be passed out in an hour.'

Even for Clay, this was harsh. He was obviously jealous of the attention his girlfriend was receiving.

Recently, his movie career had been rocked by a series of flops, especially since he'd stepped out of his box and turned actor/director. Personally, I could see no difference in his performance: it had always been the same one, the hero with a deeply troubled soul fighting for justice. Maybe it had just gone out of fashion.

'What about you, babe, missed me?'

'Not really. I've got my own life to lead. I've been busy. Like you, I guess. If you mean have I been sitting around missing you, the answer is no.'

'Darlin', that's what I dig about you: you bite back. Still, you haven't stopped loving me, have you?'

'What do I say to that? What do you want me to say?'

'I'm serious.'

'OK, we had some amazing times – not many, but some. I think you're right, we connect on some level, but I think it's unfair to ask me a question like that. So I'm going to say yes, I have. Stopped. I'm not sure that's what it ever was anyway. Are you? Lovers, yes. Love? Well, that's something else isn't it, something a little more enduring, don't you think?'

'Toots, Pocket, babe, you know I endure. I can still feel it. We endure.' He laughed, waving with one hand to the blondes from earlier who were leaving as he spoke.

'God, I hate you sometimes. However, I think you may have been right about your girlfriend, she looks like she might need to go to bed.'

Kirsten looked like she was about to pass out. Probably nothing a light meal wouldn't have cured, but women like that never got the chance to find out, existing instead on a calorie-lite cocktail of cigarettes, drugs and alcohol.

Clay looked at her unemotionally and directed his attention to Dan.

'Hey, Dave, is it?'

'Dan.'

'Dave, take her to bed, will ya? Make sure she doesn't choke on her own vomit, stick her head over the side. Here's the key, and here's another for the lift. Take it to the top floor, you'll need to swipe it.'

'Come on, Dan, I'll help you,' said Jo.

Jo and Dan stood up and led Kirsten by the arms. Kirsten stood up suddenly, wobbly on her feet like a newborn Bambi, and leaned over to Clay to kiss him goodnight. 'I'm going to bed.'

'Kirsten, let the guy take you up. Don't fuck around, don't kiss him. And listen, there's a room full of people here, so try and walk in a straight line until you get to the lift.'

'I hate you,' she said, teary-eyed all of a sudden. 'I can walk myself. You are cruel, so, so cruel.'

'Yeah yeah. Night night, darlin'.'

'That's two of us hating you: not your night, huh?' I said to Clay.

'Darlin', you don't hate me. You love me. So does she.'

'Yeah, the whole room loves you too, huh!'

'It's all true, babe. All true.'

He was right, in as much as half of me was in flux, my feelings confused. Almost like it would be rude not to give him the attention, the love in the room. And he was still deadly attractive. His cruelty towards his girlfriend might have been partially for my benefit, or sour grapes because she was the rising star now. To take the spotlight was to take the love away from him. All he'd ever known.

'So what are you doing over here anyway? Are you here to check out the sights and sounds of New York?'

'Does Brooklyn count? I'm only here a few days,' I said before thinking.

'Yeah, Brooklyn counts. I've got a place over there; it's a cool area. So I've only got you for tonight, is that what you are saying?'

'No, that's not what I said.'

'Come on, what about we go somewhere where we can be alone?'

Logically, this was probably the last thing I should do, I knew. But reason never came into things as far as Clay was concerned. Tangled up inside, knowing I'd betrayed him. Maybe what I'd done was even worse. Wanting to appear normal was hard, my mind confused, questions running through my head. Did I want him or the story? Did I need him to keep the story? Did he suspect me? Would it help if I had sex with him? Would it make me feel better? Could I just do it anyway?

I looked around me and realised everyone else in our party had dispersed. Nick had gone to bed.

The bathrooms at the Four Seasons were fairly plush, marble surfaces and all that. Not as mind-blowing as you might have thought. Still, you would have expected the condom machine to work, given the wondrous selection of flavours and colours. The mirrored surface of the cubicle door reflected my guilty face back at me. Unnerving to watch myself having sex: you have to be an exceptionally confident kind of person and able to suspend your self-consciousness, hard enough without the added complication of a famous person in the same reflection also having sex. With you.

But it was the Four Seasons. With a Hollywood film star. High-calibre sex, if not in location then at least in the quality of the performer. One of the performers, anyway, the other, me, looked a bit B-list. I pulled Clay over a little so I didn't have to look at myself any more.

Afterwards, sitting on the floor of the empty cubicle next to Clay, sharing a cigarette, I thought of Lily Sue. I remembered how she'd known I was one of Clay's girlfriends when we'd met earlier that day. What was it about me that looked the type?

As Clay passed me the cigarette I noticed something on his wrist.

'I've always meant to ask you, what is that?'

'Latin.'

'Wow! Did you study Latin?'

'Nah.'

'So?'

'So what?'

'What does it mean then?'

'It's personal, it's about being the victim of your own shit. You know, like my old man,' he said.

The mention of his father brought back the interview in a horrible flash. Then I remembered the tattoo on Lily's arm. Was it the same? Clay moved his arm away. The conversation with Lily Sue seemed so long ago, even though it had been just a few hours since we'd met. Her face kept coming back to me, those eyes pleading for understanding. In a strange way I didn't really care quite as much about betraying Clay: he was fair game. It was Lily Sue I couldn't get out of my mind. She was fragile and helpless. An overwhelming sense of responsibility and paranoia crept into my consciousness.

'Clayton.'

He looked at me with a start. I realised I hadn't called him by his birth name like that before.

'Your name.'

'My mother's name for me. Lily calls me that, no one else.'

'I know. It suits you, though. I guess I was just trying it out, to see what it sounded like. Does it make you feel vulnerable to hear me say it? I'm sorry.'

'No.'

'What's the matter then?'

'Well, I'm just wondering why the fuck you're thinking like that, babe? That's what's up.'

'OK, calm down, will you? I'm sorry, it was just a thought.'

'Was it?'

'Yes, of course.'

Clay's tone had changed. He began putting his clothes on hurriedly. Although I'd been at the receiving end of his rudeness before, I'd never heard coldness in his voice like the way he'd just spoken to me. It gave his face a harsh edge, ugliness.

'Listen, babe, you better not be fucking with my head, OK?'

'Hey, don't speak to me like that. What's the problem?'

'Where did you say you were yesterday?'

'I told you.'

'What were you doing there?'

'Sightseeing, checking out places.'

'In Brooklyn.'

'Yeah, I told you. What's wrong with you?'

'Don't fuck with me, Toots, OK? I've told you, you don't want to fuck with me.'

'I'm not, you're being paranoid. Why are you acting like this?'

'I'm going to say goodbye now, Toots. You know, I think maybe it's time we stopped meeting like this. We wouldn't want things to go stale now, would we? Because, you know, we had a good thing here, and if we're not careful that beautiful thing might start to taste pretty sour.'

For a moment, I was stunned; the initial impact of Clay's parting words stung me. Then I became nervous. I saw my hands were shaking, I felt sure I'd given myself away, that he suspected me. The menacing note in his voice had been a threat. Examining my face in the bathroom mirror, my reflection looked wired and dishevelled. In what way could a quickie in a hotel toilet possibly be deemed exciting or romantic? I asked myself. This was, as Rachel might put it, 'beyond closure'. Not good in any way, but maybe an overdue and necessary evil. Nodding now, I smoothed down my hair, ready to leave. It had been neccessary to get to this point to have the clarity to move on from Clay. I just worried I might have made it impossible to do that. Whatever I chose to do now wasn't going to be easy.

I couldn't sleep that night. Got in in the early hours, time ticking, knowing in five hours or so I'd have to get up again to leave for the airport to go back to Roddy and all the choices that entailed... My brain was on red alert and wouldn't shut down. Restless and anxious, apprehension about the story hovered in the dark corners of my mind. Clay's cold reaction played over and over in my head. The way he looked at me: did he know what I had done? Had she told him?

On the way back to the hotel I'd seen an advertisement for a new film starring some beefcake Hollywood action hero, the new Arnie, Van Damme or whoever. Behind him were the burning buildings of a city under attack. The all-conquering hero was defeating the enemy. The domineering image was so mighty, so American, it made me smile. Reminding me of Clay's arrogance, I tried to laugh it off, but at the same time I felt uneasy, shaken by the night's events.

The poster must have stayed with me as I slept. I dreamed I was walking through Brooklyn but the streets were broken and everywhere had been abandoned and I was all alone.

For some reason, I reflected back to what Michael Dawson had said about me once: that I was a good person. Was I a good person? I felt sure he would say that humanity should come first. I should act in the most basic way possible and respond to needs as I saw them, with kindness and compassion. I kept thinking about Lily. The photo on her fridge. She was just like me.

27

Complimentary Peanuts

JFK Airport was a modern futuristic dome, full of the possible. It was abuzz with manic activity.

Then the atmosphere visibly changed. It turned up a notch, as though an electric current had passed through it. All eyes were focused on one spot. A new cat was in town, strutting his stuff. This one was a gorgeous tiger.

'It's him,' I breathed. Before he was even within sight, I knew at once it was Clay.

Clay's set-up was not so much an entourage as a presidential cavalcade which filed through in a sweet-scented jet stream of precision activity. You could feel the excitement as it rippled through the exhausted crowds even before you saw it. People's spirits were lifted for a moment by this glamorous demi-God.

For me it was something more. I felt that familiar heart-lurching thrill. Just to see him was a tonic. He was, after all, there to be admired and enjoyed. But this time there was a detachment I hadn't felt before. The pain of his words last time was still fresh. I was enjoying the spectacle, sure, but I wasn't enchanted in the way I once might have been. The humiliation of the five-star toilet shag had sobered me and I wasn't sure the spellbinding quality of Clay Allison would ever work on me in the same way again. His coldness had seeped into me and self-preservation had finally kicked in.

The Coquettes had positioned themselves provocatively in Clay's path, fiddling purposefully with the gold zips on their wheelie cases. I felt sure he was going to stop and pick one of them off like a ripe, low-hanging fruit, which he'd whisk into the cubicle of his Gulfstream, Hendrix-style. But he kept walking, faster, with purpose, whispering something in the ear of his assistant before splitting off from her and heading off on his own determinedly. It was then I realised he was heading straight for me.

'I think someone wants to talk to you,' said Adam, raising his eyebrows. 'I'll leave you to it,' he added, disappearing from my side before I had time to respond.

'You again, then?' I said to Clay. It was the first thing I could think of saying, and a shudder passed through my body as he moved closer to me. I could feel his warmth again, permeating from his body. 'So are we going to wish each other well, say our farewells politely this time?'

I couldn't look at him as I spoke, because I could hear my voice cracking. I was afraid that the emotion of the last few days would rise to the surface and I wouldn't be able to hold it together.

'Hey, Pocket.' Clay moved my chin so I was looking at him. Up close under the stark glare of the airport lighting, I could see the creases drawn around his eyes. Beneath the tanned skin there was a person, a human who looked a little tired, who was ageing more than his youthful disguise let on. 'I apologise Toots. I just go crazy sometimes. I lose it, my survival instinct... But you, you're a rare flower, Toots. You wouldn't let me down.'

He looked at me and raised his brow, his eyes glinted.

'Hey, you could come with me if you want to relax for a couple of days, or if you need anything?

'No, I don't think so,' I said, not daring to hold his gaze. 'I'm due on a flight and I've my team with me,' I said, gesturing towards Adam, who was standing by the window pretending to adjust his camera.

'Listen, I'm not short of space, sweetheart. I've got my own plane right out there on the tarmac. You know what they say, what happens in the sky stays in the sky?'

'No. They don't, do they?' I laughed 'It's a lovely offer, but you know, I think what you said the other day was right. It's time to stop. For this to stop.' I was as near as I was going to get to fronting him now; he needed to know I hadn't forgotten. I wanted him to see I wasn't prepared to be treated that way, whatever he thought.

'I was offering to help you out, Toots, that's all.' There was a softness to his voice then and I knew he meant it. It was heartfelt and shook me a little. For a moment, I didn't know what to say. It was too much.

'Not sex at 12,000 feet then?' I smiled.

'Well, it's my plane, so I make the rules... And that is one of the rules.' Clay roared with laughter at his own joke and his face became boyish again, charming. He was charming.

'Suppose it goes without saying, really,' I said, thawing despite myself. 'I mean, if you have your own plane it would be a little bit disappointing if you didn't spend your time enjoying a few decadent perks here and there. It should be a rule, if you're the captain.'

'It was a genuine offer.'

'I know it was, and thanks, it's an incredible one, but I need to get my head straight to go back. Believe it or not, I think economy class has a sobering way of bringing a person back down to earth with a jolt, which is what I need.'

Clay pulled a face that signalled curious disbelief, but then nodded in agreement. 'I suppose you're right.'

'I do know some other people who might be interested, though,' I said, gesturing to the girls, who were eyeing us like predatory birds. 'And they are called the Coquettes, sounds like your kind of cabin crew, very serviceable I'd say, the perfect trolley dollies, that sort of thing.'

'I don't think you appreciate just how exclusive my offer is, Pocket.' He paused. 'Actually, I don't think you appreciate just how much I'd be prepared to do for you.'

'Really,' I said.

'Which is ironic, considering you're one of the only people who has never asked me for anything.'

'So refreshing?' I answered sarcastically, perhaps more sharply than I'd intended, because his words had struck a chord with me.

'Listen to me. It's not easy, you know, but I've trusted you like no one else, Pocket. There's something about you. I know it sounds like a cheap line, but it isn't. You're authentic. I don't know, it's like you bring out something in me, a part of me I don't show to many people. And because of that, I'm not sure I've been fair to you, because I know some of the shit I've landed on you is just too much.'

'It's OK,' I answered.

'I suppose part of me was playing with you a little bit, seeing what you would do with it. But the other part of me, Toots, the part you inspired in me in the first place, that part just wanted to tell you who I am. That's all. I guess it's up to you now.'

I was conscious that Clay was speaking from the heart, but at the same time I wasn't stupid enough to trust him entirely. I was confused. Was he pleading with me not to tell the story, or did he mean what he said? I knew we'd had something, and that what he was saying was at least partially true. But, as I'd not admitted to meeting Clay's mother and wanting to turn it into a story, I wasn't going to commit myself to the same line of confession.

'I'm sorry. I understand. I mean, I understood that all along. I get that, and you're right: it's been special, it's been amazing. I'll never forget that and of course I'm glad.'

'So this is goodbye.'

'This is it.'

'Love you Pocket, babe.'

Oh my God, he'd said it. There he went again, knocking the breath right out of me. How long had I been waiting for him to say those words, and he'd said them right when I didn't need to hear them any more. He'd chosen the moment of maximum dramatic impact, like the pro he was, and I wanted so much to believe they were true. I felt like Ingrid Bergman in *Casablanca*. I felt like crying, 'No, you can't leave me like this Rick – sorry, Clay – we were meant to be together, kiss me like it's the last time…' But I pulled myself back. This wasn't the ending.

'No you don't,' I said.

'I meant what I said,' Clay replied, grinning.

'Which part?'

'All of it, babe, all of it. I told you, I make the rules.'

'You were always arrogant.'

'You love it.'

'Goodbye, Clay.'

'Goodbye, Pocket.'

And I wanted to kiss him hard on the mouth and jump in the plane and shag his brains out above the clouds – champagne spilling all over me, caviar showering down, and those little complimentary packets of nuts too.

I turned my back and walked away, dragging my shitty little suitcase behind me, being as dignified as I could manage, which was hard considering one of the wheels had had it.

It was only after I counted to 112 that I allowed myself to turn back and look at him disappearing.

And true to form, he was behaving as disreputably as I could possibly have imagined: one Coquette on one arm, two on the other arm, bouncing along next to him, heading across the airport to his private jet's parking place.

I couldn't help but laugh out loud at the absolute audacity of the man and, yes, I loved him for it a little bit.

'Every cloud…' I muttered.

'What was that?' said Adam.

'Nothing, just talking to myself. It's time to catch our plane though, isn't it? I can't believe we're actually going home.'

As we waited for the plane, a strange normality ensued. Bought some coffee. Ate a cheese sandwich. Then eventually we boarded our flight as if it were any other. It wasn't until we took off and were safely above the clouds that a sense of relief took over.

'Back to normal then,' I said, turning to Adam.

'We're not going back the same, though, are we?' he replied, and smiled. At least he smiled. I wondered if he was right.

I stared from the window as the plane glided through the clouds and remembered the last time Adam and I had returned to Britain, after my interview with Clay. It seemed so long ago.

'What will you do when we get home, Adam?'

Adam took off his headphones and looked at me seriously. 'It probably sounds trite…'

'No, go on, tell me, Adam.'

'I've been giving it a lot of thought, more than ever over the past few days – I owe the Red boys and their banal little high-energy friends a favour. I've OD'd on this stuff Toots and I've decided, I want to do this job the way I set out to. Cover news, war, natural disasters, I dunno. I'm sick and tired of doing all this bollocks.' He smiled. 'No offence Toots. I want to do something better than bubblegum-blowing shots and fake smiles. What I mean is, the things that actually matter. I'm going to try to sell the pictures I took in New York, I mean the stuff I did on my own, the street stuff. See what happens, see where it takes me. See, I told you it was stupid.'

'Far from it, Adam, you will be excellent. You *are* excellent. It's an admirable ambition.'

'It's not admirable; it's just what I think I can do. I want my photographs to be a record of something that takes a place in history, to tell a story. I want to make a record of it, that moment, I mean, that's where I need to be.'

'I'll miss you,' I said.

'I know.'

Adam fidgeted in his seat. I knew him well enough to see there was something on his mind. He rummaged in his bag under the seat and drew out a small Jiffy bag, one of the ones I'd seen him use for his film canisters. He looked serious.

'Toots: there is something I want you to have. I didn't know what to do with them. I was going to get rid of them, but I thought better of it.

'In the end I thought of you. And I might not see you for a while, so I want to give them to you now. You might not need them. But then again, you could do. One thing I've learnt over the past week is you never know what's round the corner. You never know what's gonna hit you and from what angle. And after all that's happened, I thought long and hard and, in the end, I thought I should give them to you.'

He held up the bag. 'They're photographs.' It was self-evident and he didn't need to say it, but I could tell what he was really talking about was what was on them. Those kind of photos. The kind that aren't admired but used.

'For you,' he emphasised. 'I want you to have them. It's kind of an insurance policy, if you like. Please, don't open them now. Have a look when you get home. Then put them away somewhere, only use them if you need to – you'll see what I mean.'

A million thoughts were running through my mind. My imagination, outrageous at the best of times, was conjuring up all sorts. I opened my mouth to ask what they were, but Adam anticipated it. Typical me. Adam sensed it. 'Not now, OK,' he said quietly, fingers on lips. 'Hold fast this time, Toots. We've had enough drama in the last few days, let's just relax.' He handed me the bag, and on it I recognised the beautiful, unmistakable scrawl I was familiar with, which looked more lovely against the dreariness of the brown bag. 'Personal Insurance Policy! From Adam. X,' it said.

'One thing, Adam.'

'What?'

'I want a postcard every six months, something like that. Let me know you're out there somewhere, OK. Deal?'

'Deal.'

And we opened up our little packets of non-complimentary, economy-class crackers and chewed on our thoughts.

28
Frankenstein's Monster

Now I was back, Roddy's patience had evaporated like alcohol from the day before. He was hell-bent on finding out the details of the story. The big one, the showbiz world-exclusive he was counting on.

I spent the day after we landed avoiding his calls in the hope he'd just go away and forget it, which I knew he wouldn't.

I told Rachel everything. Clay's story, Lily Sue, my part in it all: the lot. It all spilled out of me the night I returned from New York. I needed to tell her, to start afresh. Not telling her felt like betrayal. Rachel was my friend, and that was the thing that mattered now. We were trying to figure out how to handle Roddy's latent hunger.

'Anyway, Toots, you still haven't told him, so you don't need to worry. All you've done is told him you have a big one. Just find another and you're off the hook, Toots. But can we talk about something else? Talking about Roddy makes me sick, OK? What we need is something to help us lighten up. Let's go out to that pub on Fulham Broadway, next to the station: it's got a three-for-two on the drinks; ignore the sick smell in the loos.'

'Talk about back down to earth: that place is the pits, Rach. And the sick smell isn't just in the toilets; it's in the walls, it's in the carpets...'

'I know, darlin', I know that, but I always think that's kind of a good thing if you want to think: think in the stink. It'll be dead now anyway, and I'm in the mood for something skanky, just me and you, like old times.'

An hour later, in the pub, Rachel's turn on the jukebox came on, the thrusting intro to *Sympathy for the Devil*.

'C'mon, Toots.' She grimaced, pure Mick Jagger.

Usually it was a call to the dance floor. That day, my head

slumped into my pint and I felt like it was a voice from the heavens.

'It's him again, tugging at my heartstrings. Why should I care? Clay was just a product of the environment he inhabited, no more no less. And I'd got close. As close as anyone, I believed him when he said he loved me…' Of course I knew I could never do that.

Rach gave up on her solitary dance routine, which was drawing stares from the clientele of alcoholics and dropouts, their liver-coloured complexions inflamed. It was late afternoon and the pub had that depressing half-lit shroud over it. Like visiting an elderly relative in the middle of the day when the curtains were closed and the heating was on, even though it was sunny outdoors.

'Yeah, but Toots, what you have to consider is this: if what's happened between you and Clay comes out, it will be you who looks like the shitbag. You will look like you only did it for the story, and people will hate you for it.'

'Thanks, Rach, I feel a whole lot better now.'

'I'm just saying it wouldn't do you any favours either.'

'It's not even me: it's his mother, Lily Sue. I can't get her face out of my head. She's been done over all her life, and I would be feeding her to the lions once again. She just seemed so fragile somehow, it would be her who would have to suffer the most for it. But her suffering, well, would that be any worse than the suffering my mum's had to endure all these years? I mean would it?'

'I know Toots. I do know. But one doesn't cancel out the other, does it? Life's not like that. Why don't you just ask Clay for the money to help your mum?'

'I would never ask him Rach. It would make me the same as everyone else. Even after everything, it's a question of trust. I know what he was doing when he told me about Lily Sue. He was daring me not to betray him, don't you see? He explained that to me at the airport, never mind that he's a maestro when it comes to breaking promises. It's like a mad game of control: by telling me this incredible story, he was saying, "Look, I'm giving you this on a plate, free of charge and you can make your name, thanks to me. Go ahead: do your worst."'

'Exactly. So what?' said Rach. 'What do you do? He wants you to do the story so he's the one in control? Or he wants to know he can trust you? Or he wants you to know his story and care enough to keep quiet? That's weird. Or do you think he actually wants it to come out so he can punish his mother? Something all bonkers and Freudian like that. God, I'm lost. All I can tell you Toots is what I know. Tough decisions are easy enough to take. Living with the consequences is the hard part.'

'You're right Rach, I know you are, I'm sorry. I don't know, I guess it was just the idea I might be able to change things. I never really intended to do it. The only two things I know for certain are this: Lily is the victim no matter how you look at it. She comes off worst. The second thing I know is, if I don't deliver an amazing story to Roddy to justify my trip I'm going to be the victim of the unemployment statistics.'

'Another pint, Toots. That's the answer. It's the only answer I can think of.'

'Yes, Rach, that does make sense.'

'Hey this might cheer you up. That Michael guy phoned up a couple of times while you were in New York. Left a number.'

'Oh. He did? Did he say why? Is he going to call back? I mean, what did he say exactly?' I tried not to sound agitated, but it felt like a lost chance I might not get back. I wanted to speak to him. 'Maybe he sensed it,' I muttered to myself.

'What?' said Rach.

'Oh, nothing really; it's just odd that he should call. He kind of cropped up in my thoughts a few times while I was away, that's all. Did he say anything else?'

'I don't know really; he just asked you to call him. Asked if I knew where you were staying. I said I didn't and he said he'd call Roddy. Then he hung up.' Rachel smiled at me suspiciously.

I let the thought of Michael calling back soothe me for a moment then my phone went again. Roddy. Tomorrow, tomorrow, I'd face him tomorrow.

I looked down at my phone, and sure enough, there was

Roddy's number again, flashing impatiently. I knew I would have to take the call. Make the decision. Face the music.

I would face him. Just not yet, that was all. Now, now I would dance.

At the *Incite* office, big plans were being unveiled for the expansion of the brand and Roddy had been in and out of meetings with various suits all morning. Ad men, city financiers, TV satellite moguls. Excitement charged.

A staggering, eight-foot cardboard hoarding stood outside his office. I walked towards it obliviously. It was a picture of a sexy woman in high heels, digging one of them into a man lying down on the floor. In the corner of her mouth was a pencil, and she was holding a notebook and wearing a wry smile. Corny as hell. It was only as I got nearer and it came into full focus that I realised, with a creeping wave of horror, that it was a picture of me. 'Hot Incisive Opinion, Hot Incisive Television – coming your way.'

I stared at it for a minute, mouth open. My cleavage was awesome, but I hadn't ever encountered it on the body I inhabited, that was for sure. Who was that surgically enhanced me? I glanced over at Stephen, who clocked me looking at my bizarre reflection. He sat up proudly in his chair and kissed his thumb to his finger in a note of perfection. He was acknowledging the part he'd played in the Photoshopped me. I took another look at my cardboard doppelgänger and then took a deep breath, and my stomach turned. What kind of monster was Roddy planning to turn me into?

At one o'clock it was my turn for a slot with Roddy. He'd emailed me in big red letters to say so – INCITE MULTI-PLAT-FORM BRAND STRATEGY DELIVERY MEET – with a short note underneath nailing what he wanted from me.

'Toots, can't wait to hear the launch story in full, better be fucking brilliant too. Immense Confidence Riding on this from them on high. Rods.'

Holy shit. My heart sank.

Marisa sidled up to me. An assault to the senses today in a spaghetti-strap vest with the repeated image of Kermit the Frog all over it like a deadly rash. She was holding out a plate with cake on it. (In our office, every sentiment, every occasion, was marked with cake.)

'Hey, Toots, we all just wanted to say how glad to have you back and that and we are all really excited.'

She placed the plate down next to me. I looked at the squashy piece of brown squashy carrot cake and nearly spewed. 'Thank you, Marisa, but I'm not hungry.'

I tried to busy myself by looking at Stephen's proofs for the exclusive launch edition studiously, with marked-out blank pages for my exclusive like big white lies.

As 1.15pm approached, I was in the darkness of the office supplies room and in my hand was the wrap of coke, or whatever the hell that yellowish powder was, that Rach had got for me last night from that fella in the pub. I turned it over a few times in my clammy hands but put it back in the pocket of my skirt again. I wanted to stay in there all day. Just me and the printer paper and the pencils. They smelled so nice, like school. It reminded me of being little. Then I remembered I needed a pee, talk about regression.

Sod that. What had happened to me? Standing there in a stationery cupboard relying on a wrap of cleaning product to get me through the day? I would never be that woman with the perfect breasts on Stephen's poster. To go on telly and try to be her was the road to hell. It would almost certainly kill me. Thank God for Clay, thank God for his mother. It all made a weird kind of sense to me now: their story was my story, if I let it. No. Simple. That wasn't me. This was not it. Resolution. Thank you, Lily Sue.

'You see, you change when you get famous, the rules of the game change. The shape of you, you aren't you any more. You are whatever your audience wants you to be.' Who had said that to me? I didn't know. Was it Clay, was it Lily? Were they my own words? I couldn't be sure any more who had said them, but I knew them to be true. That much I did know.

The downside, of course, was that you couldn't turn round and go back, even if you wanted to. So no matter how much you wanted to grab that piece of you, formerly known as your soul, your heart, whatever, you couldn't. It no longer existed. Deal with the devil, she was right on that. I went for a piss.

'Roddy will see you now,' I heard Ange's voice echo in my head.

I was ready for him. I marched into Roddy's office at 1.22pm. Slam. Door shut tight like a steam room. The cardboard cutout of the TV version of me, outside the door, fell flat on her perky bosoms.

Roddy's expression was insolent, like a boy who'd been caught out, on purpose. He was just seeing how hard he could push it. My nerves kicked in. Fleetingly, I felt myself falling under his spell, as I'd been conditioned to: the familiar feeling of wanting to please him, show him how good I was at my job. But this time, I nipped the temptation in the bud. Stopped it dead in its tracks.

'Why the fuck didn't you answer your phone yesterday?' His opening gambit was trademark Rods. Lightning war, aggressive. But by now, I'd learned that all that shock 'n' awe crap was just that. Emotional smoke 'n' mirrors. Psychological warfare. Sticks and stones...

'I wanted to update you in person,' I teased him, down cold.

'Go on then, shoot,' he snapped.

What was this? A cheesy Seventies cop show? Who said stuff like 'shoot'?

But I complied anyway...

'I'll tell you the story, Rods. One that will blow your brains out,' I shot back. 'Story of your life.'

And I did. I told him. Everything about Clay and me. There and then, every jawdropping, mind-blowing bit of it.

'What, seriously, you never...' he stuttered, several times.

I told him about the affair: how it started, how it ended, all the sexy detail I knew he'd drool over.

When I get to the bit when I told him about Clay's mum, he slid back in his chair, like he'd been hit by a wave of mind-bending wonderment. It was too much, orgasmic, overwhelming.

Then he looked me square in the face.

'But you know I knew a hint of it all along, don't ya, Toots? Can't get one over on the old demon. Little minx in Cannes, weren't you, Toots? You think I would have let expenses like those go through otherwise, sweetheart? But this, this stuff about his mother. This is even better, and hearing it from your little mouth, darlin', that I like. Well played.'

Fuck. The realisation struck me. Who the hell had been talking to Roddy? Paranoia descended like a darkness. Undermined. I no longer felt like the woman in control. Who could it have been? Simon? No. No way. But he was the only one who knew about Clay and me in Cannes. Surely not? Had Simon been playing all of us at the same time? Confirming the story, spurring me on, all the while knowing I would never do it?

Roddy was still going, not waiting for a response.

'Wow, this is a great story though – it's a fucking whopper.' Bubbles of saliva were forming at the corners of his mouth. His fingers started tapping on the desk excitedly. He got on his feet and started pacing around the room as ideas flooded into his head. 'Probably the best I've had the pleasure of in all my years, love it. A corker, a total corker. Tell you what the best bit is, that little old dear sitting there in her flat with her little doggy-woggies, that bit kills me. You couldn't make that stuff up. Lily Sue her name is, are you sure? Sickly sweet, straight out of the movies. Dollywood Daydream, excellent. We have to get a picture of them, her with the dogs. Got to hand it to you. This is going to rock the world, Toots.'

As he was talking to me, he was simultaneously priming his phones, emails and video conferencing. To let the world know the full impact of the story – or, more accurately, the world behind the scenes: the plethora of back-room staff, support operations and senior subcontractors that shored up every world-class media operation. Like an old hand, he knew that if he got in early, he'd get a better deal on the huge volumes that he'd barter with. On another phone, he was lining up a chat with his media agency ad sellers to bump up the rate card – and stress no discounts. He knew that it was there, amid the grime of the printing works and the biro-lacerated phones of the salespeople, that the profit would be made.

'I'm going to be talking to my guys down in advertising, we're going to need to get a little taster on the telly for this one, the day before, you know, you giving it a flavour of your incredible story, how you are going to lift the lid on one of the biggest names in showbiz, whet their appetites, get them licking their lips.

'Don't worry, hon, I won't feed you to the lions.'

'This time!' I answered drily, flashbacking to when he'd turned me over in the papers for my frock horror faux pas.

'Babe, it was a learning curve, all that party-girl stuff, but this is different, this is big time.'

'Yes, it is different,' I nodded.

'That's what I said, Toots, keep up.'

'I didn't mean it that way, Roddy: I mean really different.'

I waited for a short while, enjoying the impact, relishing the look on his face, like he was a kid with a ticket to Disneyland and a pocketful of lollipops. Drawing in a deep breath, I felt a sense of excitement, but also indignation at what I was about to say. Then I delivered my punchline.

'I'm afraid so, Roddy. You see, the thing is, it is going to be very different because I've been thinking and, on reflection, none of this is going to be necessary.'

Ignoring me, he carried on drumming numbers into his phone.

'Roddy, listen to me, there's really no need to trouble those advertising people.'

No reaction.

'Rods, listen to me: you know you can't publish any of this without me. So forget about the printer lads. It's a waste of time. It's all over. I'm not doing it.'

No reaction.

'Listen. I don't think you're getting this. It's not happening. It's my story and I'm pulling it, here and now.'

No reaction.

'Without me there is no story, it's simply hearsay, impossible to prove without a taped confession I'd say, given the might of Clay's lawyers.'

I knew that was true. The story I'd given him was patchy to say the least, and he wouldn't be able to go near it once Clay's legal team shut the whole operation down. All of it rested on my taped confession from Lily Sue. Clay's birth certificate and birth name would be impossible to trace. Roddy would never be able to prove it.

Carrying on, enjoying myself, relishing the look of dumb-foundment on Roddy's face, I said, 'I've thought about it and I've made a choice. I choose life, like George Michael said, but not that sort of life, no. The opposite in fact; not glamour, like Wham.' I was thinking on my feet now. 'Not like *Trainspotting* either, none of that self-annihilation shit, I'm not going on heroin, I don't need to go on a programme, I haven't lost the plot. Something else. Something better. I choose my life: my pedestrian, normal, boring life. Me. Mine. Toots Silver. See, I told you when we met, Roddy, I believe in everything and, what's more, I believe in me.' (I might have got a little carried away with myself – a bit Oprah – but fuck it, this was my big moment.) 'Without me, there is no story. I quit. Thanks for the opportunity. Goodbye.'

'Toots, you fucking idiot. What the fuck are you talking about? You can't just pull out like that! This is your big break. This time next month you'll be the most famous magazine editor on the planet. The girl who landed the biggest showbiz exclusive since god knows when. Sure, I know you're going to get cold feet. Sometimes we have to do things in this business that we don't like. But we can talk about that. Don't throw your life away.'

'I told you Roddy. I'm not doing this story.'

No more Roddy patter. A volcanic explosion from behind his desk as he launched out of the spring-loaded chair. Now for the real Roddy.

'You know me, don't ya?' Walking up to me, so his face was an inch away from mine. I could smell his lunch, the red wine on his breath, fuelling a hot, dangerous cocktail of alcohol and anger.

'What?' he carried on. 'You think, somehow, you get to walk off into the sunset?'

Roddy raged on, his contorted face and unruly fringe making him look psycho now.

'You think you can leave me sitting here, thinking, "Wow, she really beat the life out of me, that one. Maybe it's time to hang up my desert boots." Think you've got me, eh? That's what you think I'm gonna do, is it, just drop the story?' He paused for a moment and went over to stand with his back to me, so he could take inspiration from his hall-of-fame gallery. Sucking up strength from his self-image for the final attack.

'OK! Have it your way,' he blasted.

'But if you're not prepared to stay on board for the big win, then I'm going to have to steer the ship all by myself. I'll do the story anyway without you.'

'What? You'll cobble together a spoiler,' I interrupted, playing along. 'May I ask how?'

From under his desk, he pulled out his cherished, limited-edition microcassette recorder, half the size of a normal one and faux gold plated.

'I've got every word you've just told me on tape. The affair, your little trysts here and there, all the sentimental Lily Sue bollocks, the fucking lot.

'It might not be as good as the story I wanted but it'll do. It's all there. I'll throw in a few of Adam's old pics of you in the pool with him in LA.'

Deflated by this onslaught, I had no reply. A spoiler? How naïve I'd been not to think that one through.

Sensing victory, Roddy rolled on with a final assault. One last ambush to see me off. This time it was personal.

'Listen, darling, what skills you've got, you *had*, even, I gave them to you. What contacts you've got, I gave you from my fucking book. I threw you a bone when you'd just landed from some shithole up North. Now I'll take them right back off you. D'you think anyone who's anyone is gonna talk to you now? From this moment on, Toots, you're an unperson. You're showbiz suicide, Toots.'

I knew his game. It still stung but I was ready.

He carried on, 'See this wall, there'll be pictures of me with your daft celebrity mates, toasting my success. Those celebrity mates I gave you, by the way, Toots. D'you think they lined themselves up with you cos you were some hotshot Lois Lane? 'Fraid not, Toots. There'll be letters from them, on the other one over there, thanking me for turning them over so nicely, telling me their life story and keeping it nice in my nice magazine. Business as usual. Don't you worry about that, Toots.' Finally he shook his head, making a big deal of the pay-off he was lining up. The *coup de grâce.* 'You know, I credited you with a little more intelligence than this, I really did.' Nice – he'd finished off with an understatement. Real nice.

He didn't think I'd come back. Banking on a knockout. Roddy didn't like to win on points. And to be honest, I'd hoped it wouldn't happen. But I looked him in the eye this time, before I started to speak. I wanted to look into his soul. Then I launched into it.

'You're right, Roddy. I was being naïve. I guess I hoped you might let me go – let the story go, I mean – without a fight. Maybe I thought you cared about me a little bit, enough to let me get on with my life. But you have taught me so much Roddy, more than you realise.'

I paused to let my rebuttal sink in. Then I hit him with it. 'That's why I kept something back. I really hoped it wouldn't come to this. But seeing as my back's against the wall now, I guess you're right. Maybe it is time to show what I'm made of. I mean, there's no point being too nice, is there? Specially in this game…'

Roddy looked puzzled, slightly perplexed even. It was time to ram home my counter-attack.

'You remember Alice Caufield,' I said, 'the girl we had here on work experience, don't you, Roddy?' I gave him a second to think. 'Well, I say "girl", I mean she looked a lot older than her age. You remember the posh public school one, English rose… She was here on a gap year before going off to Oxford to study. I'm right, aren't I? Isn't her daddy on the board of directors or something? Yes.'

'I remember her, got her to serve the drinks at our launch party, didn't I? Nice little waitress, as far as I know, Toots. If she drank the fucking cocktails, got a little bit tipsy, I can't be held responsible for that now, can I?' He cocked his head to one side and shrugged.

I continued to look him in the eye, and I could see a suggestion – just a glint – of something that looked like doubt there. He was sussing me out – how much did I know? The million-dollar question. I didn't even need to say it.

'You think you can hang that on me? Not saying I never thought about it, but come on, Toots, what do you take me for?'

'But you did more than think about it, didn't you? I mean, that's you, isn't it Roddy? Like you said: you want something, you get it. I'm right, aren't I?'

'You'll never get me on that, Toots.'

Roddy was distracted, not so verbose as normal, that was for sure, but still defiant. But he was on autopilot. In survival mode. The thought of Rach popped into my head, crying on the couch after her brush with this bastard.

'Like I said, Toots, you can't prove anything.' He was struggling. 'Fuck off. I don't even know why I'm bothering to go there, because there isn't any evidence anyway. You've got fuck all on me. How could you have?'

'Unless there were photographs. Someone saw you, Roddy.' I put my hand into my bag and drew out the hard-backed envelope that Adam had given me on the flight back from New York. I nudged the photograph inside an inch upwards so that a corner poked out a little. Holding a single print up to Roddy, before drawing it three-quarters of the way out of the envelope. Just enough for him to see exactly what I was talking about.

'You probably didn't see the man with the camera. I guess you let your guard down. I mean, it was the exhilaration of the launch; we thought we were invincible, didn't we, eh? But the thing is, no one's invincible, are they, Rod? Not you, not me, not even the Hollywood stars – no one.'

Tantalisingly, I pulled several more photos completely out the envelope. Black, white and grainy. Retro-ish, to the point that you could tell they were seedy without even looking closely at them. Trust Adam to shoot them artistically.

'So I guess it's up to you now, isn't it, Roddy? It's your shout. The thing is, Mr Caufield might be an investor in your magazine now – I heard his lordship and his City mates were in this very office this morning. What was it? The £10 million bond issue to float the relaunch.' Gazing out of the glass window at the secretaries' desk to let him know that I had my intelligence sources, too.

'But he may not be so generous if he knows you've been investing your energy in his daughter. And I'm guessing it might not be the best thing for your career prospects, Roddy, if something like that appeared in the papers.' I looked up at him. 'Remember, like you said: I learned from the best.'

Roddy's face was contorted with confusion. Picking up the photos, he leafed through them one by one. Him and her going up the staircase to his room. Him with his hand halfway up her Little Black Dress. Him and her in the corridor. Him all over her. Him and her on a sofa chair in a cosy alcove. Him with his trousers around his ankles. Her half-naked. The soft, Philippe Starck downlighters illuminating every bit, in too much detail. Signature Roddy – so coked-up that he couldn't even wait till he got inside his room.

But mostly, as he fingered the celluloid, shaking his head, breathing out stressfully, he looked like he'd just been robbed. The shock of it; I doubt something like this had ever happened to him before. Finally the edges of his mouth turned up, and he spoke, softly at first.

'OK, I guess you win,' he said. 'Now fuck off.'

And before the impact even had time to hit him properly, with him sitting there dumbfounded, I turned and walked out the door. Shut it behind me, only pausing to pick up the cardboard-cutout version of myself from where she'd fallen. I stood her back up, dusted her off a little.

The tiny inscribed tattoo on Lily Sue's wrist had said: 'Quod Me Nutrit Me Destruit.' That was the thing that kept coming back to me. I couldn't get it out of my head: 'What nourishes me destroys me.' I walked away to preserve myself.

I held it together until I got home. First came the shakes. Then, even though I'm not one for passing out or being sick, suddenly I felt nauseous. Retching and vomiting in the toilet. I still felt exhausted. I was sick again the following morning, a pattern that would repeat itself for the next 11 weeks.

Epilogue
Stardust

St Paul's Cathedral, London, March 2007

Clay's Funeral

I feel the grip of the small fingers holding my hand, curling round mine and tightening. Fear. Then the rotten maternal guilt, in the knowledge that his fear is of my doing.

'Don't worry, darling. It's just men with cameras, being silly. It's a game they have to play.'

'But Mummy, why do they want to take pictures of us?'

My hand shields his face forcefully, that beautiful, pale, innocent face, which is mine. Not for human consumption. I'd never told him the answer to that question, to protect him. As long as we could give him all the love he needed, keep him safe, why should I expose him?

At the bottom of the steps, when I'm closest to the press pen, I plead with banks of paps lined-up on stepladders: 'Please, not the boy, leave him alone. He's a child.' But my words dissolve in the sparkle and crackle of the flashbulbs.

This isn't a game he wants to be part of. I'm aware that I have to be. Can't go to pieces. I need to keep my composure. Stay dignified.

Looking down the lens, I'm defiant, but inside I'm in pieces. I can't hold this facade much longer; my expression is going to crack. Not sure if I will cry, or laugh, or break. Standing here with Ray, it all comes flooding back to me.

This is his father's funeral. The dad he never met. The one he will never know. It feels like such a long time ago. I feel fragile and anxious. Suddenly, none of this seems like such a good idea any more. I've made Ray vulnerable. The thought is too much to bear.

I'd come to say goodbye, respectfully; now the situation is out of control.

On the opposite side of the road, in the shaded depths of an old walled garden, I spot the big, powerful road bikes parked under the London plane trees. The leather-jacketed bikers, smoking and moping around, but keeping a lookout discreetly. A skinny, well-groomed man wearing a designer racing jacket, an incongruously colourful helmet in his hand, smiles and makes a subtly protective gesture directed at me.

'Are you OK?' he mouths, as if to say, 'Do you need us to get you out of here fast?'

Simon – Clay's secret fixer. His confidential emissary. His invisible representative on earth. The executor of his master's every wish. The mysterious Simon, who was the link, *the only link*, with Clay's nebulous past, and with the people who'd taken him from Lily Sue's arms into a different world. Even now, when Clay had left this plane, his job wasn't done.

Comforted, I smile back at Simon, and make a gesture that says, 'Don't worry. I'll be OK. I'm in safe hands.'

'Thank you,' I mouth to him.

In the days after he died, the newspapers examined every detail of Clay's life over and over. My heart stopped every time I saw his name, the thought that this time it could be our story. Game over.

Since I'd walked away, I'd never breathed a word. Except to one person, and to Rachel, of course – she knew everything. But other than us, no one knows the whole truth, and since then he's done everything within his power to protect our privacy. But they can't change Ray's DNA: it's there in the corners of his eyes when he laughs, the wave of his hair, the unmistakable pout of his lips when he's cross. Sometimes I feel like hiding his face away, it feels so obvious.

Suddenly the lights stop flashing and it's over. I realise they have moved on. I take a breath; perhaps it wasn't just us after all. They're pointing at someone else. Is everyone in the frame? Are they taking no chances?

There is a sudden stir of excitement as a car arrives, preceded by

a police escort. The cameras are redirected again. It's a minister-
ial Mercedes, slinky black and old, with heavily tinted windows,
Kremlinesque. The vehicle pulls up in front of us and an elegantly
dressed man gets out. A man we all recognise and respect.

The sight of the back of his head – smooth, dark, close-shaved
hair meeting his contoured neck – is at once familiar and comforting. But it causes another frenzy of excitement amongst the paps.
Immediately, he takes command. The photographers are ushered
out of the way.

'No more pictures, that's enough for today, respect please, gentlemen.'

Then he steps towards us, firmly guiding my boy, then me, into
the cream-leathered warmth of the waiting car.

Relief hits me like a wave. I know I'm safe. With him.

'What took you so long?' I gasp.

'I said I'd come. I'm here.' His reply is cold, businesslike. He is
detached from all this.

'Relax. It's all over,' he adds, more warmth in his voice now, as
though to signal a change.

'Is it?'

'Yes, that was the end.'

I relax a little and shift my weight in the slippery seat, shimmying up to my boy.

'We've come a long way, haven't we? You always stepped in,
picked up the pieces for me, Michael. Why do you do that?'

'I'm the better man,' he laughs deeply.

And it's true. This I know in all certainty: he is kind, decent,
honourable. He loves me.

'Shh. Don't worry. I told you, it's all over now, no need for
that.' Michael whispers the words, so as not to alarm Ray, but Ray
is already plugged into his Nintendo DS: fingers tapping madly,
brain disconnected, oblivious to everything else, with no sense of
the momentousness of today's events in his life.

Leaning in closer, I whisper to Michael, reaching to take his
hands in mine.

'Do you think I should have told him why I brought him here

today? Do you think I should have explained to him? He deserves to know, doesn't he?'

His response is calm but definitive.

'No, because that's not his story, is it Toots? We are his story. We are what's important, the family we are. The life we made for him. You brought him today, that's the most important thing... He is happy, he is loved.'

I stare out the window, looking at the camera flashes machine-gunning the car. For a moment, a million stars explode into twinkling prismatic colours across the glass. It's like looking at the world I've left behind, the one I didn't choose – stardust.

My mind is racing. As the rays of light continue to cascade into the car, it feels momentous. But he is right – this isn't even Ray's story. Instead, I keep the thoughts to myself, reflecting on what Clay had said. 'You lose the choice when you do the deal,' he'd told me. When you cruise 'the superhighway', as he'd called it, 'You can't go back. Not really.'

For a moment, I reflect on my own choice. In the end, I'd decided to say no. Another bank of flashes explodes. And with it, memories of Clay come flooding back, as though he is sitting right next to me in the car. 'You reap the riches, Toots. But you can't have back a bit of what matters when you choose to. You know, that special connection, that indefinable thing, it'll be harder to nail it, and that's if you know what made you in the first place.'

I nod. 'You're right.' I'm just about to shoot back at him with a smart answer: 'The soul can't conveniently divide itself into bite-sized pieces, can it, Clay?' But I check myself before the words come out, and I keep looking out of the window, watching the sharp metallic rays bounce off the wing mirror.

Michael turns around fully on his seat now and looks at me emphatically, unequivocally, the look of a man with integrity burning through him. The look of justice, truth, courage, the look that won him the position in the Cabinet; oh, and me. Ha.

'Always was,' I say. 'You've always been such a good father, the best Ray could wish for.'

'I love him. He is my boy, end of.' He stops dead, thinking for a moment, looking at me, pressing home the point.

'Dad, can we go home now? I'm hungry.'

His gaze shifts from mine to the hungry face staring up from the small screen.

'Pancakes?'

'Yeah, chocolate and syrup please, and yummy stuff.'

'Oh yes, the real deal, has to be the real deal,' Michael says, smiling widely.

'Fill him with sweet stuff then?' I look at him, smiling, full of hope. 'You have always been the better man.'

'You just want my pancakes.'

'Like I said, the batter man!'

I look at him affectionately, and I drink in his calm. I need to feed off his tranquillity, come back down.

'Switch the radio on, Michael.'

'Sure,' Michael nods. He fiddles around, racing through the stations to find one that satisfies me.

'No, no, keep going, no,' I say, until eventually I urge him, 'Stop.'

The deep voice growls the words of the song.

'No, you were never normal, now I see,' I mutter to myself. Clay didn't get the choice, not like my boy. Then I smile, for the first time today, then throw my head back and laugh because it's him, the voice could be him, only it's Clay's father and he's singing the words to me. He's talking to me.

'It's the end. This is the end.'

Later when we're home, safe and fed, I feel a pervading sense of peace flooding through me, relief to be home. I go out into the garden to look at the sky. The evening is clear and refreshing; the stars are bright. Michael wanders out and puts his arm around me.

'Let's sit down for a bit, try and relax now.' He leads me over by the back door, where it's light enough to read. We sometimes sit here around this time while Ray sleeps. Michael steps into the kitchen and comes back, handing me the cut-glass dish I like, with its rose-coloured base. It's not the first time it occurs to me he's always giving me something: food, love, security, pistachio ice cream. He eats his from a cone. 'Like a boy,' I laugh, like I always do at the sight of this formidable man with his juvenile treat.

When Michael and I finally found each other I was already carrying Ray. I told Michael I was having a baby and he stood by me. It was a monumental risk, especially to him, to his career.

I hadn't known about Ray until after I'd told Roddy where to stick his job, and for weeks afterwards I'd put the morning sickness down to stress. By that time, my finances were a mess. I was in debt and couldn't pay the rent on our flat any more. It was ironic, as by this time *Incite* was becoming the multi-platform success Roddy had said it would be. Stephen's 'fat bums' looked set to go global. I was skint. But despite the poverty, the fear, everything, I was glad to be out. Away from Roddy.

I went back up North for a while and told my family, who insisted I should stay at home and let them help me. I felt so stupid. I was meant to be the one helping them. I couldn't face going back there.

But after all those days of bailing Rach out, she came to my rescue. She rang me up one day and told me to pack my stuff. She had a two-bedroom flat in Hoxton, where she'd always wanted to live, and let me move in. She said she would pay the rent. I vowed I would pay her back every penny when I could. I had no money and no job, but I wasn't going back, baby or no baby.

Our lives had taken us in different directions now, with Rach finding the success she deserved as a stylist. Her love life was still haywire, but workwise she was in control. She advised everyone from stateswomen to pop stars, actresses and TV personalities, never standing still for a moment. She was brilliant when Ray came along too, he loved her so much. She was part of my romantic beginning. We started our journey together and in that way she would always be bonded to my heart.

It had been Rach who had connected Michael and me. She

was styling a shoot with the new front bench and he was one of them. He asked Rachel about me and she orchestrated a meeting. I would never have agreed to see him otherwise, given the state I was in. I hadn't quite had the confidence to return his calls when I'd returned from New York, just dialled the number a couple of times and then stopped myself. Rach read my feelings for him better than I could. The spark I'd felt when we first met was still there. But to begin with, I insisted on taking it slow. I needed to know he would still feel the same way when the baby was born.

After Ray came along I was more settled, and by that time moving in with Michael was inevitable. Michael and I got married on Ray's fourth birthday. It was a double celebration, a magical day. I started ghostwriting, writing other people's words for them, happy to be behind the scenes. Michael had helped me get started in my new career, had arranged for me to write the biography of one of his colleagues. It was a success and so I did another. Who knows? Maybe one day I could write Clay Allison's story. It makes me smile to think of it. Michael had waited for me. He loved me unconditionally. And I'd realised what I felt for him was real. The feelings I'd had when we were first together had never left me. I'd taken it for granted then, only to be left wanting until we found each other again.

I hear Michael's voice, bringing me back to the present.

'You know, a long time ago, I read something that made a lot of sense to me. Made me realise why none of this is important.'

'What's that?' I ask.

'Look up there,' he says, pointing up to the dark sky.

'Sometimes it's worth reflecting what small a part we play in all this, remembering what we are made of.'

'What do you mean?'

'What we are about, the grand design, where we came from. Listen to this: "Every atom in your body came from a star that exploded. And the atoms in your left hand probably came from a different star than the atoms in your right hand. It really is the most poetic thing about the universe." Beautiful, isn't it? Or, to put it into showbiz language for you, it means that we are all made of stardust.'

This isn't the sort of thing Michael is prone to saying; abstract concepts rarely feature in his rationale. My face must betray me, because he goes into politician mode, so the conviction behind his words is in no doubt.

'Hear me out, it's important. It stuck with me, especially when I think about Ray. Really, the master of our collective destiny, and our son's, was something far more magical, uncontainable and overpowering.'

I think about what Michael's saying. I try to get my head around it. He's wrong to think I'm dubious: that's not it. It's something else. I'm thinking back to the words Clay's brother read out today at the ceremony, Clay's words – then the realisation comes to me that they are the same. I'm struck by a sense of weird, lovely, off-beat symmetry between the two. His two dads: biological and real. Wasn't that what Clay had said? 'We are stardust.'

I look up and examine the clear night sky above us, a multitude of raucous lights are dancing, partying and I'm certain one of them is Clay Allison winking provocatively at me.

'Every atom in your body came from a star that exploded. And, the atoms in your left hand probably came from a different star than your right hand. It really is the most poetic thing I know about the universe: you are all stardust.'

Lawrence Krauss, Canadian–American theoretical physicist, professor of physics, Foundation Professor of the School of Earth and Space Exploration and director of the Origins Project at Arizona State University

Acknowledgements

Thanks to all the kind supporters who got behind the book without whom it would not have been possible.

It has been a pleasure to work with the excellent people at Unbound. Especially big thanks to Xander Cansell for his calm wisdom. Thanks to Mark Ecob for his brilliant design and to John Mitchinson.

Thanks to the wonderful editorial team, Craig Taylor for his exceptional guidance and good humour and huge thanks to Andrew Chapman, Cressida Dowling, and Derek Collett.

Thanks to AJ Murtagh for her counsel, reading those early drafts and for her continued encouragement and conviction. Thank you to Richard Scrivener at the Creative Rights Agency for his support.

Thank you to Julian Burgin for lending your masterful photographic skills.

To the Mail on Sunday for depositing me in Cannes and for paying my expenses, all those years ago. Thanks to the Sunday Mirror for giving me my first break in London.

Thanks to Nigel Kennedy for the master class.

I am indebted to Palm Dog founder, Toby Rose and of course to Mutley, gone but not forgotten.

A special thank you to Michael Gains, with his film star friends and his smooth good looks.

Thanks to Graham Johnson for his support and for being my first reader.